Keepers
Searching for Sam

LAUREL HUGHES

DEDICATION

To disaster survivors and responders everywhere

ACKNOWLEDGMENTS

This story is the final product of over ten years worth of false starts and salvage operations, with input from so many I've little doubt I'm about to forget someone. If I haven't mentioned you by name here, my apologies. Know that your help and encouragement are appreciated nonetheless.

Special thanks to disaster mental health buddies Bob Porter, Rob Yin and Becky Hauserman, who reviewed early versions and helped keep it real.

Much appreciation also to all the professionals whose feedback on this work helped me break into the craft of fiction writing: Holly Lorincz, Jessica Morrell, Sabrina Parys, Molly Tinsley and Lorelle Van Fossen.

Thanks to all the others (especially for their patience) who provided feedback on the many fledgling attempts: Jo Ann Hongslo, Bill Hughes, Stan and Barb Thatcher, Evelyn Wagner, Lynne Waldher – as well as fellow participants in all the meet-ups and critique groups who shared their observations over the years. Sometimes it takes a village.

Cover design by Elizabeth Harrington

Photo by Susan Frost Photography

CHAPTER ONE

Monday, June 2ⁿᵈ

Leave it to Dad to just take off, and not tell a single soul where he was headed. In the middle of a flood, no less. And it was so like Nate to bellyache that her proximity to their hometown made her the better candidate for trying to track him down.

For once, just once, could either Dad or Nate consider how his actions affect everybody else?

She didn't have time for this. Even if she were in search of a little R&R, Marshland was hardly the destination of choice. Thankfully the trip was halfway pleasant in the spring, the highways neatly lined with green rows of sprouting crops. The remaining months of the year offered little more than dead or dying stubble as far as the eye could see—an adequate precursor to the excitement that awaited visitors in the town it led to: Marshland. Every bit the allure of spending the day watching a tree stump rot.

Bleary-eyed resolution was the only thing keeping her Miata centered on the deserted stretch of highway. Except, of course, the occasional farm equipment blocking the way. At least it did something to interrupt the monotony of the drive.

Driving half the morning was the last thing she needed. She'd only been home herself since the wee hours, thanks to airport storm delays.

Now she was back at it again, leaving behind the cozy comfort of a barely slept-in bed and watching scenery pass. Only this time the sun was hardly up, and those few hours of sleep were working overtime to keep her eyes open. The suitcase never even made it out of the trunk.

Thankfully, the conference was one for the success column. Her presentation on complicated grief reactions had been well received. A few new avenues for private practice referrals even turned up. Sarah had hoped to spend a little time basking in the glow of self-satisfaction, but the sound of her brother's whiny voicemail shattered the prospect completely.

"We don't even know if he's still in Marshland," Sarah had told Nate. Not to mention that the very thought of enduring another clash with their father was enough to make her brain want to freeze over. "He could be anywhere by now. Maybe he's heading your way as we speak."

"He would have called first. Look, for you, it's only a few hours away. For me . . ."

"I just got back. I've been gone all week. I have disasters of my own to pick up after. I have clients to think about."

"You're the people expert, not me. You'll be better at figuring out what's going on with Dad. I'll get out there as soon as I can work it out."

Sure, Nate. Just like you follow through with everything else.

"We both know that any interpersonal skills I might have don't seem to apply to Dad." Suggesting anything at all to Dad that reflected her background in psychology only added fuel to the fire.

"I doubt that's important to him right now. His whole world is upside down."

True. But it didn't make the ordeal any more appealing. Especially in view of the nightmarish scenario Nate had described. Marshland, flooded out? Much of the old neighborhood simply washed downriver? Impossible. Nothing like that ever happened around there. Nate had to be exaggerating. Or maybe Chet had blown it out of proportion when he called Nate to tell him about Dad's disappearance.

Getting an accurate picture of what was going on in this mess would help move things along. Obsessing over family issues certainly wasn't getting her anywhere.

She switched off the vibrant oldies and tuned to a station with nonstop detailing of flood impact. Damage and closures, pretty much everywhere. The steady recital of closed highways and byways was nowhere near as helpful for keeping her alert.

As the dismal details piled up, it was harder to shrug off. Piece by piece, the gravity of the situation became real. Chet's description of the chaos in Marshland was no exaggeration. In some places, water was still high and dangerous; many bridges and stretches of highways were down or foreseeably inaccessible. Maybe Dad really had been at risk. Perhaps he still was. What if he was stuck somewhere in his pickup?

On the outskirts of Marshland, a tacky rendition of the Can-Can interrupted her disturbing thoughts.

I've got to do something about that ringtone.

She slowed onto a waterlogged shoulder, the view of a muddy culvert looming well below. Her mind flickered with realization of how high the flow must have been the night before. She shuddered. Where did so much water come from?

She scoured the briefcase for her cell phone. Nate's caller ID greeted her.

"I heard from Chet again," he said.

"So Dad turned up. Thank heavens. I knew Chet was making too much of it."

"Well, no. Dad's still missing. But there's more. I thought I should call ahead and let you know." There was a pause, a couple of coughs. "After the flood, Dad told people at the shelter he was going to spend the night at the shop apartment."

Silence followed. Her free fingers curled around the steering wheel, gripping it with increasing tightness. "So, what's going on, Nate?"

"Well, you see, Chet went into town this morning. He was checking Dad's hangouts again. Apparently . . . there was an accident last night. A fire."

She felt her belly stiffen to concrete.

"It was the body shop. Chet says it went up like a tinderbox because of all the grease and solvents. Dad's truck wasn't there, so nobody thinks Dad was in there, either. It doesn't sound like the fire chief really knows anything for sure yet. At least, that's what Chet said."

She finally exhaled. Nate's tense tone and hesitations had her heart ready to pound its way out of her chest. "Do they know what started it?"

"Not really. Probably that old wiring, when the electricity came back on. It's a good thing you're already on your way. They need a family member to take charge, since Dad's not there to do it."

"Why not Chet? He knows that shop better than either of us."

"He's not legal family. Besides, you know Chet. He's probably in over his head as it is. I'd be there myself, but we're in the middle of a shoot."

As Nate went on embellishing his excuse, the initial shock wore off. Logic moved into its proper place. There probably wasn't reason to get too worked up over the fire. Yes, the fate of Dad's shop was sad, and yes, it would be a major blow, especially on top of his house being flooded. But Dad had retired years ago. Caring for that old building was more likely a nuisance than a desire to maintain an investment.

His disappearance was probably not such a big deal either. Dad was so private and independent it would have been more surprising if they actually knew where he was.

As good a rationalization as any. Sarah blinked away beginnings of tears as she prepared to reenter the highway.

What if Dad and his truck got washed away? The water had risen all the way from the culvert to the highway. It could easily have happened. People made those kinds of mistakes all the time, thinking they could make it across a flooded road.

Stop it. Dad always landed on his feet. He might be cantankerous, but nobody could say he was stupid. He'd come through it. Wherever he was.

She gave the car a little gas. All this accomplished was wheel spinning.

Blast. She got out for a look.

A spray of mud decorated the rear side panels of her showy car. More gravel and loose dirt made up the shoulder than first met the eye. Hopefully her finish hadn't gotten scratched.

Never let it be said she wasn't prepared. She retrieved kitty litter from the trunk, which she'd squirreled away for snow and ice catastrophes. No reason it shouldn't work for mud.

She poured liberal piles of it in front of the tires and climbed back in to give the pedal a few gentle nudges. It worked; she felt slight movement, then more, quicker movement.

No. No No No. The car was going down, and not out onto the street. The right rear was dropping.

The shoulder was sinking, collapsing. She froze in disbelief, the possibility of dropping into the culvert too absurd to consider. On impulse she floored it.

The car careened sideways. It would roll if she didn't do something quick. Against all instinct, she steered downward into the steep decline. The car cooperated, staying upright. But it bounced and jostled as it joined the flow of mud heading for the culvert.

What now? Her briefcase slid to the floor, its contents flying everywhere. She closed her eyes and held on tight.

She heard brush swiping against the car, slowing the descent. It jolted to a sudden stop.

She opened her eyes. The car was caught up in a copse of elderberry. Noisy churning continued while the last of the mudslide passed, splashing into the dirty floodwater below.

She sat a moment, stalled. The feeling and sound of shifting ground were definitely over. It was eerily still, other than the trickle of water below. And the pounding in her ears.

The radio was still going. An announcer rambled on about dangers of travel in a flood zone, that people should stay put until authorities took care of this or that hazard.

A bit late for me, guy. She turned off the ignition and took a deep breath while considering her predicament.

"Hey! You down there! You okay?"

Sarah strained to turn and look back at where the shoulder used to be. A couple of people were peering down at her from the now jagged edge of the highway.

She took stock of her condition. She seemed okay, despite being rattled. Thanks to the shrubbery's assistance with this undignified parking job, there was hope for the Miata too—once she figured out how to get out of there. She pulled at the door handle and pushed with her shoulder.

Nothing happened. The dirt pile had jammed the door shut.

She rolled down the window and waved at the good Samaritans. One of them waved back, pointing at a cell phone in his hand.

A piece of heavy equipment revved up. There was the clunk, rattle, and jolt of a chain. The Miata slowly backed away from the elderberries and rolled up and out onto the highway. She got her first good look at her rescuer.

It was Stewy, an old friend of her father's, with his Green Gertie. Both he and his dragster-looking tractor appeared worse for wear. They'd probably been at it all night, helping others who'd been similarly shortsighted.

"Well, look who's here. Sarah." Stewy gave her a bear hug.

She melted into his steadfast anchoring. Her shaking seemed to be over with. But her legs were wobbly, not feeling particularly dependable.

"You want a ride into town?" He kept an arm around her while she steadied her legs.

"I'd really like to take my car if I can."

He scratched his head as he stared at the car. He circled it, giving it a cursory once-over. Finally he got in and tried the ignition. Its friendly purr started right up. "Not much wrong, there. It needs a good look-see to be sure. Let's get her into town and take a closer look."

Green Gertie towed it to the car wash. After hosing it down, Stewy had a look at the engine, the underside, the grill—everyplace the town fix-it guy would know to look. How fortunate to run into good old reliable Stewy, always ready and able. Rolling up his sleeves and getting down to business, even in the middle of this.

"You got lucky. Only a few scratches and dings to your paint job. Sam can probably buff them out for you. Do a little touch-up."

"Have you seen him since the flood? That's why I'm here."

"Nope. I've been on tow duty. We got us a whole lot of mess back there in town."

"Did any cars get washed away?"

"Water was mostly slow-rising. It did get deep in a few places, but no heavy current to speak of. I mostly helped people who were stuck in it.

He had given her another reason to be thankful, in spite the last few hours. She could cross off at least one horrific possibility about Dad. "Thanks for helping me out. I really appreciate it."

"Don't mention it, hon'."

Sarah paused, considering the bigger picture. "For now, can this stay between you and me? I wouldn't want it to somehow get to Dad and have him worry. Not before I get a chance to talk to him."

In truth, it had more to do with not wanting her mishap to turn into the latest source of local gossip. Let them wag tongues over someone else's misery. She was there to do what she had to do: find Dad and make sure he was safe. Get in, and then get out.

Stewy nodded. "Sure thing. Now be sure and say howdy to your Dad when you find him. And let him know we're not canceling poker night this weekend. It's still on. We're gonna need it by then."

Further into town, flood damage was harder to miss. Low-lying homes sported waterlines. Piles of ripped-out carpeting and discarded furniture already fronted some of them. Lakes appeared in places where there once had been fields. Occasional mud-brown trails made known where floodwaters had succeeded in crossing streets. Actually seeing the extent of the river's assault on civilized Marshland made the radio reports sound almost apathetic.

Dad had to deal with this? He would not be considered elderly, but he was up there in years. Could he handle such a crisis landing in his path out of nowhere? A flood of this magnitude had never hit Marshland, at least not during her 28-year history.

Would Dad know what to do? How to stay safe? She'd certainly blown it at watching out for herself. Would he do any better?

She pulled up to the one and only motel of Marshland proper. An assortment of emergency vehicles and maintenance rigs were either sitting idle or jockeying around in the parking area. The Lone Pine was packed.

"No, Sam ain't staying with us." An exhausted-looking registration clerk glanced up from her monitor. "I heard about folks along the riverfront, though. Hope your Dad's place got through it okay."

"Is anybody else from Riverside Drive here? They might know something."

"Most of the flooded-out folks are at the shelter, or staying with friends and family. Or left town altogether. We're full with out-of-town folks. Mainly linesmen."

"That's just great." She leaned into the counter; its pocked surface grated against her elbows. She attempted to massage her face into a more alert state of wakefulness. "I mean, yes. It's great they're here getting things up and running again. All the same, I need a place to stay, too."

"Gonna hang around and check up on things, then?"

"Nobody seems to know where Dad got to. Word has it his house is uninhabitable."

"Seems like half of Marshland's that way."

"Are you sure you don't have a room to spare?"

"Nothing. Everything's spoken for."

Beyond the registration desk, an open door exposed a room that was clearly empty. Inside it a hassled-looking employee darted about tidying things. "What about that one?"

"That's handicapped accommodations. I got strict orders on it. We got to keep it available."

"So what are the chances you'll get any handicapped linesmen?"

The registration clerk mulled it over. "I guess you can have it for now. That could change, though, with the weather. Been a bad spring for storms. They say they're still coming, too."

Sarah slid the signed registration card across the counter. Her energy-draining morning had fully caught up with her. A nice, long shower would certainly help.

But time was of the essence. "Is there an open breakfast place anywhere, or someplace to get coffee? Is Shelley's open?"

"The diner's flooded out. Same with the deli. There's our continental breakfast, but it's pretty picked over by now."

At least it was some form of sustenance. It would have to do.

She crossed the lobby and inspected the buffet. The remains consisted of various combinations of over-processed carbohydrates, salt and lard. The best she could salvage was a dried-up white bagel, a packet of semi-cool cream cheese, and soupy-looking coffee.

She found her way to a chintzy table. The compact vintage television nestled in a far corner was tuned to flood updates. Despite the chaotic damage parading across the screen, local landscapes were immediately recognizable.

Dad was hanging out somewhere in that mess. Maybe he was settled in someplace, starting up a game of cards. That would be his style.

Clues. How are clues found when you don't have a client sitting in front of you?

"You're looking for your father?" At the next table sat a prim middle-aged woman, surrounded by an entourage of well-worn travel gear.

"Sorry. I didn't mean to think out loud. We're trying to figure out where he got to. You looking for family, too?"

"I'm here for disaster relief. Just got off the red-eye."

Yes, all those traveling disaster relief bunches the radio announcers had kept talking about, rather than getting to something useful. She stepped up efforts to peel open the stubborn packet of cream cheese. She stopped to check the expiration date.

"People scatter after disaster." Her breakfast companion got up and filled a dented travel mug with coffee dregs. "They keep heading further out, until they find a vacancy. Or stay with people they know. It's almost always very temporary. Most go home as soon as they can. Even when it means completely rebuilding."

"It's just as well, as far as Dad's concerned. I've tried to talk him into building something new for years. Last I saw, his house was practically falling apart around him. It's a great lot, there on the river. He could have something really nice if he tore it down and started over."

"There are websites where people can post their disaster status. Have you looked yet?"

"Dad thinks computers are a bunch of 'hooey'." The lukewarm coffee passed her lips. She grimaced. At least it was caffeine. "He doesn't even use email."

"Could he have decided to go your direction? Where you live?"

No way. Dad would never lower himself to enter "Sodom and Gomorrah," no matter how desperate the situation was. "He'd call first."

They continued to track the flood programming as they finished their meals. The stream of new footage seemed interminable, peppered with reruns of the most dramatic scenes. Thankfully the media hadn't been around to record and broadcast her own misadventure.

"So many homes," said Sarah. "Nothing this big has happened around here—that I know of, anyway. Those people they're talking to . . . they're all the same. In a daze."

"That's usual, after a disaster."

"You do this a lot?"

"It's my specialty. I'm helping the locals with their mental health response.

"Small world. I'm a clinical psychologist. Sarah Turner."

"Lacey Wilson." They clasped hands.

Lacey was slow to release; a wave of scrutiny passed. Sarah couldn't shake the feeling she'd passed under some kind of barcode scanner, that somehow her inner turmoil was now out in the open. She swallowed. "Um, is there anything else I should know about finding a missing evacuee?"

"I understand there's a shelter up and running. They might know something."

Getting there was more of a challenge than anticipated. Detour signs, roadblocks, and standing water ruined any chance of simply following her nose along old habitual routes. Lacey's vehicle was still visible in the rearview mirror, creeping along. Though by now, Lacey probably regretted taking up Sarah's offer to lead the way into town.

As they rounded a corner a large U-Haul came into view, backed into an empty lot. A couple of yahoos were unloading things out the back. Townspeople milled around, watching and kibitzing.

She scanned the crowd for Dad. He didn't appear to be among them. He'd fit right in, though. Putting in his two cents always was right up his alley.

A honk sounded behind her. Lacey was signaling to turn into the lot. Sarah sighed and turned in as well.

"As long as we're passing through, I'd like to get the feel of things out here," said Lacey. "Once I'm tied up at headquarters, I might not get another chance."

It was too hot for sitting in the car and waiting. She should probably head to the shelter on her own. There was no telling how long Lacey would want to hang around. She didn't seem the type who would have trouble fending for herself.

But something about the scene attracted her. Something she couldn't put a finger on.

Sarah got out and followed Lacey, joining the crowd clustered near the truck.

A small scrappy-looking worker with a paper nametag—"Steve" in big block letters—was peering into the truck. "I seen some shovels in here before, if you can wait for me to get back a ways," he said to somebody. He disappeared into the truck.

It would likely be a long wait. Steve seemed like a nice enough guy, ready with good intentions. Too bad he made his way about it with the speed of a tortoise.

The sun beating up the back of her neck was relentless. It was going to be a scorcher.

How did I get myself into this? She stepped away, seeking shady reprieve. The old lot was different, more level than she remembered it. Almost completely defoliated as well, no doubt thanks to the previous day's inundation. The sun drew a putrid smell out of the mud, a reminder of the pig farms upriver.

Then she saw it: that old snowball tree, alive and well. The one Mom was always sure to point out whenever it went into bloom. That was what had beckoned her out of her car, and dragged her into a pointless stroll.

She never did figure out what Mom saw in that tree that was so fascinating.

Mom. She ignored the tug of her heartstrings. Yes, she still avoided it. She didn't deny how she stuffed feelings about her mother's passing, even though it had been almost two years. But it happened right when she was finishing up her schooling, getting licensed, and setting up a practice. If she'd allowed grief to have its say, everything would have gotten off track. Maybe fallen apart altogether. Mom would not have wanted that.

She turned away from the tree and refocused on activity near the truck. The supplies looked mainly for cleaning purposes: Clorox, brooms, rubber gloves, buckets. A nearby table was piled high with snacks, bottled water, and other drinks. Some token gesture fruits and granola bars were thrown in for good measure.

Sarah opened a bag of Cheetos and nibbled. The surrounding neighborhood felt so familiar. Yet at the same time, distant. Not just because of the flood damage. Everything felt like a caricature of home, as if she had landed in the middle of some Looney Tunes version of her reality.

The Cheetos tasted like sawdust. She gave up and dropped them into the plastic garbage bag. There was a tap at her shoulder.

"Come on." Lacey gestured toward their vehicles. "We're just getting underfoot here."

The high school looked quiet. Out front, Elspeth Goode was sweeping the stairs. When she noticed them the broom stilled. She folded her arms and stiffened, her gaze locked on the disaster vest Lacey had put on.

So Elspeth was still a pain in the butt. *How fitting to run into her first.*

"What can we do for you?" Elspeth stood at attention, as if guarding Fort Knox.

"Hello, Elspeth. It's me, Sarah."

Elspeth paused and blinked, apparently needing time to consider such a claim. She pushed her glasses up her nose and looked Sarah up and down.

"Why, Sarah Turner. You're back! Look at you, all grown up now. So styled-up, I didn't even recognize you."

"This is Lacey Wilson. We met at breakfast this morning."

"Nice to meet you, I'm sure." Elspeth forced a smile, still clinging to the broom positioned between them.

"Perhaps you can help me out, here." Lacey acted oblivious to the undertones. "I'm looking for the disaster headquarters."

"It's at city hall, right down Main Street here. You can't miss it. It's not like it's Los Angeles or something."

Lacey followed Elspeth's curt gestures, glancing toward the main part of town. "Have you been assigned here long? I could really use more detail about what's been going on the last few days."

Elspeth took the bait. As always she had plenty to say, and little hesitance in saying it. Lacey and Sarah listened with dutiful attention, asking questions here and there as Elspeth went along. Unfortunately none of what she was saying would help Sarah get any closer to finding Dad.

While Elspeth continued her monologue, Sarah's gaze drifted toward the school grounds—they seemed so friendly, and familiar. Yet a million miles away.

Why does everything seem so unreal?

When her thoughts returned to the present, she noticed that Lacey had scribbled all over a notepad. Somewhere along the line, Elspeth had thawed into animated enthusiasm.

The standard interviewing tactics Lacey was using were fully recognizable. Seeing them applied this way—under the guise of gathering practical information—was something new, however. Dual purposes served. It made sense. Practical, even.

Making such an observation felt somehow settling, reestablishing her within the familiar: her profession, and the drive to heal that had sustained her over the past eight years.

She was back on track.

"You've been very helpful." Lacey flipped shut her notepad and dropped it into the front of her disaster vest. "Looks like you've got a first-class operation here. Are there any bumps in the road I can help smooth over? What do you have for mental health support?"

"Paulson Forbes comes every evening. He lives here, too. He's doing a wonderful job."

A local mental health professional? There'd never been health care providers of any sort in this out-of-the-way hamlet. Not in recent history, anyway. A piece of local scuttlebutt to catch up on.

Elspeth went in search of contact information for Paulson. As they followed her into the building and neared the shelter area, voices could be heard—a couple snapping at each other, a child crying—not unlike what had appeared in the morning television clips.

Sarah recalled some of those interviews. Many people had been too upset to choke out an entire sentence. She braced herself for the worst.

But instead of finding a sea of traumatized victims, the shelter contained only a sparse scattering of residents, far fewer than the thundering hordes she'd anticipated. Where was everybody?

Making an assessment without looking too obvious was no easy task. Casual observation scoped a few people who looked somewhat dejected.

Eventually a sense of their uncertainty filtered through, becoming almost palpable. Empty stares here and there reminded her of her own clients. The flood victims would likely face similar life struggles, especially as they slogged through early stages of loss. It didn't matter whether it was the loss of a home or the loss of a loved one; a loss was a loss. Had there been any deaths because of the floods? She hadn't heard of any yet.

An especially distressed child eyed her, sniffling and clinging to her mother. Otherwise, the scene felt absurdly low-key. Most residents didn't even take notice of them.

And why were there so few? Especially with reports of so many residents being chased from their homes. There were only a couple dozen people on site, at most.

The weirdness of it threw her off. Plus, there was no crowd to disappear into. She felt exposed, so out in the open in the large room. How should she act, what was she supposed to do, when entering a place like this? Crisis situations, crisis intervention—that was doable. She could help with it, if need be. This was just . . . whatever it was.

Lacey advanced like a deer entering a meadow—ears at attention, sniffing the air for smoke or predators.

"Is this how shelters usually look?" she whispered to Lacey, following close behind. "The ones on TV are more crowded. People are more . . . active, and noisy. Really upset. Nobody here looks particularly panicky."

Lacey gave a sideways glance. "I suppose it depends on what you call panic."

"You know, running around and screaming. Not knowing what to do."

"Panic can happen during the more active stage of the disaster. But what you're talking about—that was more likely frenzied behavior than panic."

"There's a difference?"

"Yes. You can feel frenzied and still be effective, or goal directed. Panic is more of an empty-headed state; it's all limbic system. It comes up in crisis situations when people don't see solutions, or feel hopelessly trapped. The immediate threat is, for the most part, long gone for these shelter residents. Right now most are probably out finding solutions to their predicaments, or tending to day-to-day needs. Taking care of business."

Right. "That's not how it is on TV. Or the Internet. Everybody always looks too overwhelmed to go on. I see a little stress, here and there. But

KEEPERS SEARCHING FOR SAM

unless you look closely, this doesn't seem all that different from setting up for a bake sale."

"Panic sells." Lacey looked away, her brow knitted. "That's why we hear about it. It's an unfortunate reality of disasters. The behavior of those who don't cope well stands out, even without the media there to accentuate it. In fact, some people do panic during these situations because they're led to believe it's the normal reaction. But panicking can mean tragic consequences—the big screen doesn't tell that story. If a panicky 'the sky is falling' instinct were the natural human reaction to crisis, how did our species survive this long?"

Lacey's proposition made sense, even if it did run contrary to intuition. It further complicated the growing challenge of gaining solid footing. She'd been misled, somewhere along the line. What else did she believe about disaster that was only myth? *Blasted media.* This one deserved a Facebook post.

"People are resilient," Lacey continued. "In truth, all of these people are heroes, not victims."

"Have I just walked into a lecture?" It was an attempt at humor. A last resort, given she was beginning to feel too far out of her league to contribute anything intelligent. But it came off as rude. That was not what she had intended. The whole thing was getting to her.

"There's plenty more where that came from." Lacey went on as if she hadn't noticed. "Right now, I need to get checked into my assignment. Stop by headquarters later on, if you'd like. They might have some information about your father."

"I'm going to check Dad's house first. He might be doing clean-up by now." At least there was a headquarters she could consult with if the riverside visit didn't pan out.

Overall, the few hours spent with Lacey were unsettling, a mixed bag. Sarah felt even less prepared to take a look at the old neighborhood than when she'd started out. Not just because of possible dangers, but because of her new uncertainty about instincts. Which ones could she trust?

At the cafeteria door she turned, stealing a last look at the disaster survivors. They were still mostly sitting around, waiting for God knows what. Such a long, tough road lay ahead of them.

It was beginning to look like it might be the same case for her.

CHAPTER TWO

"Sarah, wait up! We've got years of catching up to do." Elspeth bustled down the walk after her.

Definitely not on the agenda. "I need to work on finding Dad. Where's Chet? Is he back at his house yet?"

Chet's tract house had been a ramshackle fixture across from Dad's for all of eternity. As far as Sarah was concerned, it could go any time, flood damage or not. It was situated further up the bank than most, so chances were he had escaped the worst of it.

"He's probably there. Tell him hello for me. Now, don't you be a stranger."

The delight Elspeth seemed to find in the chance encounter was bewildering. She'd always been the town busybody, sticking her nose where it didn't belong. She'd endlessly harassed Sarah and her buddies when they were youngsters. They couldn't get away with much of anything. Mom would receive a phone call long before Sarah got home with a twisted spin on how things played out.

Could it be Elspeth wasn't aware of what she thought of her? Or how she felt about the entire community, for that matter. There were so few secrets to be had in that in-grown town.

She jostled along over the potholes, eventually finding her way onto the one lane detour into the old neighborhood. As the bottom of the hill approached, she slowed down.

Carnage burst into view. The closer she got to Green River, the more dreadful the evidence of spillage. Memories of her friends' houses, childhood play areas, and hide-and-seek cubbyholes were now only that—memories.

Uneasiness curbed the curiosity that had gotten her this far. She had not mentally prepared for so much destruction. Nor had she expected it to matter. Soon, the status of her own childhood home would loom before her. What would she find?

She changed course and instead drove onto the gravel leading into River Rest Park. It wouldn't hurt to make a quick stop at this former play setting. At least that was the rationale that sold the idea. She knew she was only delaying.

The once beautiful nature reserve, however, was now a sea of mud-coated lawn. Random piles of tree remains dotted it as flotsam, blocking most of the view of the river. The sputter of a chainsaw occasionally interrupted the silence. The eager beavers tending to debris removal looked both miniscule and ineffective given the mammoth task before them.

She got out of the car and made her way to the shoreline. The humidity, the light breeze, the feelings of expanse and adventure—those were all as remembered. But everything else was off. Her eyes refused to believe the sight before her. Somehow she'd tumbled into the hole of the White Rabbit.

She looked across the river. On the opposite shore, a dingy sea of brown swept across the once-familiar panorama. It looked almost like someone had sketched a new shoreline and then messily erased it. The side of the river she stood upon probably looked the same from afar.

Such devastation. Such mud-spackled despair.

The lack of natural sounds was eerie. Even the calls of waterfowl were absent. Apparently they had moved on, the habitat too inhospitable. Only an occasional breeze broke the silence, winding through the hollows and whistling between sweeps of hills that had failed to keep Green River within its bounds.

As she rounded the bank, she caught a glimpse of a familiar rocky bulkhead. As it jutted further into view the "Monolith" became the first sight to grant her any feeling of homecoming.

She lowered herself onto a smooth indentation near the water's edge, a platform where she and young friends had so often frolicked. The sun-warmed rock oozed strength, its stability so dependable.

Thoughts of the hollowed-out area directly behind it stirred a grin. So many different roles it had played, especially in the midst of teenage shenanigans. It was an invitation to daydream. How things used to be.

Thanks for the staging area, old buddy. Her fingers rose to her face, brushing against her lips. Her first real kiss. Jimmy Orton, ninth grade. *What ever happened to Jimmy? And what about his mother, Sylvia?* She lived so close to the river.

"Good morning. How's it going?" A man and woman were making their way toward her. They wore disaster vests similar to Lacey's.

"Okay, I guess." She swatted at a pestering insect. "Nice morning. Except all this."

They exchanged chitchat common to strangers making friendly in a strange setting, until the newcomers switched gears into semi-formal questioning. Sarah continued to come up with polite responses. But as the grilling progressed, she found herself observing them as intensely as they appeared to be examining her.

What in the world were they after? Lacey had been a lot more hospitable.

"I see you have an out-of-state car license," said the man. "What brings you here?"

"I grew up just down the road. I'm checking on family. Have you seen Sam Turner? His shop burnt down. He's my Dad."

Their formal reserve evaporated. Neither of them had seen Sam. An awkward silence followed.

"Sorry about all the questions," the woman finally said. "During big disasters, looters tend to turn up. It's like they make a regular living of it. We've already had break-ins around town."

As if these people didn't have enough on their plates. On the other hand, it was yet another collection of complete strangers turning up in the middle of nowhere at the drop of a hat. Helpers and looters, both.

Don't people have lives to tend to?

Yet it did raise a new concern. Was she at risk, wandering around in a torn-up and largely deserted neighborhood? Burglar types could be dangerous, if she happened to run into one. She'd been gone so long she couldn't say for sure who belonged there and who didn't.

"We wish we could make it all go away, but of course we can't," the woman said. "So we do what we can to make recovery go a little easier."

Or was it more like not being able to pass roadkill without sniffing it over. What motivated people to do this? It was one more piece of oddness in this situation, something previously unheard of that she could not easily make sense of.

"There are responders here helping with family situations like yours," said the man. "There's one going around in this neighborhood. We only just met him ourselves. He seems nice enough. He's a counselor. Do you want us to send him your way?"

She brightened at the idea. Anyone who did counseling in a given area would be likely to have in-depth understanding of what was going on around town. Finally, someone who could help her gain a little traction.

"Please. Send him along." She told them which cross streets to look for.

After they left, she wondered if the street signs would still be there to guide them. In fact, in view of what she'd seen so far, it seemed doubtful anything that flimsy would have survived.

Stop stewing. They surely had some way of figuring out how to get around. At least, hopefully somebody around there knew what he or she was doing.

As the Miata reentered the mangled roadway, the wind picked up its forlorn howl, battering against the convertible soft top. By the time she pulled up to the parcel of land that supported her first home, riverbank houses were nowhere to be seen.

Including Dad's.

Gone. All that was left was a spear of foundation sticking up out of the mud. Right about where her bedroom had been. That was it.

As she scanned the river's edge, it took her a second look to accept that the great willow was truly gone. It had been there forever, a primary fixture in their day-to-day lives. She'd seen many photos of it throughout the years, the earliest depicting the tree as a shelter for romantic picnics.

After she and Nate toddled onto the scene, it served as a support for swings and, as they grew older, became a Tarzan-style diving apparatus. Practically a member of the family. Now there wasn't a trace of it, not even the piece of bank that had supported it.

Even those old photos were probably gone now, washed somewhere downriver.

The sight was repulsive. There was nothing for instinct to take hold of, to reconnect. Just about everything that had ever been on the stretch of Iowa riverbank was gone. Forever.

A large form lumbered into view.

"Hey, Sarah. That you? Sam never said you got a Miata. Sure is pretty. Fire engine red. Bet it put you back a few G's. Well come on, you gonna get out of there, or what?"

The sudden surge of affection for her informally adopted brother brought her back to the present. Still, she felt numb as she stepped out onto clay and gravel, almost as though she were walking in a dream.

"It's great seeing you." Chet circled her car, running his hand along its side and over the trunk. "Nate told me you were coming. He's been real worried, you know, with Sam missing and all. What a great car. A little on the small side. Okay for a person your size, anyways."

How Chet got from one topic to the next was an ongoing puzzle. It was as if everything that went through his head simply printed itself off and rolled down off his tongue, like some kind of miskeyed cash register receipt.

"Have you heard anything more about Dad?"

"Nothing new here. The fire chief . . . he still doesn't know what started that fire." Chet dropped to the ground and began inspecting the car's underbelly.

"But it sure burned hot," he called from below. "About the only thing left is the storage room. By the time the firemen got there, the rest was too far gone to do nothing."

Chet pulled himself up and put a hand to the hood release.

"You mind?" He popped it open without waiting for a response.

"Mostly they had to keep the fire from spreading to that old warehouse," his voice echoed from under the hood. "That's where they're keeping supplies for flood victims. We got us a real big-time production."

She glanced at the time. Between his fascination with her car and the collection of flood stories he'd most likely stored up, she could be standing around all afternoon. There was no way she could interrupt. It ran the risk of having him start over from the beginning. She waited for him to run out of words.

"How about Dad?" She strained to try to see whatever was producing the shrill screeches coming from near the engine. "Where have you looked so far?"

"I been all over, every place I could think of." Chet slammed the hood and turned the bill of his Cavaliers cap to the rear. Sticking his head through the driver's side window, he began to manhandle various bells and whistles. "I talked to Stewy this morning. He doesn't know nothing, either."

He leaned in further, completely filling the small window.

God help us if he gets stuck in there.

"It don't make no sense." The small car his upper body was now wearing muted his booming voice. "Sam would tell somebody if he was going to leave town. Wish he had a cell phone, but you know Sam. I couldn't live without mine."

He interrupted the vehicle appraisal mania to search for an archaic handheld, prying himself from the car with unexpected dexterity. He held the phone out to her, glowing with pride.

She strolled away with the piece of electronics and tried to look interested in it. The bit of redirection worked. He followed her onto the muddy lot, rambling on with his accolades for the miracles of modern technology. Interspersed were reports of people he'd talked with, and places he'd looked for Dad. In spite of his haphazard approach to problem solving, it sounded like he'd hit all the bases. At least, everyone she had thought to get in touch with.

Why was she even here? It was becoming more and more ludicrous. Was there anything more she could do, other than bother the people Chet or Nate had already spoken with?

Where are you, Dad?

At river's edge, they suddenly noticed a shovel sticking up out of the ground near a dug-up area.

"Well, I'll be." Chet wrapped pudgy fingers around the handle and peered into the hole. "I bet that's where Sam found that piece of junk he was hauling around."

"Piece of junk?"

"When he stopped by the shelter last night. He had it stuck under his arm, like a prized piglet or something. Looked like everything and the kitchen sink, all welded together. Never did figure out what it was. I took a picture on the phone."

Sarah pulled up the photo. There he was. Dad. A little less of that silvery hair than when she'd last seen him. Those grey-blue eyes, same as hers, except for his trademark stoic look—his idea of a smiling expression. He had on the same style of blue denim coveralls he'd labored in as far back as she could remember, his own personal uniform.

If only I'd gotten here sooner.

In front of him, Dad was holding out a strange-looking contraption. It looked wet, the way its metal parts sparkled in the sun. The mechanism was attached to a rectangular wooden base, maybe a foot and a half long. The medley of metal gadgetry looked to be a similar length in height. Off on one side was a handle-type device. She couldn't figure out what it was, either.

"That . . . that was the last time I saw Sam." A quivering lip silenced Chet.

Sarah stood on tiptoe and gave him an overdue hug.

Guilt pangs stabbed at her. She'd been so wrapped up in her own concerns, she hadn't even considered how Chet might be handling Dad's disappearance. He depended so much on Dad, essentially Chet's substitute father. Dad had informally adopted him many years ago, choosing to support this seemingly abandoned young man—who was admirably managing to get along okay in spite of his marginal developmental disability.

While comforting Chet, she spotted a man walking along the shoulder of the road. He appeared to be looking at them.

"Somebody's coming. Do you know who he is?"

Chet looked uphill, sniffling and wiping away moisture. "That's Paulson. Paulson Forbes. Hey, you ought to get to know him. He does counseling, like you. Except he goes door-to-door. Helps anybody. Everybody. Can you believe it?"

Weird. She'd never heard of such an approach to community mental health. How in the world did he handle informed consent? Something sounded off about it.

As the man got closer, she made out a scruffy-looking hippie type. He wore minimal disaster signage. A beat-up pack was slung over one shoulder.

This, apparently, was the local mental health support. *You've got to be kidding me.*

"Hey Paulson! This is Sam's daughter, Sarah."

She kept her guard up, simply returning what was offered as a warm handshake. Paulson looked a little older than she, by maybe five or ten years. His smile seemed genuine enough. Though the scraggly hair and uneven growth covering the lower half of his face didn't leave her inclined to take him seriously. The glob of sunscreen still clinging to the back of his wrist didn't help too much either. Overall assessment: a professional train wreck. If he even was a professional.

"I understand you're looking for your father," he said.

"Yes. You know him?"

"Sam was one of the first people I met when I moved here. He talks about you and your brother all the time."

I can imagine. A wave of uneasiness passed. It was that invasion again, her personal status coming under scrutiny—this time, even more intense than Lacey's barcode scanning routine. He had such penetrating brown eyes, so dark and deep. It was as though he were looking directly into her head, or her soul. It kind of creeped her out.

"I was there at the fire, at his shop last night."

She came to attention. "You saw him? He was there?"

"No. But I was at the shelter when the fire first started. He could have been at the shop early on, then left. I can ask around, if you like. Someone will know."

His accommodating manner didn't set well. It was like he was almost too friendly.

Misgivings took the place of the idea of teaming up with him. He would take time to figure out. Was he really a counselor, or maybe some kind of con artist? He could even be a looter for all anyone knew.

It siphoned more mental energy than it was worth. She had enough mystery to figure out.

"Well, thanks anyway." She turned to Chet. "Can I borrow your washer? I was out of town when this happened."

*****

Sarah turned down their offer to lend a hand. They watched in awkward silence as she struggled to get a large designer suitcase out of the small trunk. She dragged it along on its squeaky wheels, dodging the chunks of asphalt, puddles, and potholes leading up to Chet's.

"You ain't heard nothing?" The concern gushing out said more than Chet's words. "Nothing, at all?"

"Lots of theories and gossip. Nothing you could hang your hat on." Paulson continued to watch Sarah walk away. She looked so stiff, so strained. Floundering.

"I wish there was more we could tell her. Here she's come all this way." Chet's eyes continued to plead. He looked more like an expectant five-year-old child than the mountain of a man Paulson had to shade his eyes to look up at.

"I know you're all worried about Sam. But there's absolutely no sign he was in that fire. They've been sifting through ash all morning. They would have let you know by now if they'd found anything. They're also checking to make sure it wasn't arson."

"Who'd want to go and do that?" An indignant scowl joined the pleading. "Go and burn down that poor old man's building. He just lost his house."

"Ruling out arson's probably standard procedure. All the same, be ready for gossip. Some think it's the work of the Schwartz brothers, or maybe some other trouble-making kids. Others think Sam got careless with candles or kerosene. Then, of course, there's the 'burnt it down for the insurance' theory."

Chet fisted his hands into cannonballs before landing them at his hips. "Sam loved that place. He'd never burn it down."

"Don't give it a thought, Chet. It's just gossip. But I thought it might be better if you heard it from me—before Elspeth or someone else gives you an earful."

Chet's hands slowly dropped, his shoulders sagging, nothing like his usual unsinkable enthusiasm.

Getting him up and moving around wouldn't hurt a bit. "How's cleanup going?"

"Just a little mud, is all. Others got it a lot worse. Sylvia lost almost everything. Roy took the squad car out to her house, did you know? When that flash flood came. He rescued her out of there, just in time. She didn't want to go. Kept saying that house was all she had. Figured she was going down with it, I guess. Can you believe it? That's what Mildred said, anyways. Mildred has a big mess at her house, too. What with Harold's bad back and all, it's going to be a while before they get things set to right again."

"Maybe you could lend them a hand. It's certainly a worthwhile way to pass the time. It might help to keep busy while you're waiting for word on Sam."

He cheered up as swiftly as he had dropped into the dumps. "That's a great idea. You know what? Maybe by now, they've heard more about Sam."

Chet prepared to climb into his pickup. "Wait. What about Sarah? Can you let her know?"

Paulson watched Sarah through the grimy garage window. He knew very little about the petite woman. As he watched her fill the washer, he wondered why she hid her natural beauty under so much big city coif and makeup. She didn't look much like Sam, save for her blue-grey eyes. Her chestnut hair must have come from her mother's side.

Sam had told him she left Marshland to pursue her career a few years back. How much had urban living changed her from the girl she used to be? It was clear that this was still her home by the ease with which she interacted with Chet. Yet at the same time, her obvious uneasiness with strangers, such as him, suggested a level of distrust that was hard to believe had always been there.

He tapped on the window and waved. Sarah looked up. She visibly sighed, completed what she was doing, and opened the door. Distracted coolness met his eyes.

"Chet said to let you know he's at the Heesackers' helping with cleanup." The message sounded rushed. *Could have done that better.* He added a quick nod as a goodbye, and would have been done with it then and there. But then an alternate Sarah sprang to life.

"Aunt Millie was flooded? Are they okay?" The suddenness and intensity of her outburst—it sounded more like the panic of a child finding herself abandoned in a strange place.

"They're fine."

She'd revealed to him a vulnerable side, completely out of the blue. He held back the urge to place a hand of comfort to her arm. It probably would not go over well. "You know them well?"

"All my life. Mom and Aunt Millie were like sisters."

A flurry of questions spilled out. He told her what he knew. Once she was satisfied about the Heesackers, she went on to ask about others who lived by the river. She certainly didn't have any difficulty with assertiveness, at least when it came drawing out whatever information she was after. But, at the same time, she also seemed sensitive, and caring, especially as they talked about common acquaintances. He liked her. Yet below the surface this unease, or irritability continued. Like she had some kind of chip on her shoulder. More like a plank.

Of course. She's city folk now. Here she is, standing around in a garage with a man she's never seen before, in a deserted disaster area. "It's a bit dark and musty in here. Your laundry seems to be going okay. How about if we move outside?"

They found seating on a pile of rockery and continued to trade information. But the change in venue didn't do a thing for the distancing. She was attentive, and polite. Tolerant. Otherwise, a million miles away. It almost felt as if she were living out life in her clinical stance. It wasn't hard to see she was a mental health professional. She so naturally took a pulse of the town.

Yes, their collegial connection. That's the ticket. "I hear from Sam you're a psychologist."

"Yes, Dad does have his ideas, doesn't he?" Her back went ramrod straight, her eyes hardened. The snap of the transition could have knocked him over.

What had he just stepped into? He hurried through a mental review of their conversation—what he had missed, or done wrong.

She continued to bristle, as if preparing to fend off an ambush.

He took care with his words. "He didn't tell me about the type of work you do." Maybe she was a rat psychologist, or number cruncher, or something else other than a clinician. "What's your specialty area?"

"Bereavement. I'm affiliated with a hospital." The terse response made clear that his lost ground was only drifting further into the hinterland. Her rigidity held fast, if anything intensified.

"Uh . . . that would sure come in handy working with disaster survivors." Surely they had common ground in there, somewhere. "What have you noticed around town?

"Actually, I've been thinking more about how to find my father." She stood. "You know, I think I'll go check with the fire department. Thanks for filling me in." She forced a mechanical handshake, turned, and left.

Went over like a cow pie at a bake-off. Maybe he'd have another shot at it later. There had to be something to crack through that shell. She was clearly hurting. She did have plenty to be worried about. There was no reason to take her aloofness personally. Even if he did feel slighted.

He checked in with his team leader and jotted down a few notes about the next referral. Thoughts of the shaky conclusion to the encounter with Sarah lingered.

Since when did he ever have such dismal failures to connect? Professionally, or personally.

That was it. A blow to the ol' ego. She was in fact attractive, though she'd look better if she didn't work so hard at it.

It was just as well. With everything else going on, that kind of complication would only get in the way. Especially with someone whose personal charm was more like burnt toast.

*****

He didn't deserve that. She veered the car away from Chet's house and moved onto the damaged roadway.

Whatever Dad might have said about her wasn't Paulson's fault. Actually, once he started talking, he didn't seem as suspicious as his dubious appearance suggested.

How did he manage to fit in, anyway? Chet seemed right at home with him. Then again, Chet was like that with anybody.

She rejoined Main Street and crept the length of its mundane skyline. How many times had she skipped along that old plank walkway? A quarter hot in hand, off to see what kind of treat she could buy at Uncle Harold's store.

The old Baptist church, the Hidey Hole (a local beer joint), Vic's Antiques and Collectables (aka the junk store), and the single-pump filling station, recently inherited by Elspeth—so many familiar sites coming into view as she drove further into town.

Flood-streaked vehicles were nosed up against the curb. If she were lucky, Dad's pickup would appear somewhere in the lineup. She slowed her car down as she passed the hardware store, the Grange, and anywhere else Dad might have stopped in. Once that faded tomato-red relic came into view, the mission would be completed. This disconcerting trip down memory lane would come to an end.

At Harold's Grocery and Deli the "Closed" sign dangled in the window. Paulson had mentioned it was only because of the flooded grounds. Uncle Harold planned to reopen soon.

Paulson. Once again a reminder of him had interrupted productivity, distracting her from forming an effective search strategy.

His very presence in Marshland . . . what on earth was he was doing here? Yes, there was mental health work to be done everywhere. But why move to Marshland, a half-empty hole in the wall? Was he a masochist at heart? Coming here to practice meant practically hiding out from civilization, from professional society. Though this was probably the only place in the world that would let him get away with his concept of professional demeanor.

And if he's such a write-off, why is the hand he touched still tingling?

She lifted a sweaty palm from the steering wheel and gave it a good shaking out.

Just creeps me out.

*****

"Stash 'em, and we'll get 'em later. Real great idea."

"Give me a break. It went fine until that geezer came along. How was I supposed to know he'd lock it up?"

"*Easy pickings* you said. Yeah, real easy. Except we can't even get at any of it now."

"Relax. We'll find a way. Things will settle down, then we'll make our move."

"What about the old guy? There's word around town he's missing. His name's Sam, Sam Turner."

"I already know who he is."

"Anyways, there's talk going on. What if somebody thinks to hook up what we been doing with that? I didn't plan on that kind of rap."

"People like to gossip. Let them."

CHAPTER THREE

The scene at the shelter had painted such a haunting portrait. Memories of it refused to stay tucked away. The charged atmosphere was certainly understandable. The pit of her own stomach rippled with every new piece of disaster fallout she stumbled into. The shelter residents had actually lived through it as it happened.

It reminded her of a client, Mrs. Abernathy, when she was early on in her therapy. She was well-transitioned now, thanks to over a year's worth of hard work. For both of them. The Abernathy's financial situation became a nightmare when her husband passed. She'd lost much more than her life partner. Especially after her black sheep of a cousin turned up and raided the house for photos and family heirlooms. Squabbles over the spoils ruined relationships that otherwise might have served to support. Sarah sat through hours of tears that year, listening to Mrs. Abernathy repeat and update the impact of her losses. Working it through, then working it through again from yet another angle, as life predictably found its way of revealing gaps where something once had been part of Mrs. Abernathy's life.

It had been one of her most difficult, yet rewarding cases. Both she and Mrs. Abernathy had risen to the challenge. The client moved on. And she got to revel in the fact that therapeutic intervention does, in fact, make a difference in people's suffering.

But the emotional carnage at the shelter—this was a community disaster. The whole town was reeling in loss of one sort or another. How do you know where to step in, or how? Was there something different about how to proceed? Maybe that was what Lacey had been doing with Elspeth. Was that a standard procedure? As far as that went, what constitutes appropriate standard of care, especially when the entire support system is affected?

The Can-Can sounded even more ridiculous while cruising downtown Marshland. It was Nate. She parked in front of the fire department and gave him her progress report, or lack thereof. Nate said he'd already been in touch with both the fire chief and the sheriff. Nothing new to report at his end, either.

So stopping at the fire department was just one more piece of redundant effort. *Blast it all.* There had to be a more efficient way of getting this done and over with.

"They went ahead and listed Dad among the missing, but don't seem particularly worried," said Nate. "Marshland had plenty of time to prepare before the flood, so there were few physical injuries, certainly no known deaths. And it's only been half a day since he was last seen."

"How do they know there aren't deaths, if everybody's not accounted for?"

"They say it's normal to take a while to figure out where everybody is. That most missing people are usually unreachable because they're holed up somewhere until the chaos is over."

The sheriff and chief of police were probably right. But from what she'd seen here, not to mention her own private episode of the *Perils of Pauline*, there was no way she could just set it all aside and go home. She needed reassurance first. She needed to find Dad alive and well. That was the first priority—despite feeling increasingly annoyed with his inconsiderateness.

"I saw Chet," she said. "He's asked around at usual haunts. It sounds like he checked all the nearby motels, too. Where else could he have gotten to?"

"Beats me. They say they'll notify us if they hear anything. I guess we just wait. With everybody wrapped up in flood work, I suppose it'll be a while."

"Nate . . ."

"I know it's got to be frustrating out there. Sorry about that. I'm scared about what happened to Dad, too."

"It's more than being scared. It's . . ."

"But it's a relief to know you're there now, to take care of things."

She swallowed her anger, allowing herself to enter the flow of the full picture. Yes, this was Nate. The one who had always depended so on their parents for guidance and ongoing emotional support. Losing Mom had been tough on him, as it had been for her. But for Nate, losing Dad would be an even bigger blow.

Mom . . .

She shook it off. "I'm worried about my clients. Most of them already missed sessions because I was gone for the conference. I can't continue cancelling on them—they'll lose ground on the progress they're making." She did have a business to tend to.

"So send in a substitute."

Sarah sighed. "You can't do that, Nate. I've got someone on hand for emergencies. But he can't just step in and pick up where I left off in the therapy process. It doesn't work that way."

"Don't worry, I'll do what I can to get away. Then you can get back to your clients."

Right. She ended the call.

She was no further ahead than when she first arrived in this godforsaken mess. She had no idea what to try next. Making clients put treatment on hold when her presence here did nothing to further the situation was becoming questionable. Not to mention unethical. So far, phone calls from home could have established anything she'd learned.

Across the street from the fire station loomed city hall. Large signs and banners describing the disaster relief operations in town hid most of the concrete façade. Lacey was supposed to be in there somewhere. Perhaps by now, she'd circulated enough to find out something useful.

Stepping inside, she immediately put a hand to her mouth, resisting the urge to laugh aloud. The meager city government building was blanketed with the same assortment of disaster signage that had been plastered all over the high school shelter. It was like watching *Star Trek* with her mother, those episodes of the Borg coming to roost.

Go this way to find that. Go that way for this. Do not pass "Go." Do not collect two hundred dollars.

Lacey sat at a corner table. A young man was hanging an enormous "Disaster Mental Health" sign overhead. Somebody lying on the floor was hooking up a hard line.

"What do you think?" Lacey motioned her over. "We're up and running."

"I certainly didn't have any difficulty figuring out where to find you." Sarah kept her eyes on the precarious enterprise laboring above. The dilapidated ladder next to her wobbled in concert with the worker's efforts. She grabbed one of its legs and steadied it.

"When lots of people are coming and going, those signs up there are lifesavers. Wait'll you see what headquarters looks like tomorrow, with incoming milling around."

"I was wondering if you've heard anything yet that might help find my Dad." She continued to hold the ladder, but relaxed some. It wasn't as rickety as it had originally appeared.

"I'm still getting up to speed on preliminary assessments. We've certainly got a job ahead of us. Most of the population of Marshland had damage of some sort, or was evacuated. Or both."

"It was an eye-opener, what I saw along the river," said Sarah. "It's no wonder people at the shelter were so overwhelmed."

Somebody shouting a question from across the room stole Lacey's attention. She responded with an exaggerated nod and wave.

They seemed so tightly woven, functioning as a unit by means of mere gestures. Yet she was clueless about what exactly they were coming together to create. It again brought on that feeling of being out of her element, even within her field of credentials. A proverbial fish out of water, in spite of the professional bond she had forged with Lacey. The oddly labeled disaster relief stations added to her sense of disorientation and aimlessness. Some of the tables even sounded rather dire—D-Mort? What was that here for? Bodies? Maybe the report of no deaths was just drivel for the masses.

The busy collective seemed formidable, perhaps even intimidating, so purposeful yet so mysterious. It was as if invisible threads tied them all together, ones they could grasp and maneuver as needed. While she could not.

Snap out of it. Yes, she'd spent the last several hours having the rug repeatedly pulled out from under her, in ways she never would have expected. But all she really needed was to get her feet back on solid ground. That would help her move forward.

This disaster mental health idea—a chance for intervention before pathology settled in—at least that made sense. Intriguing, maybe even fascinating, if she found time to take a look under the hood. After this fiasco was over with, she'd make a point of looking online.

But then, what about the mission of finding Dad? Would it be too late, waiting until she got home? Clues may lie within the field itself, ones that point to Dad's possible whereabouts. Lacey had referred to the operation as the "information pipeline." If so, the notion of making time to look into it had considerable merit. It could be a conduit, a pathway to her goal—and she would be helping those who were suffering. It sped up the process for all concerned. *Get in, get out.*

"So what comes next for you?" Lacey asked her. "More checking around for your father?"

Bringing it up felt awkward. Perhaps there was an indirect way to go about it. How did people pull this off?

"This waiting around is getting frustrating. I sure could use something productive to do." She moved away from the ladder to make way for the descending worker, the sign above now solidly in place.

Another young man brought over a cube-like trunk. He dumped it next to Lacey's table; a harsh thud followed.

"If you have a license to practice in this state, I'd have no trouble finding something for you to do. Just sign on as a local volunteer." She lifted the trunk's lid and peered at the contents. "There'll be out of town volunteers coming in, including for mental health. There won't be enough to go around, though. These storms laid waste to about half the plains states."

"I'd need to know more. I've heard a little about what you do here. Once, a trauma psychologist presented at my practicum. He mentioned disaster mental health. But I don't have any real training. What exactly do I do? I know grief reactions. What I see most here, though, is trauma. Fresh trauma, not what's still there later, when people decide to seek therapy."

"What we do with it is not the same as our private practice, either." Lacey set out an unending succession of office supplies. "Unfortunately, just as you experienced, it's not standard curriculum for most graduate training." She set a stapler on top of a stack of file trays.

"If it's a specialty field, what does someone like me do?" It felt risky. Well-intended efforts that are off the mark could do more harm than good.

"I have materials that describe the differences." She tore open a cello-wrapped packet from the trunk and slapped a manual onto the table between them. "If we run into heavy lifting, we refer to local health care. Our job is to be supportive, to teach self-care. Keep an eye out for crises. Step in if it makes sense. But like I said earlier, resilience takes care of most of it."

Sarah skimmed through the manual. Basic, clear-cut stuff. Band-aid therapy. Hard to believe it was enough to do any good. "At the shelter, they did look in need of a listening ear. Even a few of the responders did."

Lacey lifted a goofy-looking stuffed monkey from the trunk. She paused to smile at it.

"Yes." She set the toy on the corner of her table, facing outward. "This mission is not for everybody. You could run into survivor issues of your own, especially with your father missing. People around town will want to talk about your situation. You need to feel comfortable with that."

"I grew up here. I'm used to lack of privacy." Though in all fairness, she hadn't considered that angle. In Marshland there would be no hiding out in anonymity when she needed solitude, the way she could in the city. Her life would be an open book again.

Lacey leaned in, muting her voice. "It's only fair to warn you. I'm going to keep very close tabs on you. It won't take long to figure out whether this agrees with you, or if it's too much. It may even feel like you're doing too little. That can be the more difficult of the two."

Lacey abandoned the unpacking. Her barcode scanner appeared fully reactivated.

It was probably hard to keep much secret from Lacey.

"My mother insisted I get licensed here. We were close, you see, and she . . . she always hoped I'd come back here someday."

The newly installed telephone jangled into service.

"My first call. We really are in business now."

Thank heavens. The disruption of the test call gave opportunity to swallow the surge of sentiment that always bubbled up at the mention of her mother. Lacey was right. There was emotional baggage. Even if it wasn't the type Lacey was thinking of.

She had never been in the middle of mass crisis, either. What was she supposed to do, with whatever it was she found? Not just for clients. What about her own unpredictable emotions?

Until now, her field of practice and her place in it had felt so safe, so certain. Her job had been clear: just do what fits the current standard of care and help hurting people. But in this strange and chaotic setting, would she get it right? Or would she do harm?

Maybe this was a mistake. She should study disaster relief more first, on her own.

No. She had to find Dad. This would help lead the way. She certainly couldn't think of much else to do to succeed in this task.

Then there were those survivors at the shelter—their neediness, how some had looked so lost. This wasn't happening in the impersonal big city, with multiple resources and ongoing strategy for inherent challenges. It was in her own hometown, where the community had less. Where Dad was, somewhere. At the very least, joining in held out a thread of hope for finding him. She needed the inside track of the relief operation.

Sarah gulped. "You know what? This is just what I need. How do I sign up?"

"Thanks for volunteering. We're fortunate to have you, with your background."

"In some ways it feels like an adventure. Something really different." No sense in trying to hide feeling like a novice. Lacey would figure her out soon enough. If she hadn't already.

"It is really different. For you, my greater concern is whether you feel settled with it yourself. It's an issue of competence."

My mental health competence? "It's not a problem." Sarah fixed a steady gaze on Lacey. "If I wasn't here, I'd be practicing back home. I'm fine."

"Good." Lacey offered a thin smile that lacked much conviction. "All the same, know that if it gets to be too much, you can always back out. Life happens, personal reactions happen. It gets in the way of our 'A' game. While you're at it, keep in mind that the need to make that kind of judgment call crops up more quickly in disaster."

When she turned up the driveway, Chet was pacing and talking to himself in his open garage.

"Sarah!" Obvious relief. "Good. You can take care of that laundry. I just got back from the Heesackers'. They sure got themselves a job there. Mud everywhere. Their sliding glass door got shoved right out. It's unbelievable."

It didn't take long to figure out the reason for his disheveled look: she hadn't finished handling her clothing. Especially her "delicates."

"I'll take it with me and finish it at the motel. I'll need it tomorrow. I'm going to help out with the disaster operation."

"Hot damn, Sarah. That's great. You know, I was thinking the same thing. I met some great folks so far. At lunch, I met up with some boys from that warehouse. Most of 'em didn't even know each other before they got here. The way we was all jawing and laughing, you'd think we'd known each other all our lives.

"This guy Steve, down there at the flood station, he gave me a new shovel. No charge. And all the Marshland folk that already knew how to help out with disaster, before it even got started. Who'd have thought? It's amazing. There's something for just about everybody. If you don't mind getting your hands dirty."

"Gee, Chet. Maybe you should consider volunteering, too."

Chet's wheels turned in predictable directions. "You know, you talked me into it. Thanks, Sarah." He went inside to finish cleaning up, strutting with the sureness of a man on an important mission.

Don't mention it. She gathered laundry from the washer and replaced it with the assortment of gamy-smelling clothing Chet had dumped in front of it.

Afterward she offered to fix Chet a home-cooked meal. Kicking back and enjoying a little downtime sounded sublime. Not to mention it was a chance to get used to the dramatic change of scenery outside of his front window—Dad's almost empty lot. She could sit, relax, and let the past several hours settle. The memory of that roller-coaster ride into the elderberries was still giving her the willies.

Unfortunately, Chet had his heart set on the shelter cafeteria. "Everybody can come eat there, anytime. You should meet these guys. They're great! A lot of people you know will be there. Didn't you and Shelley's kid hang together in high school? Shelley's doing the cooking, you see, with the diner flooded. Everybody'll be excited to see you. And, I'd sure like to have a ride in that car of yours."

A grand reunion with the greater masses of Marshland was hardly her option of choice. There was also the issue of whether Chet would fit into her small car's passenger seat.

She was exhausted. That briefcase full of disaster relief materials Lacey wanted her to look at was still sitting there, too. But she was hungry.

The cafeteria was full. Chet squeezed in with a group of disaster workers congregated at a far table. Abandoned, Sarah looked around for the possibility of a table to herself. No such luck.

She circled aimlessly with the supper tray, uncertain where to land. It seemed oddly haunted—high school days intruding into the present, eyes persistently drawn to places she and her friends had typically sat.

I never should have come here.

A hand waving from the center of the room caught her attention. It was Lacey, bringing her back to current reality. Sarah eased through the dining hall and took a seat across from her.

"Sure is a full house." Sarah raised her voice to be heard above the echoing chatter.

"The shelter residents are back. Visiting disaster workers are turning up. Apparently this is the only place in town that can deal with so many people at once."

Sarah sampled the food. Spaghetti and meatballs were not a bad choice for feeding a crowd. Lil's mom, Shelley, hadn't lost her touch.

"I've been giving thought to where to place you tomorrow. In the afternoon, there's going to be an informational meeting for anybody who's interested. Always hard to say who will turn up. These community meetings can get really spirited. So we're sending a few mental health people to hang around. It'll be a good opportunity to assess how people are doing in general. I'll send another worker or two to go with you. What do you think?"

"It sounds . . . interesting." Hopefully those handouts Lacey gave her were thorough. What exactly did a mental health professional do in such a scenario? There wasn't likely to be privacy. Therapy, in the middle of a crowd? How did that work?

Before she could comment further, the empty chair to her right slid away. A beat-up backpack hit the floor next to her.

Paulson set down his tray. "So you got the special of the day: Spaghetti Monday. Just like the diner. Pretty good, huh?"

She scooted aside to make way for him to wedge in. As if she had any choice.

"Paulson and I connected at headquarters a while ago," said Lacey. "He's been bringing me up to speed. Operation leadership says he's been doing a real bang-up job."

Sarah forked up hurried bites of the remaining pasta.

"I've assigned Paulson to the meeting tomorrow as well." Lacey's eyes flickered, her bar code scanner blipping in the background. "He's got good rapport here. He's giving a self-care talk."

Sarah called up a suitable show of polite professionalism. "I look forward to hearing it."

"Opportunities for this come few and far between," said Paulson. "I'm looking forward to it, too. I'm glad you're joining us. People have heard you're in town. I've run into a few who said they'd like to say hello. Some of them are here now."

Sarah obliged him, reluctantly looking up from her plate. He was right, of course. A number of familiar faces dotted the crowd. But the idea of being caught up in a homecoming ritual felt more like making time for a root canal—without the Novocain. Especially after Lacey had pointed out, rightly so, that some would want to talk about her father. There was so little she could say. These days, they probably knew more about him than she did. It would only mean repeated episodes of those useless conversations with Nate.

Yet there was always a chance a clue about Dad would turn up. Even if she was wiped out, she shouldn't pass on the opportunity. *Whatever it takes.*

By the time they finished their meals, she'd led Paulson into believing he'd shamed her into a quick tour of the room. She made the best of it, poking around for anything useful regarding Dad's ill-mannered disappearance.

"Hey, Sarah. Your daddy ever figure out what the heck that contraption was?" Bob Asher asked. He and his wife, Dora, were long-time "river rats," as she and friends had always referred to the trailer park residents.

"Not that I know of, Mr. Asher."

"Too bad about his shop burning down the way it did."

A heavy arm suddenly landed across her shoulders. "So where you been all this time, hon'? You get yourself some of my pasta?"

Sarah whirled around, finding herself up against Shelley's plump but sturdy frame. Her return embrace burst from within, with not a hint of hesitation. How alarming, that it still felt so natural. Shelley's steadfast strength was so comforting.

"How are you, Shelley? And Lil. How's Lil?"

"We're doing good, all things considered. You're here helping Sam? I heard about the misfortune with his house. His shop, too."

"We haven't hooked up yet. Do you know where he's staying?"

"No, I've been pretty tied up here. Cleaning up at the diner, too. Took on a bit of water. I'll keep my ear to the ground, though."

As the guided tour continued, others shared similar sentiments and offers. As an information-gathering strategy, it was a waste of time. Nobody said anything she didn't already know. As predicted, they all seemed to expect her to provide grist for the rumor mill—which from all outward appearances had shifted into overdrive. Thank heavens she'd had the foresight to ask Stewy to keep her own mishap under wraps.

They eventually arrived at Chet's table. After tolerating lengthy introductions to his dinner companions, including sensationalized testimonials of how great they were at disaster relief, she and Chet left.

*****

Paulson returned to Lacey's table.

"Okay, so what was that about?" Apparently Lacey couldn't even sit through dinner without deteriorating into supervisor mode. And she hadn't missed a trick.

"What?" He blinked at her with a half-baked show of innocence.

"When I asked about taking Sarah under your wing, you didn't mention there was some kind of discord going on. What gives?"

"When we first met she was . . . lukewarm. Brittle, actually. Guarded. I'm not sure what it was about. Could be disaster stress. Maybe she's just a loner. Time will tell. I'd still like to help her out. I thought taking her around to say hello to a few people would be a good start."

"She didn't look particularly receptive." Lacey ran a doubtful eye over his failing subterfuge. "Are you sure this is going to work out okay?"

He squirmed in his seat. "Sure. I've dealt with much tougher customers than this."

"For now, I'll take your word. In the middle of all the *sturm und drang,* however, please keep in mind this one has an edge. She's one of us. If you do anything that looks like digging around or 'therapizing,' she'll see right through it." She paused, other obvious doubts rattling around unsaid. "Post-traumatic growth is what I predict for this one, not pathology. Let her work it through. I don't have to remind you this is an unusually sensitive situation you're picking your way through. Do I?"

"No worries. I'll watch my step." Though it wasn't going to be easy, between Sarah's crispness and Lacey's invasive scrutiny. Not to mention his lame ability to manage his attraction to Sarah. Once again it had had him fawning over her like a schoolboy.

"Please don't make me regret this," said Lacey. "I do agree with your approach, though. She could use a few buddies right now."

Evidence of a full day of appreciation littered the corner of the cafeteria set aside for play. A couple of children still occupied one cluttered table, caught up in a coloring project. Paulson, halfway under the table, had twisted himself into a pretzel to join a boy propelling a metal hotrod with racing noises.

"Paulson, guess what?" Excitement carried Bob Asher's voice across the shelter. "We're going home!"

He and a few staff members were supposed to get the evening off so they would not end up putting in another fourteen-hour day. In fact Lacey insisted on it during her condescending lecture on early burnout. She'd assured him that a newcomer was lined up to cover for him that evening.

But as the supper crowd thinned and the shelter culture reemerged, the temptation to hang around was too hard to resist. He was part of it now, a piece of their story, working through their horrible experience and getting on with their lives. Leaving the shelter without checking on how they were doing would leave too many loose ends.

"They just told us," said Bob. "The water's gone down. We can get through. Still don't have no power, but what the hey. Not that hospitality here hasn't been great," he quickly tacked on.

Paulson pulled himself off the floor, brushing away dirt mixed with food crumbs. "No offense taken. Who'd want a cot in a crowded room when they could be home in their own beds? Does Dora know?"

"Not yet. She'll be so excited. She's been fretting about her houseplants, of all things. Have you seen her? We need to get a move on before dark. Otherwise there'll be a heck of a time seeing our way." Bob scanned the room, his eyes not lighting on what they sought. "This ain't right. Where in the world did she get to?"

Out of nowhere, Elspeth was in their faces, as no one else would dare. "Well, you could ask me. I'm the only one who keeps track of anything around here."

"You know where she went?" said Paulson.

"Why, of course. She said the trailer park entry was open. She was going to check on things by herself." She folded her arms and glared at Bob. "Seeing as 'Bob was still out gallivanting around somewhere'."

Paulson leaned out a cafeteria window and scanned the collection of parked cars for the Ashers' battered pale blue Chevy. It was nowhere to be seen.

"I wish she waited. We don't know if our trailer took on water or mud or what. Who knows what she might run into?"

"When did she leave?" Paulson asked Elspeth.

"It's been a while. An hour, at least."

"I can run you over, Bob. If you don't mind the open-air seating." A chance for a spin on the dirt bike while also doing a good deed—it didn't get much better. Lacey's observation about his needing a break was not just her paper-pushing fancy.

"I'd be obliged. I hate to think she might come up against something. Maybe the road wasn't so safe after all. What if she got stuck?"

They set off toward the river. Dodging multiple detours, Paulson gave up and took a short cut over open terrain. By the time they reached the trailer park, the excursion had them as beat up and mud-spattered as the rest of the flood aftermath.

The Chevy was parked in the strip of gravel above their lot. It fit right in, flood grime not differentiating the car much from its usual state. Bob hurried down the dirt path toward the aging singlewide he shared with Dora. Paulson followed.

The door was already open, swaying in the surges of humidity. The garden gnome that usually stood sentry at the base of their rickety porch had rolled a few feet down the rocky slope. He gave in to a whim, taking time to gather it up and return it to its station. He stood back and admired the result, appreciating the sense of getting things back in order. The gnome itself appeared undamaged. Those things were practically indestructible—kind of like the spirit of these river residents. It was little wonder that half the lots in the shoddy trailer park had one out front.

By the time he got to the doorstep, Bob was already inside and calling for his wife.

"You in here, sugar plum? I've been looking all over for you."

Paulson stepped into the stifling heat of the tin enclosure and peered down its length. In at least one respect, Bob and Dora had been lucky. There was no evidence of flood damage. But their home had been ransacked. Kitchen drawers were on the floor, upside down. Cabinet doors hung open, a number of shelves scooped clean, with contents lying wherever they'd landed.

"Bob?" The floorboards creaked as Paulson continued toward the sound of Bob's voice.

"Dora, wake up. Wake up, sweetie. Come on, now." Bob was kneeling over her, holding her hand and patting it lightly.

She was not moving. Her body lay across their bedroom floor in twisted disarray, like a Raggedy Ann discarded by a bored toddler.

45

Thankfully he could see her stomach rise and fall, a good sign. In the shadows was a glimpse of crimson, a splotch of blood. The gash puncturing her scalp was barely visible from where he stood.

He forced himself to ignore the gut punch. "Dora? You okay?" He knelt next to Bob.

If Bob had noticed the blood, he hadn't shown it yet. "I knew she shouldn't have come here by herself."

"Don't move her." Paulson looked around for a compress, and pulled out his cell phone.

CHAPTER FOUR

Tuesday, June 3rd

By the time the shelter's breakfast buffet was set, news of Dora's fate had dispersed throughout the entire community, among disaster victims and relief workers alike. There didn't seem to be much dependable information, outside of the initial discovery. As usual, the gossip tree was producing considerable fruit to make up for this fact.

Sarah got the main gist from Paulson as they made their way to the DMH desk, dodging a flock of newcomers. He looked like he'd already been there for some time. He also looked more disheveled than the day before. As he shared the finer details of his adventure with Bob and Dora, she realized that he'd probably never made it home at all the night before.

Dora hadn't regained consciousness yet. Tests were being run, and it was still unclear what had been taken from their home. Bob was holding vigil at the hospital. Other residents returning to the trailer park had discovered additional break-ins.

This new development turned out to be the main feature of Lacey's morning briefing, which increased the look of tension among the newly arrived faces.

"The investigators are considering the obvious—that Dora stepped into a burglary in progress. We're reminding everyone to use common sense. If you come to a home with an open door and nobody answers, don't go sticking your head in. Call the authorities immediately. As always, safety first."

The recruits nodded, doing what they could to digest the news.

"This is the first time I've ever done this," the volunteer sitting next to Sarah whispered. "Does this sort of thing always happen?"

"You're asking the wrong person." Sarah's first reaction had been alarm, followed by a stab of fear. Was it possible her father had been similarly attacked? But he'd been fine the day after the flood—both Nate and Chet had spoken with him. The house was already long gone by then.

Nonetheless, she'd already spent one nearly sleepless night worrying about his whereabouts: was he was safe, or injured or stuck somewhere? Now she had other terrifying possibilities to consider. What if he interrupted a burglary at the shop, and the burglars set fire to it afterward to hide the evidence? And stole his truck for their getaway?

And what about her own safety? Was it advisable to be out wandering around in this risky chaos? She'd already had one close call.

Stop being overdramatic. You're fine.

She still hadn't checked out what remained of the shop. Somehow during the day, she'd make time to get over there. That was a promise.

"Paulson Forbes was up and at 'em before the first raindrop fell," said Lacey. "He'd like to fill us in on what he's been seeing. Paulson?"

A few questioning glances passed among the group, no doubt due to Paulson's scroungy appearance.

He also looked a little pale. Dark circles underscored those peculiar eyes, which at the moment suggested they'd seen too much. He gave a heartfelt account of his activity to date.

Paulson really did appear to care about these people; he even seemed to consider them friends. She couldn't imagine what it must have felt like to be with Bob at a moment such as last night's—how hard it must have been to discover a terrible crime like that together.

The episode made her think of the shelter residents again. So dazed, and so traumatized. No doubt they too had shared numerous stories about flood-ravaged homes and destroyed lives. What was it like for him to hear about loss after loss, tragedy after tragedy, and only be able to be supportive and nothing more? Unlike her normal day-to-day routine, this mass trauma situation did not allow for delving into comprehensive work and long-tem care. And from what she'd seen, it didn't look like DMH workers got much downtime between cases.

When she first met Paulson, the very existence of his credentials seemed questionable. What he had just shared left no doubt about his legitimacy. Including how well he knew her hometown, and what was happening in it right now.

Then . . . there were his experiences with her. What had it been like for him, dealing with her? Someone who kept brushing him off? He was only being friendly. The same as he was with everybody. She was probably the first mental health colleague he'd run into since it all began. How would it feel to have absolutely no peers to consult with during something like this? Even with Lacey here to guide, she felt lost at sea in this mess.

He really hadn't done anything wrong. He was only a little different. It wouldn't hurt to be more generous. More tolerant of diversity.

It was not a choice. Her conscience wouldn't leave her alone if she did anything less.

If only she could get past those blasted eyes.

*****

Nonstop interviews laid waste to his morning. First Paulson spent hours speaking with law enforcement types, then with the disaster operation bigwigs writing up the incident, who seemed mainly interested in finding creative ways to paint his involvement as benign. Then, finally, he had to sit through yet another long phone conversation with the clinic director.

He felt like he'd told the same story about nine hundred times. When everyone agreed they were finished with him, he darted out the back of city hall, before anybody else's curiosity could coerce him into another retelling. If all went as planned, his lunch hour would be spent staring into a corner with his mind on hold. With any luck, he might even be able to sneak off for a quick nap somewhere.

After loading up his tray he scoured the cafeteria for a place to hide. The wave of a raised arm caught his eye.

Was that Sarah? Sarah, waving at *him*?

He checked behind himself. *Nobody.*

He turned back, tilting his head and pointing a finger to his chest. She nodded and motioned him to join her.

This about-face was certainly out of the blue. What had he missed?

"How did training go?" He eased into the chair across from her, searching her face for an explanation.

"Good, very informative. I follow trauma research for the most part, but I'd never heard much about how it's used in disaster. It makes all that dustbowl-dry literature a little more connected to reality."

"It reminds me of ER work." Safe conversational territory, while he figured out her sudden change in attitude. "Supporting and triaging. Getting people whatever it is they might need to get through their crisis."

"You worked in an emergency room?" The question came from one of the other DMH recruits at the table.

"I worked with a hospital for a while, up in Detroit," said Paulson.

"What brought you to Marshland? Do you have family here?"

"No. I read there was going to be a position opening up in a new public health clinic here. I decided to try something different."

Sarah's lingering gaze let him know that he not been successful in dodging the issue.

Just what I need. The one topic he'd rather avoid.

He'd started it, though. What had he been thinking? He really did need to get that nap squeezed in, before he screwed things up beyond repair.

"Your ER experience explains why you kept such a cool head last night," said one of their tablemates. "I probably would have lost it, right then and there."

"There sure are a lot of people here," said another. "All of them have homes damaged or destroyed?"

"Not everybody had material losses," Paulson said. "But one way or another, they're affected. Everyone in the community is. That's the beauty of these feeding stations. They provide both food and a place to gather. It helps people reconnect."

He shared any details coming to mind that might help them out with where they were going, or what they would be doing. By the time the cafeteria began to clear most of their tablemates had successfully tracked down their teams and gotten on their way. He and Sarah remained.

"Lacey says we're the only ones she can spare for this afternoon's meeting," she said. "I guess it's just you and me."

He momentarily froze at the double entendre. Was that for real?

Or maybe just wishful thinking getting out of hand. "We're spread pretty thin. You can imagine what it was like when it all started. I was the only one doing this."

"I would have been in even worse shape. I'd have no idea how to begin." She leaned forward on her elbows, still a different Sarah. For once she sounded sincere, maybe even interested.

"Back when I took that disaster training, I never dreamed I'd end up going it alone in a major incident. Lacey says that's not so unusual in the beginning, for isolated areas at least. I had a lot of hairy decisions to make. What's most important? Who's going to have to wait?"

"Is that what it was like in ER? I never worked that angle. For me, it's usually after the fact. Or with slowly developing situations."

He sighed. So it was only a mining expedition, an attempt to get back to the one topic he didn't want to get into.

"Most of my work involved patients who'd already been through triage. You know, we really should talk about our game plan for this meeting."

Her ears pinned back at the abrupt change of topic.

That came off pretty damned blunt, dude. He pretended it was nothing and forced a smile. "How should we manage it? Should we stand together and greet people in a specific designated place? Or separate and monitor different parts of the auditorium?"

"We split up." She gathered up her emptied dishes and eating utensils. "Makes the most sense to me."

"Works for me too."

She got up and gave her chair a shove toward the table. "Sounds like a plan." She picked up her tray and was gone.

*****

"What'd you have to go and hit her for? She was just a dizzy old housewife, not hurting nobody."

His partner leaned back in the rickety wooden chair. He propped his feet on a stack of boxes and let loose a stream of cigarette smoke. He studied the cloud in silence, its end swirl looking like a nuclear explosion.

"Cute, real cute. Doesn't none of this nag on you, at all?"

"I didn't mean to hurt her. I only meant to push her away before she saw me. Then get the hell out of there. I had no choice. She would have recognized me the second she turned around."

"Why didn't you put on a hoodie or do something to hide your face, like I told you? That way you'd only have to run."

"It was too hot out. Besides, the park was on mandatory evacuation. Nobody was supposed to be there. Who'd I be disguising myself for? Security? If one of them turned up, my goose would be cooked anyway, disguise or no disguise."

"What if you killed her? This is getting crazy. When I said I'd help, the worst you said we'd do is mess up a few homes—just a little B&E. FEMA and house insurance would take care of everything. Why weren't you more on top of goings on?"

"So why weren't you? I brought you into this because of your supposed experience."

"I been trying to tell you what's important, but you're not listenin'."

"Look, things happen you can't predict. It makes no difference what business you're in. Don't worry about it. She'll recover, and when it's all said and done, that trailer trash will come out further ahead than they ever were."

"What about Sam? What happens with him?"

"You're still checking in on him, right?"

"He's staying put. But who knows what he saw? You fixing to do him in, too?"

"One thing at a time, Mother Teresa. Don't borrow on trouble that doesn't even exist yet. You've a point though. Too many people are around now. It won't hurt to start thinking up an exit plan."

*****

The trickle of attendees began to arrive a good half hour early. Paulson stood near the right-hand entry. Sarah stayed to the left. They greeted those who entered, introducing themselves and making small talk.

Between arrivals Sarah paced, not so much because of task anxiety as feeling disgruntled over her attempt to connect with Paulson. All she did was ask about his hospital work, one of the things they had in common. It was a natural conversation topic. In fact, he was the one who brought it up. Yet her innocent questioning sent up a barrier as formidable as a Klingon force field.

It had to be his past. It was obvious something was there, something he didn't want to talk about. At least, not with her.

She sighed. Standing around and watching people enter felt like being a greeter at Walmart. Was her presence truly going to help any of them? Nobody needed professional skills for this. Maybe she should be doing more.

But she'd bite off her tongue before she'd seek clarification from that bundle of contradictions loitering across the lobby. She'd received the message, loud and clear, back at the cafeteria.

She briefly considered the option of asking everyone who came through if they'd seen her Dad. But if that didn't constitute conflict of interest, what did? She was there to support them, not the other way around. Lacey's concerns about the state of her mental health were becoming painfully obvious.

Newcomers continued to trade polite greetings and move on. Thankfully at least a few asked questions about Dad. It gave legitimate openings to surreptitiously probe for more information.

On Paulson's side of the lobby, real conversations started up. He was right at home with everyone, and segued seamlessly into whatever people wanted to talk about. Everyone in town seemed to know him. Even some of those coming in on her side of the lobby were eventually drawn his way.

It's as if I'm not even here. The longer it went on, the more it grated.

She was the one with the extensive background in grief and bereavement, not Paulson. As far as that went, she was also the one who grew up here, the legitimate Marshlander. What about all those years she'd been the star pupil, won the science project awards, got voted into student leadership? Not to mention she was one of the few in the area who'd gone on to do graduate work. Had she really changed so much that she was unrecognizable?

She glanced down at her conference garb—a smart combination of one of her better business suits, a silk shirt, and her classiest black heels. Paulson had somehow found time to change into serviceable Levi's, an olive green polo that had seen too many washings, and high-end athletic shoes. One step up from the dusty scrounge look.

She thought back to the newcomers at the training. They had been dressed down as well, more casual than standard office attire. Maybe she should forego the blazer.

She took it off and hung it over the back of a nearby chair.

An excited Chet appeared and headed toward Paulson before noticing her. When he turned her way, he puffed out his chest and pointed at his official paper nametag.

"Guess what? I'm helping out at that warehouse now. What a great bunch of guys. Great boss, too. He goes around doing this all the time. You wouldn't believe everyplace he's been. Even Puerto Rico. Twice, he says. And I found out my forklift certification's still good. I get first dibs at the new one."

"It sounds wonderful."

"Now you're here, too. Never thought we'd both work for the same outfit. You get to work with Paulson, too. Isn't he great?"

"He's been . . . very helpful." On short notice it was the best she could do, as far as saying something both socially acceptable and truthful to describe their increasingly odd relationship.

"I figured I should come on down and hear this. Maybe they can help me with my shed. It got washed away, all together. Even all the tools. No sign of them. They might be able to help with Sam's house, too. With it being gone, you know. Since you're here now, you can let Sam know what all to do when he gets back."

His bright-eyed simplicity shined back at her. Apparently somewhere along the line, he'd found a way to assure himself that Dad was fine, and would soon return. She, on the other hand, was increasingly less certain. How easily Chet made peace within himself—in complete denial that anything bad might have happened. Perhaps he was right.

However, his comments raised new concerns. Was Dad's house insured? Surely it was.

Well, no, she didn't know that for sure. It was something else to bring up the next time Nate called. There might be good reason to listen in on this talk, rather than go nod off in the car until it was over. "I may join you, once they get started."

"You bet. Come sit with me."

"Of course." It was a good excuse to not sit near Paulson.

New arrivals continued to crowd the cramped lobby. Most were taking advantage of the opportunity to compare notes with neighbors. She did what she could to make her spying on Paulson inconspicuous. However, her eyes immediately shot up when he and a group of young men looking just off the field all burst into laughter.

Why in the world was she so bothered? She couldn't think of any situation where she felt so aggravated over nothing.

"Little one. I can't believe it's you." Her second mother was beaming at her.

"Aunt Millie." She wrapped her arms around her.

Uncle Harold, strolling in from behind, extended his considerable breadth to give the two of them a second-layer hug. "Welcome home, hon'."

"Chet told me you were here," said Aunt Millie. "Just look at you. All grown up and professional looking. Your mama would be so proud if she could see you."

Her throat tightened. The last time she'd seen Aunt Millie had been Mom's memorial service. She gulped at the swell of emotion. Then stuffed it back where it belonged. Professional demeanor went on autopilot while they exchanged stories of flood damage.

"You'll have to come by soon. After I heard about your parents' house, I looked around for some of my old photos. I found pictures of it. Some others, too, of your family over the years. I'll make copies. I ran across some fun ones of me and Jane in high school. So you come. We'll go through them. And you can get us caught up on this exciting new life of yours."

"I'd really like that. I'm working with the disaster, though. I don't know exactly what I'm going to be doing yet."

"Whenever it works out. All you have to do is call."

Before Sarah could bring up the topic of Dad's whereabouts, somebody turned up the microphone in the auditorium.

"We're getting ready to start." The voice of Mayor Schwartz boomed over the clamor. "Y'all out in the lobby. If you're joining us, come in and get yourself a seat. There's still plenty of room."

Sarah and Mildred quickly exchanged phone numbers, as the three of them moved into the seating area. Sarah worked her way down the aisle until she spotted Chet.

"See, what'd I tell you?" Chet slapped the back of the empty seat next to him. "Sure glad you're listening in. Anytime ol' Mayor Schwartz gives a speech, all I hear is a load of backslapping and handshaking, except with a bunch of fancy words, instead."

She smirked in agreement with his highly accurate estimation of their long-time mayor.

Luckily for participants, the mayor had decided against revamping the forum into a campaign for his latest reelection bid. Before he introduced the FEMA rep he delivered a rah-rah spiel about how Marshland was going to come back from the brink of ruin and soon would be better than ever.

Eyes rolled among those sitting nearby. Grumbling arose here and there, too. There had to be a story behind this. Something to quiz Chet about, later.

The rep's presentation mainly focused on the details of federal disaster assistance. Sarah was surprised to learn that standard home insurance generally didn't cover this type of damage. Those who didn't have flood insurance probably weren't covered. Another disaster after the disaster. Hopefully Dad had had the good sense to prepare for it. Nate would know.

As the speaker moved on to implications for businesses, she shot occasional discreet glances. Where had Paulson gotten to, what was he doing? She finally spotted him on the opposite side of the auditorium, toward the back. He was standing in the aisle and leaning against the wall, arms folded. Looking around the room, just as she was.

She snapped to attention, materials reviewed during the wee hours coming to mind. *Of course.* She was supposed to be doing mental health surveillance, not just sitting around.

Just then he caught her eye. He nodded, releasing a hint of a smile. She looked away and tried to appear occupied.

Blast it all. What was it about that guy that kept getting to her? It was those darned eyes. Somehow they always left her feeling naked.

This is ridiculous. She shifted uncomfortably in the squeaky theater chair. She checked the time.

The speaker opened the floor for questions. Several hands went up.

He pointed to Harold, who then stood up and began speaking. "Most of the hard-hit homes were downriver from the end of the levee. People in the Highcastle neighborhood did just fine. Are we finally going to get some help extending that levee?"

"What happens in the way of rebuilding depends on what your community decides is best, and what your local government applies for."

The auditorium-wide grumbling returned.

"What is everybody so unhappy about?" Sarah whispered to Chet.

"It's those developers. They got their own ideas about the riverfront, and who all ought to be there. Folks know they got the mayor in their pockets. Ed Schwartz and Todd Goode go way back. Sam always calls them 'the Muhammed Ali's of self-interest'."

Sounded like her father. Leave it to Dad to call them like he sees them.

As questions waned, the speaker introduced Paulson and the self-care presentation. Paulson stepped up to the podium amid polite applause. After an unsuccessful attempt to adjust the microphone, he removed it from the stand.

"Thank you." He moved about freely, no sign of nerves. "Now I know most of you have already heard much of what I'm going to say. No fancy new rocket science. What we're dealing with here in the flood aftermath is simply a unique situation, something foreign to Marshland. But by all pulling together, we can cope just fine, the same as always."

He went on to deliver standard messages on caring for self and others during times of stress. Some of it sounded like it had come from the materials Lacey had given her.

However it was his presence that brought it home. He was a master at holding the audience's attention. At times they seemed almost hypnotized. They laughed after he said something about Stewy's pigs breaking loose, an incident that surely had a story behind it. It would have been nice if he'd elaborated. She could use a good joke about then. Something else to ask Chet about.

His connection with the town again underscored her feeling of disconnect with it. She was now more an outsider, looking in. She felt almost as though she no longer belonged there.

As he began to wrap up his speech, she excused herself. She returned to the lobby and prepared for the post-meeting traffic.

.

CHAPTER FIVE

She had a long wait. Following the mayor's closing remarks, side conversations took over. The audience was slow to make its way to the exits. In fact, Paulson had elected to stay behind and mingle in the auditorium. One more judgment call she'd apparently blown.

She could always follow his lead and traipse back in, to where the people were.

But, no. The lost sleep was catching up. She was tired, perhaps too tired to trust herself to do right by anybody. Especially if it meant applying a form of intervention she had yet to figure out how to do. Fantasizing about tiny motel soaps and cable TV options had considerably more appeal. It was time to call it an early evening. Maybe she'd get lucky, and the cable at the Lone Pine would oblige her with a few classic reruns. That would settle her nerves.

Eventually people drifted into the lobby. The talk about financing disaster recovery did not appear to have instilled much hope. If anything, they seemed more uptight than they'd been to start with. The laughter and light-heartedness of their arrival had evaporated, replaced by somber discussion.

Voices at the other end of the lobby rose above the general murmurings. She moved closer to their origin as the dispute continued to escalate.

"This wouldn't have happened if you'd listened to us." An angry farmer stood nose to nose with Mayor Schwartz.

Some older teenage boys, including the mayor's son, were clustered just outside the entrance. They perked up at the sound of the exchange and gravitated toward the action. Others in the crowd gradually surrounded the mushrooming discord.

"The committee members reviewed all the engineering reports before we built that levee." The mayor had adopted a stance of diplomacy—about as well as he was able to, anyway. "This shouldn't have happened. But flash flooding is different than regular flooding. Flash floods make water move in ways we can't predict."

"So why weren't you planning for flash flooding?" The woman's eyes shot daggers at the mayor. "We spent our whole lives building up our property. Now it's nothing but ruins. You could have prevented this."

"I'm really sorry to hear about that, ma'am. We'll do what we can to set things right again."

"No doubt about that," said the first man. "By chasing out the rest of us."

"And good riddance." The mayor's son, cronies in tow, moved in from the periphery.

"You're a fine one to talk, resident psychopath." Another group of questionable-looking teenagers filed into the limelight.

It was looking to get ugly. People on both sides—they all looked just short of a fistfight.

What now? Lacey had sent her and Paulson there because it might get too "spirited." What in the world were they supposed to do? She wracked her brain, going back to the wee hours, what those training materials had said. Clarity was not forthcoming.

She had to do something. Keep from getting caught in the crossfire, if nothing else.

Options. What were her options?

Try to defuse the situation, yourself. That sounded dangerous.

Get Paulson. Let him handle it. Just swallow your pride and ask him what to do.

Call building security. Whoever and wherever they were.

Before she could pursue any option, one boy shoved another. Somebody struck out.

The situation deteriorated into a free-for-all. Screams and angry shouts spread throughout the lobby. People were running and shoving. Some were attempting to get out of the way; others appeared to be moving in for a better view.

She dug out her phone and dialed 911. The emergency dispatcher told her someone else had already called it in. Help was on its way.

Safety first, Lacey had said. She at least remembered that.

She moved along with those choosing to avoid the altercation. As she made it to the vicinity of the exit, somebody crashed through. He pushed between Sarah and the others, jumping headlong onto some combatants wrestling on the floor.

She did an abrupt spin, her head knocking into the doorjamb. She dropped to her knees. She tried to get up, but couldn't, suspended by wooziness. A pounding sensation thudded in her skull, accelerating. There was a warm trickle on one side of her face.

She glanced down. Red dots decorated her favorite silk shirt. An iron taste fouled the inside of her mouth. She clung to the doorjamb as she willed herself to get under control.

The sheriff turned up out of nowhere, with a couple security guards.

Just then an arm appeared and a hand took firm hold of her waist, pulling her up and away from the manic scene. Her knees wanted to buckle. She leaned into the rescuer as he walked her out of the building.

*****

They stopped at the maple tree in the far corner of the school's front lawn.

"Here, sit here." Paulson helped her to the ground. *Don't pass out. Don't you dare pass out on me.*

Sarah obliged. She lay back on the mound of grass and stared upward into the leafy branches. Puffy breezes were softly rustling them.

The retreat into nature was a welcome release for him as well, given what it had taken to push through and get her out of there. He was still out of breath.

He dropped to the ground to help her lift her knees. "Are you okay?"

"Apparently not." She pointed at blood smeared on his shirt.

"Darn. Never did like this shirt, anyway. You don't have any weird diseases I have to worry about, do you?" A little humor—it might distract her from her injuries.

She produced a weak laugh. "Not since I last checked. Unless you count the malaria, beriberi, and that flesh-eating disease they have yet to figure out."

She was making jokes, too. A good sign.

The fire department made its entrance with sirens blaring, soon followed by an ambulance or two. Crowds parted to make way. As the first responders spilled from their vehicles, Paulson waved one of them into their direction.

"Hanging out with you is dangerous," said Sarah. "Though I seem to be coming out of it better than Dora."

Thanks, I really needed that. At least she was coping through humor, a higher-functioning defense. That was good.

He briefly filled in the EMT and stepped away to let her do her job.

He let out a long, slow breath. There was no way around it. Protocol was surely to call Lacey and check in. He had to find out exactly what it was the higher ups wanted him to do next.

Just call me Typhoid Paulson.

*****

"You don't get a choice in the matter." Lacey shoved aside the paperwork piled up in front of her. "You're both off tomorrow."

They had just filled her in on the afternoon fiasco. As per Lacey's instructions, Sarah and Jenny—the staff health nurse—had visited an urgency care clinic in Willsey. Paulson had insisted on tagging along. The small butterfly strip at her hairline called attention to the ultimate result of the day's mishap. But she'd be fine, after a good night's rest.

In spite of what they'd just been through, she, and seemingly Paulson as well, were anxious for reassignment. Though it sounded like chances of that were diminishing rapidly.

"First of all—Sarah. Staff health says you're not fit for duty right now. It's their call. Jenny told me to ground you, for at least one day. I agree. There will be plenty of opportunity to help out later."

Sarah opened her mouth to suggest otherwise, then reconsidered. Exhaustion overpowered the urge to object. The last week had been a nonstop whirlwind, and those muscle relaxants were making her loopy.

"Just don't forget about me. What I saw out there today was . . . profound. So much turmoil. I know I can do something to help. Besides, it's still probably the only way I'll run into anybody who knows where Dad got to."

Lacey's response was motherly and patronizing. "I think your father would want you to take care of yourself right now."

Sarah couldn't recall functioning under such scrutiny since graduate school. Yes, her performance with this DMH business couldn't be described as stellar per say, and her feelings of inner ineptitude at times made her feel like a child. But she didn't need to be treated like a five year old.

Just one more opportunity to prove herself—that was all she needed, just one more. To do something—anything—that actually helped these people, rather than caused new problems.

It could wait one day. "Fine. I'll be here bright and early, Thursday morning."

"Thanks." Lacey turned to Paulson. "Now you, sir, began the day marginally fit. Those double shifts are catching up to you. I had hoped that after your presentation, which I've heard great things about by the way, I could force you to rest. Instead you flung yourself into the middle of the action again, playing superman. Paulson, you've gone above and beyond. You, sir, you need a break."

Paulson gawked back at her in disbelief, despite his obvious exhaustion. "But we're spread so thin. More so tomorrow, without Sarah. You haven't been out there. These people are suffering. That fight at the school is only the tip of the iceberg."

"I understand, Paulson." Lacey became steely-eyed. "This isn't my first rodeo. I'm not questioning your observations."

She waved toward the bulletin board behind her, which was now decorated with clusters of sticky-notes. A number of new staff names were tacked on beneath site labels that hadn't been there earlier.

"We transferred additional responders from an overstaffed operation south of here. They've been turning up since supper. We can easily spare you for a day."

Paulson leaped up from his folding chair; it collapsed and clattered to the floor. "Who do you think you are, to tell me what I can or can't do in my own backyard?" He planted his palms on Lacey's table, the veins on his neck straining.

Sarah leaned to one side, eyeing him. She had not predicted this. Paulson had an explosive, aggressive side? Until now, he had been all Caspar Milquetoast.

"I am the community mental health program for Marshland. I'm all there is here. It's my baby. God only knows what would be happening to these people if I weren't here."

"They need you to be in good shape if you're going to be of any use to them." Lacey pulled out a pad of forms.

*****

How can she be so complacent? So damned dismissive? Infuriation swelled. He at least deserved her full attention for this. "I can do whatever I damn well please, with or without your blessing."

"Yes. That is your right." Lacey started scribbling on a form, acting as if his outburst was nothing to take note of.

Headquarters had hushed.

He looked around. Countless sets of eyes now stared at him. Watching his meltdown. And Sarah—she was busy trying to disguise a look of alarm.

He picked up and reset the chair, unsure how to act. Finally he sat and caught a glimpse of the clock. Could it really be that late? Out a nearby window he noticed darkness was already setting in.

Lacey wasn't off the mark about how drained he was. He'd never had so much trouble realizing when he needed to rest. But how could he rest? In the middle of *this*? She expected him to turn all of his hard work over to a bunch of strangers, people who knew nothing about Marshland or the people who live here. On top of it, many of them were complete rookies at disaster.

His head felt heavy. He let his face to fall to his hands and rubbed his eyes.

Eventually Lacey looked up from her paperwork and acknowledged his existence. "Look, you're doing a great job. I'd like to see that continue. You know as well as anybody that you can't take care of others if you don't even take care of yourself."

"I suppose things will make more sense after I get some rest." What he really needed to do was get a grip. But a little quality sleep wouldn't hurt either. It had been a while.

"Go home, sleep in. You deserve it." She signed the form she'd been playing around with and handed it to him. "Take this to transportation over there and get a car. We need to snap up a few before everybody else gets them. Besides, you shouldn't be using your own vehicles on the job. I'll expect you two to carpool in on Thursday."

"Thanks." *I think.*

*****

"My bike is still at the school. I have to go pick it up and bring it home. Then I'll drop you off at the Lone Pine."

"Don't go to all the trouble. I can take my car."

"You just took quite a rap on the noggin, lady." Paulson was clearly in no mood for compromise. "Besides, Jenny warned you about driving with that medication. The roads are a mess. It's even worse in the dark."

"Fine." Sarah was too tired to argue.

The trek to the lot came to a halt when a couple of workers intercepted Paulson. He seamlessly transitioned into clinical mode, once again showing concern and joking around to lighten the mood. It didn't seem to matter how stressed and worn out he was. He always had time to be helpful. And others were always so glad to see him.

Why didn't she have that anymore? It was as if her entire social network had vanished into thin air. Her graduate school friends had fallen off the radar, setting up camp all over the globe. Her old neighborhood was somewhere downriver, its residents scattered. She hadn't stayed in contact with much of anybody back home, other than family. She still didn't know where Dad was. Nate was just an annoying voice in the wilderness. And Mom . . . *Mom.*

Now here she was, back in her hometown, where people hardly even recognized her. And the more she tried to help with their flooding disaster, the worse she seemed to screw things up.

Paulson finished his conversation and they continued to the parking area. She pulled a little ahead.

I can do this. The know-how is there, how to help these people. Their distress could be alleviated. She was sure of it. She could taste it.

But why did she keep turning into a liability, one more person for Paulson to attend to? A casualty to be taken care of? She had never felt so incompetent, so useless. Alone.

Her eyes began to well up. *Not now. Please, not now.*

Somehow she kept it at bay, plunking herself into the rental car.

Paulson stuck the key in the ignition and then stopped. He turned and touched her arm.

"Are you all right?" Genuine concern poured from those eyes, flowing from the very depths of his being. There was no hiding it. He so sensitively and accurately saw through to her misery.

She broke into deep sobs.

*****

Her shoulders heaved, her torment curling her into submission. He reached up and swept aside the panel of chestnut hair falling into her face—in part to comfort, in part to better to see her.

He'd been so caught up in his own frustration he'd lost track of Sarah's needs. Had he made it all the worse for her, subjecting her to that faceoff with Lacey?

As a therapist, he knew the crying was what she needed just then to get herself through whatever had bubbled up. However, professional instinct was playing second fiddle to his personal instinct—the urge to gather her up, draw her close to him, and find a way to protect her from whatever it was that tormented her. After that run-in with Lacey, the comfort found in holding someone near sounded pretty good at his end too.

He forced himself to ride it out. After a few moments passed, the sobbing died down. She sat back and wiped away tears with both hands. She began a pocket search.

"Sorry to make you sit through this." She dabbed a wad of Kleenex at where her makeup had streaked.

"With everything you've been dealing with over the last few days, I'm amazed at what you've been doing. That you've held up as well as you have."

"Are you kidding? This is pathetic. Look at me."

"We all have our breaking points."

"Not me. I'm not broken. So spare me, please."

He quietly cursed his poorly thought-out comment. This was not a good time for the sledgehammer approach. "My bike will be okay for now. I'll take you back to your motel, and you can clean up. Get some rest. You even get to be first to unload the cheesy-looking shirt good ol' blood-phobic Jenny dug up for us."

Sarah took a long look at what he was referring to—the oversized disaster-themed T-shirts that had replaced their stained clothing. "Yes, here we are. Tweedledee and Tweedledum."

He smiled at her attempt at humor, and started the engine. "It runs! Things are looking up."

*****

They traveled in semi-companionable silence. Paulson occupied himself elsewhere, negotiating puddles and potholes through minimally lit detours. Sarah did little more than stare into space, numbed by a kaleidoscopic swirl of the day's happenings.

She carefully made her way through the dark motel entry—as good a strategy as any to avoid looking him in the eye. *It wouldn't kill anybody to replace a few light bulbs.*

"I'll be back tomorrow." He handed over her briefcase. "We'll get your car out of hock. You probably have a few things you want to get done."

"Sure, why not." She hesitated at the entrance, so drained that even the thought of pulling open a door seemed a mammoth task.

Paulson opened it for her. "How about this. I come pick you up, say, around eleven or so. We'll get lunch. I've heard about this great shelter cafeteria. Or we could always go into Willsey."

She did need a ride to pick up her car. But the other business—where had that come from? "Um . . . " She glanced up at him.

His steady gaze was awaiting a response. Was that a hint of vulnerability? Until now, those eyes had always seemed so knowing, confident and tuned in, even when he was going head to head with Lacey. Then again, his day hadn't been any picnic either.

"All right, yes." She pasted on a smile. "Lunch tomorrow."

"Be sure to call if you need to go somewhere before then."

They continued past registration to her room. "I guess . . . I should thank you, for your help today. So. Thank you."

Paulson continued to stand and face her, silent, as if he too had become depleted by the exhaustion of this extraordinary day. Finally he reached out to pat her shoulder, left his hand there. "You're welcome."

Such intense eyes—how they connected, soothed. A balm for the weary soul.

It was unbelievably kind of him. Here he was, still trying to be supportive, in spite of everything she'd put him through.

"See you tomorrow." She reached up to give him a quick goodbye hug.

He came alive, the look of exhaustion apparently a mirage. Arms pulled her near. Her body answered in kind, hands and arms seeking to reach further, fully encircling those strong, kindly shoulders. That musky masculine scent—there was no way to resist drinking it in. She buried her nose in his shoulder. It was so easy to relax against him, the warmth of his very human presence.

A sigh escaped. *His, or mine?* A hand stroked her back. She pulled in closer. *Closer.*

He withdrew, the suddenness startling.

As he stepped back his lips briefly touched against her forehead. "Goodnight, Sarah."

She felt irrationally cold. Off balance. Confused. All she could think of was going back in time. She wanted to return to that intimate moment and let it go on forever.

She stared down at the warm motel key clasped in her hand, forgetting what it was for. He placed a gentle hand over hers and guided the key into the lock. It clicked decisively in place.

"Thanks." She watched his retreat through the darkened lobby and out to the parking lot. He climbed into the rental car and left.

*****

"Are you drawing attention to us on purpose? What's with this racing in and getting mixed up in all that today?"

"I wasn't going to stand around and let them beat the crap out of him."

"Maybe you should let that kid take what's coming for him every now and then. Might help knock some sense into him about the people he hangs out with. I know all about the Schwartz brothers. And their associations, too. Word is that they're just a bunch of dopers and rabble-rousers, even the ones that ain't in school any more."

"So when did you become a social worker, Mr. B&E?"

"The B&E days are long gone. I had the sense to get out. I wouldn't even be messing with it now if it wasn't for you. And good honest work wasn't so hard to find."

"Yeah, right."

"Turns out that woman that got clocked today was Sam's daughter."

"Now that just breaks my heart. As far as I'm concerned, that high and mighty Turner family deserves whatever they got comin'." He gave it some thought. "I heard she was in town. You know, there's always the chance she has the key to our dilemma. Literally." He laughed at the play on words. "Counting on Sam certainly hasn't been getting us anywhere."

"Now what? We start harassing her too?"

"Maybe you'd like it better if I went ahead and took an ax to that shed, paying no mind to the 24/7 warehouse security ten feet away."

"Course not."

"Just keep an eye on her, Steve. Play it by ear."

*****

Paulson stepped out of the longest cold shower of his life.

What the hell did he do that for? The woman didn't even like him. But there he went anyway, jumping in and taking advantage of the situation. Acting on his own needs.

He had absolutely no business getting involved with her. Not someone this vulnerable, so fragile. Even though Lacey had said "take her under your wing," she hadn't meant this kind of special attention.

It was so easy for people to let that to happen, to let the power differential built into supervisor and supervisee arrangements turn into a tryst. That was why such dating situations were frowned upon. It takes advantage of the little guy. It was one of those rules that actually made sense.

What were they, the two of them, anyway? Other than their supervisory arrangement, he had no idea what to call their official relationship. Should he think of her as merely a coworker? Who is at times also a client? A fellow community member? A friend? Or all of the above?

It had been some time since his last attempt at a serious relationship. Sarah was not the type to be interested in the one-night stand policy that had, of late, become a norm for him. She would be all business about romance—either throwing herself into it completely, or dismissing the notion as unworkable. This situation would require a lot more than a little masculine charm.

He gave up on sopping the water out of his hair and let the towel drop to his shoulders. He was chilled to the bone, in spite of the lingering heat. He sat on the edge of the bed and ran a slow hand along the pleasing softness of the comforter.

He grabbed its edge, yanked it back.

Add in another complication. Her father. What about professional boundaries?

Memories of the past few days slipped in, crowding his already disjointed thinking. He couldn't get the images out of his head, or stop rethinking his actions. Had he done enough to get people out of harm's way? What about Dora? Could he have done more?

Then what would it be like to have Sarah there, now, beside him? Someone he could hash it out with. Or who would help him set aside the brooding.

That's what it was really about. Forget the BS about professional boundary concerns. It was a tug toward something more genuine, for once.

Don't screw it up.

CHAPTER SIX

Wednesday, June 4th

Sarah awoke to the rumbling of rigs and other highway noise. Sunlight streaming through the blinds suggested it was well into morning. The room was already getting too warm. She reached over to open a window. A little fresh air would get things going.

As the cobwebs of sleep cleared, events of the previous evening surged into place. In spite of how exhausted and overwhelmed she had been last night, she had not fallen asleep right away. Instead, she had collapsed on the bed, fully dressed, and stared at the ceiling for hours.

What on earth's going on with me? The self-analysis that had tortured her all night promptly returned for morning duty, that simple question continuing to nag her from multiple angles. After a dose of much needed muscle relaxants, the speculations had come to a brief end. Now she was right back where she started.

With the cold light of morn on her side, the previous evening was an embarrassment. How could she possibly have done that? She had fallen apart over nothing, over something she could have certainly handled on her own, and—on top of that—she had done it in front of someone she hardly knew, probably the last person she would have chosen to confide in. To make matters worse, she'd been rude to him when he had tried to comfort her. And then practically threw herself at him, which, of course, made her look all the more unhinged. She could only imagine what he thought of her now.

Why was she letting it bother her? Why should she care what he thought? *Blast it all, anyway.*

Her prescription bottle seemed to be mocking her from the nightstand. It was that medication's fault in part. Those things had pretty much turned her into a space cadet.

She snatched up the container and tossed it in the direction of her open suitcase. The minimal activity rewarded her with a back spasm, the first of the day. As she waited for it to let up, she set her sights on a hot shower and plain ibuprofen.

The travel alarm said 10:30 a.m. already. She should probably call Paulson and delay him.

No. Get it over with. She hurried into presentable form, ignoring an onslaught of additional spasms. She gave scant attention to hair and makeup. Who would care anyway? It was Marshland.

She rummaged through her suitcase. Her clothing options were sorely limited. Conference garb wasn't going to be suitable for disaster fieldwork, even if the work supposedly did fall within her work purview.

She found a pair of clean but rumpled khakis and a simple shell that would get her through the heat of the day. Picking up clothes for the rest of the week needed to get onto the to-do list. Come what may, she would stick with this disaster junket until she got it right, beginning with appropriate clothing.

She wondered how her mentor was feeling about this whole thing between them. Especially after yesterday. What kind of ideas did Paulson get in his head, considering the direction taken by that goodbye hug? Was it something she'd have to backpedal on? She really did need him, at least in respect to mentoring.

She wished she had been assigned to work with Lacey. That would have worked out well. They generally saw eye to eye and understood each other, even if Lacey's ability to see right through everybody could be unnerving.

Sarah sighed. She would simply have to follow Paulson's lead, even if his independent nature and unorthodoxy did leave much to be desired. Applying this kind of approach worked well when she was with troubled clients who were still trying to understand their symptoms. She could dredge up that same patience for Paulson. Besides, after everything she'd put him through, she probably owed him as much. Once Dad turned up, and she got herself out of there, chances were she'd never have to deal with the guy again.

The rental car pulled up a few minutes early. She grabbed her purse out of her briefcase, slipped on sandals, and darted out. Paulson was already holding open the passenger-side door by the time she got to the car.

"Your ride awaits." He took a bow of mock servitude.

It was a different Paulson. Yesterday's flyaway hair was neatly slicked down and pulled back. He was no longer hiding behind sloppy beard growth, as he appeared clean-shaven. His clothes—although still trademark blasé—at least didn't look slept in. More than she could say for herself. The look changed his entire demeanor. He did clean up good.

She stood there for a moment trying to take it in.

"Uh . . . ready for a road trip?" he finally asked.

"So it's Willsey for lunch I take it?" She climbed into the car. A wadded up Kleenex peeked out from where it was crammed between the seats. She snatched up last night's meltdown evidence and stuffed it into her pocket.

"I spoke with Lacey this morning." The energy in his voice was a turnaround from his withered state of yesterday. He must have succeeded in getting a little sleep. "I mentioned to her we might come to the shelter for lunch. She said if she caught us anywhere near disaster relief activity today, she'd have logistics hog-tie us, throw us in the back of a van, and dump us somewhere in Newark."

"So Willsey, it is."

The passing scenery took her back. It could have been any spring day past: traveling to a game against the Willsey Wildcats; meeting up with Lil to hang out at the mall; watching a movie in a crowded theater and wondering how much alone time she and Jimmy would have afterward.

She glanced at her driver. The stark contrast between the cleaned up version of Paulson and her madcap evenings past with Jimmy brought reality crashing to the ground. Though it was a relief to see she had been up-close and personal with a real man the night before.

It looked to be another scorcher. Sunlight played up the picturesque sights along the highway, including occasional pockets of flood damage neither of them had heard about. They took a few detours to check them out—"reconnaissance," Paulson called it—in spite of Lacey's explicit mandate. It supplied fuel for superficial conversation about the flood, the relief effort, the weather, or anything else that might perpetuate their complicit agreement to ignore the 600-pound gorilla sitting between them.

It was pitiful. He seemed even more avoidant about where they'd left off the night before than she was. How fortunate for the citizens of Marshland that the mental health professionals had come galloping into town to help everybody with their interpersonal dysfunctions.

"Dora briefly regained consciousness yesterday," Paulson told her. "They're keeping her sedated. The skull fracture will need some kind of surgery. But the prognosis is looking better."

"You talked to Bob?"

"I heard from Lacey. I have to tell you, the information pipeline with this disaster relief bunch could give the local gossipmongers a real run for their money."

"What other news did she have? Anything about my Dad's whereabouts?"

"No news. I asked her specifically."

Conversation stalled while she considered it. She made a mental note to get better organized regarding where her search for Dad had left off. "How about that skirmish at the high school? Did Lacey have anything to say about that?"

"Most of the fighting involved a specific group of kids that are always getting into scrapes as it is. The adults eventually remembered they were adults and broke things up."

"How do parents so easily miss how their own behavior trickles down? Maybe some of them will think a little more about it now."

"There were a few minor injuries," he continued. "Bloodied noses and the like. A couple other bystanders like you got bumps and bruises. Lacey didn't know if any criminal complaints were filed. I hope not. I hate seeing kids get mixed up with the criminal justice system when they haven't even finished school yet."

"If they do finish school."

At the edge of the city limit he turned into a supermarket parking lot, which then led to a new strip mall. At the far end of the complex stood a small, half-hidden Thai restaurant.

"Where did this come from?" said Sarah. "I don't remember ever seeing Thai cuisine around here, at least not anywhere within a fifty mile radius."

"It may well be the only one. I found it when I first relocated. I was vegetarian then. This was the only place that was at all accommodating."

"But you're not vegetarian now." She thought back to how enthusiastically he'd put away that plate of spaghetti and meatballs.

"I would have starved to death. Or would have needed a lot more time for foraging. Besides, I fit in better if I eat like everybody else. It wasn't that big a deal. Fitting in was the bigger priority. Whatever helped me get tight with the community. Food is food."

They selected a booth near a window. Paulson tied up the server with questions about a new painting. Eventually the server excused himself and they were left to their menus.

"So your diet was another big change, when you moved here. I'm impressed that you were willing to take on so many changes in order to take this job."

"It was because of several things . . . going on at once." His eyes darted, not setting on anything in particular. He was beginning to look as somber as a patient awaiting major surgery. His chattiness all but disappeared.

She settled back into her seat. Maybe giving him some personal space would help dislodge whatever he was becoming so anxious about. Besides, there was no need to delve into territory he obviously preferred to avoid. Her curiosity was not that morbid. Maybe she should change the subject all together.

Before she could attempt it, he started in again. "I'd been working with the hospital about ten years. It was okay work. Paid well, after a couple of promotions. But with HMO's, PPO's, and hospital politics controlling who gets what, it became more and more frustrating.

Infuriating, actually. I was ripe to leave when this opportunity came along."

"What about friends? Family? It must have been hard to leave them behind." Someone as social as Paulson must have had a massive network.

She shuddered at thoughts of whom it might include.

"Actually, I was married. It didn't work out." He left it sitting out there, and rattled the ice in his water glass. He took a sip.

Not unexpected. Most people either were married or had some other long-term relationship by this stage of life.

The server returned and asked for their order.

"I haven't really looked at this." She scanned the lengthy menu. "You know what's good here. How about if you order for both of us? I'm easy to please."

Paulson fired off the names of a few dishes. The server nodded as if he already knew and scurried off.

She kept her mouth shut. Would Paulson return to his story?

It was a surprise when he did.

"I was still in school when we married. My ex was . . . well, a real free spirit. She's the one who got me into vegetarianism—and a bunch of other 'fringy' things, too. I guess you could say I was a bit loose and fringy myself back then."

Like he wasn't still loose and fringy now, with his sloppy *Kung Fu* wanderer approach to social work in a small town. On a motorcycle, no less. If his current status represented conventional in his book, just how full of quirks had he been back then?

"Things looked different after graduate school. You can't play supportive roles in other people's lives if you're impulsively darting off to whatever new experience presents itself. I guess you could say our worldviews parted ways."

"So you left her?"

His gaze drifted again; he fiddled with the corners of his napkin. "I had a patient suicide."

"I'm sorry."

"Someone I'd seen on and off for years. I saw it coming, full speed. When everything came down, there was nothing I could do about it. They released him, even though anyone with more than three functioning neurons could see it was a bad idea. The rest is history." He began drawing random figures on the table with his forefinger.

How frustrating, how devastating that must have been. But, telling such a personal story at this early stage of a friendship? *Definitely TMI.*

"I did a crash and burn for a week or so. My ex couldn't identify with it. She eventually packed up and left."

"I can see how you would want to start over." Why was he sharing this nightmare with someone he barely knew? Yet another oddity about this guy to sift through.

"The last straw was right after that. I had this patient who said she was getting ready for a zombie attack. She claimed there were warnings about it on a CDC website. Out of curiosity, I checked it out. It turned out to be true. The CDC had a disaster preparedness website for a zombie pandemic."

"You can't be serious."

"No joke. Look it up when you get a chance. It was tongue in cheek, of course. At least I hope it was. Looking back, I can see how something like that would help get the disaster preparedness message out to certain populations. But at the time, all I saw was the system dumping money into zombie preparedness, instead of hospitalizing a suicidal patient long enough for his meds to kick in. That was *it*. I wanted out. I wanted as far away from bigwig-driven services as my bike could take me."

Somewhere in there, there had to be a reasonable explanation for the deep mining. Why was he digging himself into such a deep hole with a relative stranger? He hadn't seemed like the type who would ignore usual interpersonal boundaries, in spite of his unorthodox appearance. Perhaps—was he evening out the playing field?

Yes. That had to be it. He was indirectly trying to get past last night's awkwardness by exposing his own vulnerabilities. Especially since neither of them had been able to drum up the nerve to address it head on. Fair enough.

"It was around then that I heard about a part-time position in Marshland. There aren't any children in the picture, so there was no need to stick around near my ex. I applied and got hired. During downtime I got to know people. Did a little private work, contractual work here and there. Lots of spontaneous house calls, lots of pro bono. Not much in the way of third party. Just connecting, and making myself available. I think it's been a positive. Especially now, with the flood."

He took a long drink of water. After setting down the plastic tumbler his eyes finally met hers, seeking . . . God knows what. Apparently, end of story.

It was her turn. "Have you talked with anyone about this?"

"Not really. Not until now. It isn't the sort of thing you bring up in a new community, especially one this conservative. Time settled most of it. I've put it to rest, built a different life. It's not something I'm particularly proud of. At least, that I ever wanted to tell anyone about."

"I imagine you're already aware you're not responsible for other people's choices." Her own experiences testified to that. Look at Dad. Jimmy, too, for that matter. And Nate. "But sometimes it's like that realization just doesn't matter. Especially when it's about people you love."

Why in the world did you go and do that? She winced. It was not the words themselves, but the passion that had succeeded in sprouting out along with them. It pushed open a door she had no interest in opening. *Double blast.*

She sat back and folded her hands over her napkin. He was still looking at her, waiting. Expecting more.

Before either of them could start up again the server swept in, carrying three steaming bowls of fragrant provisions: Pad Thai, lemongrass something or other, and another dish she did not recognize.

"This looks wonderful." A lunch this magnificent would surely sidetrack anybody from those loaded comments. She relaxed. "I'm famished."

*****

Paulson inwardly smiled. *Not a chance he'd overlook that loaded comment.*

Nevertheless, he, too, was famished. They spooned up generous portions and dug in.

"This is really good," said Sarah. "No way I'd expect to find it in Willsey."

Paulson stole the occasional glance while she enjoyed her meal. Sarah looked so pleased with herself, probably convinced she had removed the need to explain herself.

Some other time. Besides, it was a relief to be able to savor the moment. She had just heard some of the sorrier details of his life and hadn't run off screaming in horror. She wasn't the type that would, anyway. But it had been a risk. Of facing the unknown, if nothing else.

Thank God, it was over with. There had been no way around it, if she was going to know who he was. Simply allowing her to know him better wouldn't violate the supervisory relationship. That's all it was—getting to know each other.

With the session of true confession over, he could sit back and enjoy observing Sarah, the woman. She was a different person at this moment, so openly relishing her food that she seemed oblivious to anything else. A real person replaced the upright urban pawn he met a few days ago.

She looked like she had gotten a little rest. And from the minute he'd caught sight of her coming out of the motel, it was clear he was the one who'd overdone it in regards to appearance. He had expected to see her dressed the same as she'd been the last couple of days. In fact, it had taken a while to decide it truly was Sarah.

It was more than the casual clothing. Her hair was gently swept against her shoulders rather than pinned up to mimic some latest trend. Her face paint no longer resembled a department store mannequin. Just a touch of color here and there, in ways that complimented her features. She looked less severe, more approachable. Almost the same way she appeared the previous evening, after tears washed away most of the window dressing.

"As long as we're in Willsey, I'd like to pick up a few things." She spooned up more Pad Thai. "All I've got with me is what I brought along for the conference. Obviously, what I really need is something for tromping around in mud and debris."

"The mall's not far from here."

"That'll do. It's been ages since I've been at the Willsey Mall."

"Is there anything else you need to do? We may as well take care of what we can while we've got the chance."

"If there's time later, I'd really like to check out Dad's shop. What's left of it, anyway. With Dad gone and Nate missing in action, nobody's keeping track. Unless you count Chet."

"I saw what was still there the day after the fire. They did a good job protecting the back of the building. That's about all that's still standing— most of the back wall, and that small addition. Whatever's in it is probably okay. Looks pretty solid. There's a heavy-duty chain and padlock across the access. So you probably don't need to worry about looting. I could run you over, if you like."

"Thanks. It would be nice to hear the details from someone who saw it happen. You might remember something that will help me figure out where Dad went."

"So our day is filled." He scraped the bottom of his plate and examined the empty serving bowls. There wasn't enough left to bother with takeaway boxes.

Nothing like a little disaster to create an appetite.

*****

"I also need to pick up a few things. Lacey said we'd need them for fieldwork." If only she had her briefcase, with all those notes she'd taken. She missed it. Not just the notes it held, but the security of having that prop in hand. Such an odd discovery—all that time, it apparently served a secondary purpose. Like a security blanket, or an anchor. Its absence had her feeling naked again. *How annoying.* "Sunscreen, that sort of thing. Can we stop at this supermarket?"

"Whatever you need."

They traveled a few doors down. She entered and picked up a grocery basket. They went separate ways. Without him as a distraction, analysis of the morning's events was easier.

He was being so ultra accommodating. Exactly what ideas had he walked away with the night before?

She tossed a container of sunscreen into the basket. Then a tube of heavy-duty lip balm.

He probably figured she was some kind of Fragile Fran, needing to be coddled every step of the way. That would explain why he still hadn't brought up the topic of last night. Of course, she hadn't, either. True, he wouldn't have decided to tell her his life story if her behavior had scared him off the whole arrangement. Maybe she was blowing it out of proportion.

But how was it that an offer to help her pick up her car had turned into an all-day field trip, forty miles away? That part had been agreed to before she'd made the mistake of throwing herself into his arms. Then there was this business of his new appearance. Did he always do that to go to town, or was it just for her? Was that something she really wanted to consider, to sort out? *Who is this man, really?*

"Sarah—is that you?"

She turned in time to see a squealing checker-vested store employee jogging toward her.

Sarah returned an answering squeal. "Lil. I can't believe it! How are you?" She dropped the basket and threw herself into Lil's outstretched arms. A blast from the past, more than welcome.

"I'm doing great." Lil shoved at the pale brown bob gone awry, better exposing her round smiling face. "What brought you back? Last I heard, you were off looking for that Ph.D. we all voted you most likely to get."

"That's old news. I got that Ph.D. I'm a practicing psychologist now."

"Congratulations. Does that mean I call you Dr. Turner now?"

Paulson came up from behind carrying a basket filled with produce. "Who's your friend? I could hear you guys clear across the store."

"This is Lil. Lil White now, I understand?"

"Yes indeedy. And there's a new little White right here in the oven." She rubbed a hand over the obvious swell on her belly.

"Congratulations," said Sarah. "Your first?"

"Yep, our first little bundle of joy. We can hardly wait."

"Lil and I grew up together. This is Paulson Forbes. We're working the flood disaster."

"I'm so behind," said Lil. "After you left for school, it was like you fell off the face of the earth. I don't even know if it's Dr. Turner or Dr. Something-else."

She snatched up Sarah's left hand and examined it. "No ring."

"No, no immediate prospects. I had a steady back in graduate school, but we parted ways."

"Jimmy Orton is still around. Available, too, last I heard, if you're interested."

Sarah laughed. "Fortunately, I won't be hanging around long enough to follow up on that lead. I keep pretty busy."

"Your daddy said almost the exact same thing the other day. He said you were so busy with your job, you didn't make it back here much."

Dad? She glanced at Paulson, who also came to attention. "You saw Dad? When was that?"

"A couple days ago." Lil's bewilderment at their sudden interest slowed the rapid-fire chatter. "He looked a little worn out. Otherwise, pretty spry for a guy his age."

"What day, exactly?"

"It was either Sunday or Monday. Right after the storm. I'm not real sure. Why? Is something wrong?"

Sarah brought her up to date.

"Gee, I hope nothing happened. I heard about your old neighborhood getting flooded. Thank heavens your Dad got out in time. When I saw him, he was just buying groceries. I helped him find a mini tool kit. You know, those dinky things for little fix-it-ups. He said he had some tinkering to do. But he looked fine."

"Can you remember if it was before or after the fire? That would really help. Nate's just sure something horrible happened."

Lil gave it thought, but shook her head. "I wish I remembered. I had shifts both those days. I just don't."

"If he comes in again, could you let him know we're looking for him? Let me know, too, if he turns up."

They exchanged phone numbers.

"You can bet I'll be calling." Lil patted the pocket where she'd tucked away Sarah's business card. "Now that I know how to find you, there's no escaping it. You'll be hearing from me, for sure."

CHAPTER SEVEN

At least Lil's piece of news gave Sarah a bit of encouragement, or so it seemed. It helped Paulson feel better, too. Sam's disappearance was starting to seem suspicious. They should have heard something more definitive by now. The town was not that big. He could only imagine how worried Sarah had to be.

She turned silent on the way to the mall, once again disappearing into her thoughts. It seemed to come easy. To some extent, he had to admit the habit worked for her—once she reemerged, that is. Besides, he'd been quick to realize there was less meltdown behavior when he sat back and let her internally process whatever was bugging her without his side comments.

"Where would he go?" she finally said. "What in the world is he doing? Why would he leave town and not tell anyone? He's always so annoyingly independent. At the very least, you'd think he'd tell Nate. Or Chet."

"No, it doesn't seem like Sam, does it?"

An odd expression met his sideways glance. She eased up, nodding to herself. "I keep forgetting that you know my Dad. It's just so strange to hear someone I only recently met talk about him this way. That you are so familiar with him."

"Uh, some." He silently cursed. *Shut it down before something stupid flies out.* Surely there was some safe piece of conversational territory about Sam.

What would he tell her, anyway? Sam obviously hadn't confided in her that he'd consulted him about losing his wife. Maybe he didn't say anything about it because it wasn't a formal therapist-client relationship. Or, he didn't want anybody to know. All the more reason to hold his tongue.

But the reassurances he could give her, the pain he could liberate. It would take only a few, well-placed words. All of them, however, would most likely violate confidentiality taboo. He hated the fact that, for once, Sarah looked interested in what he had to offer, and all he could do was sit there tongue-tied and silent.

Finally he filled in the lull with questions about which stores she wanted to go to. She went along, retreating into superficial conversation. But it didn't hide the fact that she'd noticed the detour.

Frankly, it was a relief to have the topic left behind. But the distancing was excruciatingly miserable. Especially with yesterday's awkwardness still alive and well. Over the entire afternoon, that wretched chard of tension and uncertainty hadn't fallen away. At his end, anyway. *Which is exactly what you'd expect, you idiot, since you're not stepping up to the plate.*

What was he afraid of? Nobody could describe this woman's core as emotionally frail, in spite of last night's meltdown. At times she seemed so sturdy, he'd entertained the notion of her parents routinely sticking a bowl of nuts and bolts in front of her at the breakfast table.

He'd never had trouble approaching people who were out of sorts. *Never.* In fact he'd overheard others joking that he'd even be able to start up a conversation with a fencepost.

If only he could stop being so wishy-washy.

*****

The back roads they took to the mall returned them to the reality of the flood aftermath. It was like stepping into a different world, as if the few hours of relative normalcy had never taken place.

However she couldn't forget how he'd clammed up at mention of her father. She'd practically heard crickets chirping. *Fine, be that way.*

What exactly did he believe? There was no telling what Dad might have said about her, given how much Dad harassed her about her career choice.

A change of topic was in order. "I wonder how long it will take for everything to get back the way it was."

"Could be what we're seeing right now will constitute normal for some time. I've thought about it too, though. What it will be like when people get their lives back to normal. Their new normal, that is."

"Don't get me started on the word 'normal'." *Blast.* One more thing she did not want to get into. Not with everything feeling so out of whack. For Marshland. Well, for herself too, to be truthful.

"Why's that?"

It was too seductive to resist. "Back in graduate school, they said that after 9/11 professionals started treating the word 'normal' as verboten. The way the story goes, some survivors complained there couldn't possibly be anything normal about their trauma symptoms. It felt too awful to be normal, and was certainly nothing most had experienced before. Then the media jumped in, and there was a push for everybody to use language in a way that went along with this errant perception, rather than provide them with conceptual accuracy."

"I remember some of this. I didn't pay much attention."

"Well, you're going to love this. Instead of better explaining what 'normal' means, clinicians started saying 'common and expectable' instead—not just for this, but for anything we used to call normal. I cringe every time I hear somebody say 'common' or 'expectable'." She huffed. "What a cop out."

"They're just words." He glanced at her. "What's the big deal?"

"Everybody already knows the common definition of the term 'normal.' There's so much reassurance, such comfort people get when you tell them they're normal—it's second to none. It annihilates the secondary stress caused by such worries. And my clients have never had trouble understanding both normalcy for themselves and normalcy for grief reactions."

"Doesn't seem like rocket science, does it?"

"I've never been able to see how setting everybody up to confuse the two paradigms serves any good purpose." She noted her hands in flight, waving about in emphasis, in spite of efforts to rein it in. "It could even be detrimental for things like narcissism or self-absorption. Why make people worse off by telling them yes, normalcy is what's normal for you; you are in fact the center of the universe?"

"That's probably stretching it a bit. But I see your point."

"The general population owns what language means, not us." She sat on her hands, a last ditch effort to get in check. "The mental health field can't just claim it. Nobody died and made us God. Common definitions can't be simply deleted and replaced at will. The real world is not a word processing program."

"I suppose there could be a little grandiosity buried in there. But does it really warrant all this energy? It's not that big a deal. At least as far as helping people recover."

She stopped for breath. Autonomic breakdown peeked from beyond the horizon—heart pounding, palms sweating. Tingling in her throat, too—she'd been raising her voice.

She was saying way too much about herself.

But this deserved concern, no matter who she was talking to. The implications, the ongoing damage produced by this dilemma. Especially as it applies to mental health professionals.

"Then this whole 'common and expectable' business." Her hands freed themselves and her elbow banged against the door handle. *Ouch.* She rubbed it. "Would I want to hear someone tell me that the pain of my loss is 'common?' Or 'expectable?' It's degrading. Besides, how could that ever replace the comfort of hearing in the well-understood jargon of Main Street, USA that it's perfectly normal. How many have gone without it for the sake of childish word games?"

"You really are worked up over this, aren't you?" A twinkle sparked in his eyes.

Was he only humoring her?

Just like Dad, whenever she tried to explain anything to him.

She folded her arms and looked away. *Figures.* Apparently a discussion like this with Paulson couldn't end any better than it did with Dad. "I just wish everybody would join the real world. Does normalcy only make sense here? Where everything is upfront, straightforward and practical? Rather than brimming with the arrogance that you can simply . . . simply reassign social realities at will. As if reality could be forced to go along with somebody's intellectual exercise."

"I suppose culture plays a role in it."

How could he be so infuriatingly calm? Surely he sees how important this is . . .

And he was moving into kid gloves mode. The gentler tone, the humoring commentary. Treating her like she'd lost it again.

Get hold of yourself.

Paulson wasn't just a professional colleague. He was her mentor, her guide into this amorphous practice she was trying to make sense of. Her ticket into disaster world, where she would find Dad. If she didn't ratchet down a few notches, she could find herself booted out of the program altogether.

She gritted her teeth. *Breathe.* Your professional self. "I wonder if the trauma of 9/11 did it. Affected the professionals. Until then, therapists had no trouble explaining the difference between normal experiences and normal for conditions. They also managed to keep in mind that what's important is what a specific client thinks words mean."

"There certainly has been a lot going on in trauma psychology since 9/11."

It hit her. "Yes. Maybe it's that. It's . . . another form of disaster damage." That was a thought. A new form of normalcy, even for mental health care providers.

Yes. Like her own acting out over the last five minutes. Perhaps, just perhaps, this was in fact normal. Her rant represented something normal, even if it was a bit frazzled. She let out her breath.

"Disaster damage?" Paulson glanced at her again. "Like what?"

It was way too personal, too intimate to share, this inner conflict she hadn't recognized was there until the very moment she'd resolved it. Definitely not with Paulson. But after all she'd been through over the last couple of days, she'd stumbled into a place of peace: she was, in fact, normal.

Paulson was still awaiting a response, occasionally glancing at her with those semi-anxious, questioning looks. As if he wasn't even sure he wanted to know what was coming next.

"Maybe 9/11 did something to all those professional heroes." She paused. "It was pretty incredible, when you think about it. The most massive, magnificent mental health intervention in the history of the profession."

"You're probably right."

"Chalk up one more for the terrorists. A gift that keeps on giving." She gave in to a scowl.

He went silent. When she looked at him he turned his head away, but not quickly enough. He was definitely holding back laughter.

She felt her eyes narrow. "What's so funny?"

"Sorry about that. I couldn't help it. I haven't heard this kind of debate in years. It feels so . . . out of place. Here we are talking about something like this, while going along this peaceful rural highway on a beautiful sunny morning."

She scanned the hills going by on either side, no clue what he was referring to. Apparently something else she had missed. "What's that got to do with it?"

"Folks around here don't go for these kinds of philosophical debates. What you're talking about isn't an issue for them. What matters is what you actually do. Maybe how your day-to-day life reflects your beliefs. All this analysis . . . they're *so* not there."

She folded her arms, then wrapped them around herself. "I don't see the humor in it."

"What's important to them is as straightforward as the worldview you described: duty to family, job, community; doing your best; common courtesy, no matter who you're with; integrity; self-respect, respect for others; being a good citizen."

"I suppose next you're going to quote some kind of Boy Scout code of honor."

This time he laughed aloud.

She felt her face begin to burn. "What exactly is so funny?"

"The contradiction. You really don't see it, do you?"

Oh. She did see it. How annoying.

"Sarah?"

She pretended to be distracted by scenery. Boy Scout code and all. *Chalk up one for the* Kung Fu *wanderer.*

Sarah slammed the car door.

He obviously knew more. *More about Dad and me than he lets on.*

And he was purposely not telling her. This had to be why he was keeping himself so contained—there was something her father had said about her. Was that the real reason he'd laughed at what she'd said? Was she some kind of local private joke?

She hurried through the mall entrance as if she he weren't right there, hovering at her elbow. It was a relief when they went their separate ways. Why did she even care? It was accomplishing nothing. Her focus belonged on Dad.

Enough with the high drama. It was time to get over it and move on. Forget about Paulson and his warped worldview. Enjoy the excuse for a shopping spree. Get the ol' gray cells back on line. Then after the day's excursion was over with, she could settle into this unique opportunity to learn about the disaster business. If she could squeeze it in, she'd hook up with Lil again, too. Make the best of the rest of the week.

And the sooner she tracked down Dad, the sooner she'd be out of there.

A clearance rack held a pair of stylish dark-colored jeans that fit well, but not so tightly that nobody would take her seriously. She also found a pair of heavy-duty outdoor shoes, which were a little pricey, but they looked like they would last. She grabbed a few other recommended items, including a canvass satchel with a good, strong shoulder strap— that briefcase wasn't going to cut it for fieldwork, either. The satchel felt comforting, hanging there at her shoulder. Almost like an alternative security blanket, now that she was willing to acknowledge she needed one.

She smiled. Shopping ritual did have its way of bringing her down to earth.

"Did you find everything you were looking for?" The cashier rang up and bagged items.

A wave of déjà vu passed. She ran her eyes over these familiar surroundings, a place once so often frequented. So many memories, window-shopping with Mom. She had forgotten how they'd always enjoyed checking out the pretty new clothing. Then there were times they'd try it on to model it for each other, knowing full well there was no way they'd ever afford it.

"You do look like a satisfied customer." The cashier smiled back at her.

"I was just thinking about when I used to come here with Mom. Once she brought me here for a prom dress. I must have tried on every formal in the store. The one she liked turned out to be perfect. It was ice blue, some kind of imitation silk. It set off the color of my eyes beautifully. And the design was just right for a smaller person. I felt like queen of the prom."

It was something special they'd had, she and Mom. If only she'd had the chance to tell her.

She blinked back a tear, but smiled. How cleansing, to think about Mom this way again.

She sat at the benched area where they'd agreed to meet. If the town clock looming overhead was correct, she was early. It was better than being late.

The mall was quiet, practically deserted in comparison to years past. Some of the smaller shops were now boarded up cubes of empty space. It left no doubt about the local economy, still recovering from its tailspin. Even the pet store that had been there as long as she could remember displayed a banner: "Going Out of Business – Everything Must Go." In all likelihood, this would be her last chance to see what remained of it. She entered.

Paulson was there, discussing something with a sales clerk. She fought off her reluctance and waved at him. She did have an obligation to let him know where she was. Other than that, indifference could have its way.

She explored the rows of future pets awaiting homes. The variety of fish was captivating. Tropical species of every color of the rainbow flitted about. Some came up and bumped against the glass as if to say hello. Especially a big black one with a few white spots on its side.

"Gorgeous, aren't they?" Paulson was behind her, leaning in toward the tank for a better look. His warmth radiated against her, his body mere inches away.

A flush crept up her neck, uncooperative with attempts to shrug it off. She kept her back to him. No way would she let him see this victory of her hormone system over the power of her will.

"What's this black one?" She pointed.

"It's a domino damsel. Damsels are nice. Easy to care for, anyway."

Thank heavens he was cooperating with the bit of redirection. But it served as a reminder, the competing argument niggling all morning: this man was being really nice. He was trying to make her feel better. And she was gearing up to act like a turd again. Surely a happy medium could found between collegial professionalism and leading on this type of guy.

Tolerance for diversity, Sarah. "You know about these fish?" Going along with a relatively neutral topic would help. Especially since she was the one who brought it up.

"I have a marine aquarium set-up. I was too ambitious last time. I got high maintenance types. I got busy and, well, they all went to that giant fishpond in the sky. I heard this place was going under. So I figured I'd better see how much longer I've got to find replacements."

As they prepared to leave, her cell phone vibrated against her thigh. The number was familiar, but not immediately recognizable. "I suppose I should get this."

"Take your time." He wandered back into the depths of the pet store.

"This is Dr. Turner." She returned to her spot on the bench.

"My oh my, listen to you now. This is your Aunt Millie. Are you all right? I heard you got hurt yesterday."

That certainly hadn't taken long to get around. "I'm fine. It's just a little bump on the head. The boss made me take the day off. I'm at the mall in Willsey."

"You and your mama always were the ones for shopping."

Of course. All those times they'd made it a threesome—she and Mom rummaging through the entire store while Aunt Millie stood around rechecking her watch.

"Have you heard anything about your Dad? Chet said you were having trouble finding him."

"No, there's nothing new. Please, let me know if you hear anything."

"If he comes my way, I'll tell him to get in touch with you immediately. After I give him a good talking to for leaving you hanging this way. I'm calling to see if you'll come to our quilting group tonight.

It's last minute. We're going to make quilts and things for people who got flooded."

"What a nice idea. I have to warn you, I'm a little rusty. I haven't done any quilting since I was a teenager."

"It won't matter tonight. We're just talking and making plans. Everybody will love to see you. And you can ask everybody if they've seen your Dad. Can you come? My house, around six-thirty. I'll show you our cleanup project, too."

"It would have to be an early night of it. I don't know what Lacey has in mind for me tomorrow. From what I've seen, these people put in pretty long days."

"Come a little early, then, if you can. Have supper with us. We'll visit for a while, before everybody gets here. That way you'll get a chance to see Harold. He always disappears into the woodwork when the quilters turn up."

So much for checking out Dad's shop. But it was her first real day off in ages. The shop situation wouldn't change, if put on hold a little longer. Besides, even this brief conversation with Aunt Millie had felt heavenly. It had given a sliver of comfort, a sense of being grounded. More of it would serve her well.

After the call ended Paulson approached, carrying a fish traveler. As he drew near she made out a good-sized dark-colored fish.

"The domino damsel." Thank heavens, the very social creature was going to be rescued from who knows what. Hopefully Paulson wouldn't get "too busy" this time.

He sat next to her and held it up for her inspection. They both studied the fish through opposite sides of the clear plastic container. It wafted from one side to the other, as if sizing up the two of them.

"I'm going to call her Sarah, Jr."

Sarah tipped her head and peered around the container at him. Why on earth would he name this fish after her?

"You see, damsels tend to become a bit aggressive at times." He peeked back at her with a goofy grin, an eyebrow raised.

*****

92

Sarah practically fell off the bench, doubled over. Paulson started laughing too, even more raucous than she.

"Stop it, before I wet my pants." She pulled a crumpled Kleenex from her pocket and wiped her eyes. "I suggest you call her Junior for short. That way Junior and I won't get confused about who you're talking to."

"All right. Junior it is," said Paulson.

"That was Aunt Millie on the phone. I promised to have supper with them tonight. If we head back now, I'll have time to take care of a couple other things."

This was good. Sarah was hooking up with her important others. It would bolster her. Do something for that just-below-the-surface edginess that so rarely took a break.

But it was also disappointing. Their afternoon together would soon come to an end. Right when he'd finally found a way to cut through the BS.

She was so unique. In spite of the more awkward moments, they had adjusted to one another's quirks in a companionable way. He had fewer doubts about how well they'd be able to work together the rest of the week. It could have become a real nightmare. Still could, as far as that went.

Sarah had Junior in her lap during the ride home, occasionally holding her up to admire her. Paulson brought up stories about tropical fish he'd seen while scuba diving. Sarah talked about old times with Lil—things they used to do together, dreams they'd had way back when.

"Did you always want to be a psychologist?" he said.

"I wasn't sure what I wanted, other than not wanting to be in Marshland. Mom always encouraged me to get a good education. She watched me grow up with my nose in a book, a lot like my Dad. She liked to bring up how smart Dad was. How great he would have done if he'd gone to school. Instead, he set up a shop and started a family. I think it bothered her. That somehow, it was her fault. Dad always seemed happy enough with his choices, though.

"Anyway, she knew I needed more than what Marshland has to offer. She was so excited when I got accepted into graduate school. You would have thought she'd gotten in herself."

"I bet Sam was proud, too."

A pause followed. "I guess." Her lack of enthusiasm said otherwise.

"You don't think so?"

"Dad never understood why I wanted a career. He thought I should settle down right here in Marshland. Get married, and then sit barefoot and pregnant, eating bonbons in front of soap operas, I suppose. That isn't me. Yes, I want a family someday. But there's so much more I want to accomplish."

"Like what?"

She looked thoughtful. "To make a difference, I guess. I don't know how, or where. But the idea of hiding out forever in housewifery in a small town just doesn't cut it."

"I know what you mean about Sam. He's definitely old school. But I'll bet there's more to it than what you're saying about him. I can't help but wonder if it has something to do with being disappointed that you're not living here, closer to him."

There was silence. He risked a glance in her direction. She looked like she was truly entertaining the possibility. *Bingo.*

"I never looked at it that way. He certainly never said anything like that."

"Men have a harder time fessing up to those sorts of feelings. It could just be he's questioning a life plan that took you away from him."

There, he did it. He just broke a few rules. Saying that much wasn't going to hurt anything, though. Screw the rules.

The city hall parking lot overflowed with activity. Workers and vehicles alike had multiplied exponentially. Maneuvering back to where she'd left her car took some doing.

"I know if I were Sam, I'd want to keep you around." He helped her transfer purchases into the Miata.

"That's sweet of you to say."

"It looks like you have old friends here who wouldn't mind reconnecting, too."

"Who knows? Thanks for everything, Paulson. See you tomorrow, bright and early."

As Sarah got on her way an odd sensation settled. Strangely cold, in spite of the heat. That he was more alone in the moment than he ought to be.

His work was cut out for him, if he continued this path. Every time he and Sarah genuinely connected, she backed off. Shut almost any door as soon as it opened. Was it worth the effort?

"I guess I have to settle for you for now," he said to Junior. "Let's get you out of this plastic thing and into your new home."

As he backed out of the parking space, he caught a glimpse of the Miata exiting onto Main Street. Another vehicle pulled up behind her and did likewise.

CHAPTER EIGHT

Disappointment over spending the rest of the day alone turned to downright depressing. Any other time, the rare opportunity for peace and solitude was a treasured commodity: an opportunity for dirt biking, or disappearing into an old movie or western novel. Instead, the idea of alone time felt empty and aimless.

Time for a reboot. The first piece of business was tracking down the fish tank. If he remembered right, it had been unceremoniously dumped into the closet at his office. Getting Junior situated meant a quick stop at the health clinic.

Out of habit he turned into the space next to the dumpster. A tight squeeze, with the rental car instead of the bike. Being back again seemed unreal, somehow foreign. So much had happened since he'd darted out the back and zipped off into the swelling relief effort. It brought to mind the collection of uncompleted tasks surely still scattered over his desk.

Here I am, in the middle of a major flooding disaster, behind in everything, and messing around with an aquarium. Really must have lost it.

He used the front entrance instead of the staff door, a show of resolve that he had not come to do work. He simply needed to get the tank and leave. This time he'd do the fish justice and set her up at home. She might last longer.

The entry strategy was a miscalculation. His style of dress elicited wolf whistles and catcalls.

"Looks like someone's got a hot date tonight." The clinic receptionist never missed a chance to give him a hard time. Especially regarding his social life. "Who's the lucky lady?"

"She's right here." He held up the fish traveler. "Her name's Junior." He ducked into his office and closed the door, barricading against any other speculations his colleagues might drum up for entertainment.

In the far corner, his desk was in same condition as he'd left it—and under additional mail, memos, and messages. His clinic email had to be a terror by now, as well.

He sighed. "You're going to have to wait a little longer, Junior." He set the container on his desk. The fish circled the perimeter of her confinement, checking out their surroundings, eventually settling in to supervise.

"Yeah, you're right." He dutifully sorted, most of the mail worth only a glance before dropped into the circular file. "The décor around here is pretty lame. It came with the office."

He opened anything that looked important and made a few quick phone calls to clients whose appointments had been cancelled during the excitement. He saved a large thick envelope for last.

He slit it open. It held some bulky bureaucratic tome. Paper-clipped onto it was a pink message slip, initialed by the director: "Please take care of this. Need back by Monday."

He fanned through the thick stack of papers. It was an application of some sort. Looked like something to get funds for disaster-related mental health needs. There were countless blanks to fill in—how much damage, mental health services to date, who knows what else. Data he had no idea how to find. There had to be fifty or sixty pages to wade through.

Surely she was joking. Earlier she'd insisted his priority this week was helping disaster survivors. If he wasted time messing around with paperwork, who'd help the people in need?

And by the time he got it out of his hair, Sarah would be long gone.

*****

The pungent mildew smell drifting up from the Heesackers' basement immediately hinted that things there weren't anything like what Sarah remembered. As Aunt Millie led the way down the narrow stairs, the smell became more pronounced. Anxiety spiked, as well as hesitance to continue. It produced a haunted feeling, almost like back at the old neighborhood.

Ignore it. She continued down the stairs and joined Aunt Millie, who was already busy spot-checking and admiring her basement.

"I've used Clorox, but it's hardly doing a bit of good. Harold says unless we completely tear out the drywall, the mold will bug us forever. Chet says he'll help, when the time comes."

The second-hand furnishings that had filled the room for as long as she could remember were gone. The sliding door and picture windows were boarded up, hiding the spectacular view of river and hills. The inability to see out made the basement seem somehow smaller, almost claustrophobic. A mud-colored waterline along splotchy walls told of grimy flow at one point swallowing most of the room. Only the popcorn ceiling and light fixtures appeared unscathed.

However, Aunt Millie's vast wealth of energy and determination had also made its mark. There was no debris, mud, or floodwater anywhere. The bare concrete floor was scrubbed clean.

Rather than looking pained by the status of her daylight basement, she stood there smiling at her. Tall and proud, hands resting on hips and awaiting positive feedback. As she should, of course. She was comparing it to the mud-filled mess she most likely started out with, not what Sarah remembered about the room.

"You've done a marvelous job, Aunt Millie."

"I agree, if I do say so myself. Tomorrow somebody from the insurance company is coming by. We'll have it back to normal in no time."

"Whatever you fixed for supper sure smells good." She hurried up the steep stairway, thankful to leave behind the latest encounter with devastation.

They feasted on beef stew, green salad, and freshly baked whole-wheat rolls while Sarah talked about her hospital work. In addition to boasting about her program, she shared some of the more interesting aspects of the conference she'd just attended. They listened politely.

"Tell us about what you do for fun out there in greater civilization," said Harold. "There must be all sorts of things to do in your time off."

"Actually I don't have much free time. When I'm not at the hospital, I squeeze in clients. Private practice turns a dollar better than anything else. I've still got student loans like you wouldn't believe. Not to mention payments on that little extravagance out there in your driveway. That toy alone guarantees I'll be living in my one-bedroom walk-up a while yet."

"Surely you do something on weekends," said Aunt Millie.

"I still like to curl up with a good book. Or turn on those old shows I used to watch with Mom. Then I do whatever needs to get done before the work week begins."

Aunt Millie delivered her classic mother look. "Now that doesn't sound like much of a life for a young gal like you. Don't you have friends you spend time with? Not even a special guy to tell us about?" The last suggestion brought a sparkle to those probing hazel eyes.

"I have friends at the hospital." She scoured recent memory. Was her life really that dull? "Sometimes we get together after work. Or do a seminar together. But you're right. I've mostly kept to myself since graduate school. Once I'm better established, I'll think about that more."

"I shouldn't be needing to tell you, of all people, about all work and no play. We're going to have to do something about that. Beginning with tonight. You'll get to visit with mothers of some of your old friends. Lil's mom and Jimmy's mom both said they were coming."

"I'm looking forward to it. I remember when I used to call you, Mom, Shelley and Sylvia the 'Fabulous Foursome'."

"Sylvia's having a hard time of it, poor dear. She barely made it out of that flood alive. The house was spared, thank God. That's about all, though. Shelley's diner took on a little water. And, of course, Harold and I had that mess downstairs. In spite of it all, you could still call us fabulous. We do the same things we did when your mama came along. We sure do miss her."

"I'd probably be around more if she were still with us."

They fell silent, reflecting. It drew out pensive images of the past, a world that had somehow evaporated. Mom's second family; a sisterhood.

"Why don't we get out those old photos now?" Aunt Millie pushed a few dishes out of the way. "We still have time. I wouldn't mind another look at them myself."

Sarah cleared the table while Aunt Millie rummaged through the rescued basement items cluttering her living room. She returned with a good-sized cardboard box. She tried pawing around, then gave up and dumped its contents. Old letters, yellowing photos, and a variety of trinkets rattled and scattered across the rustic tabletop.

"These are things I saved from when your mama and I were in high school." She sifted through a pile of notebooks and paperwork until coming to a worn Pee Chee folder. "Here it is." She pushed it across the table.

Sarah opened it. The side pockets were stuffed with photo store envelopes containing numerous black-and-white photographs, featuring teenagers of an earlier era. She selected a stack and flipped through them.

Marshland High was the most frequent backdrop, a much younger version than Sarah remembered. The new wing was still a gravel parking lot. That maple, the one she'd sat under only yesterday, was little more than a twig. Packed dirt appeared to be what the sports teams played on, rather than the Astroturf and state-of-the-art track surface currently blanketing those grounds.

"Just look at these." Sarah spread out the next collection—candid images of much younger versions of Aunt Millie and Mom.

"This is wonderful." She showed Aunt Millie one of her and Mom holding comical poses in a beat-up convertible.

"That's the car my father let me drive back then."

"He must've been crazy," said Harold.

"You've probably got a point there, hon'. But somehow we managed to live through it. Marshland had a lot less traffic back then. Most of the roads were still gravel. We could only go so fast. The main hazard was farm equipment around the next corner. Well, truthfully that came second to not going so fast that we got our clothes dusty or our hair messed up."

Aunt Millie pulled out another collection. "My trusty Instamatic took these back when your mama was making plans for her wedding."

Some of them she had seen before in her parents' albums. She immediately spotted a copy of her favorite—Mom trying on her wedding gown for the first time. She had always said she was saving it so Sarah could wear it at her own wedding.

No telling what happened with that dress now. Or the album either, for that matter. Gone forever. Along with other remnants of childhood. Everything that had been in that house was gone. A twinge of melancholy passed, painful but bittersweet.

A separate envelope held a professional-looking photo of her father. He was wearing his wedding tux. He looked so young, and debonair. More than just a little nervous.

The next packet didn't make sense. Her mother was wearing her wedding gown. But instead of her maid of honor clothes, Aunt Millie stood next to her dressed in a costume. It looked like something out of *Star Trek*.

"What's this one about?"

Mildred came around to look over her shoulder. "You know your mother, how into that she was. Instead of being gussied up in traditional wedding party clothes, she wanted us to wear *Star Trek* uniforms, like in those old re-runs. Mine was from making alterations to a Halloween costume pattern. But you can imagine how your father felt about the idea."

Harold slapped his hand on the table and broke into a gut-busting belly laugh. "First chance I get, I'm going to remind him of that. You've been holding out on me with that one, Millie. Standing up there doing the nuptials, right next to Captain Kirk. I can see him going 'Beam me aboard, Scotty!'"

He let loose with a second hoot of laughter.

"It was the first time I ever saw them get into a serious argument." Aunt Millie snatched the photo from Harold, giving him a dirty look. "Actually one of the only times. Your parents truly did love each other, even if they were as different as night and day. As you might expect, your Dad won that argument about how the wedding party would dress."

What a bunch of characters. Even as young people. Sarah picked up the photo of young Sam and gazed, savoring the temporary escape from here and now uncertainties.

"Your Dad will turn up, Sarah." Aunt Millie wrapped arms around her from behind. "I know he will."

The quilters were punctual. Each received the obligatory basement tour and progress report, then situated themselves the living room with Sarah. Sarah took full advantage of the arrivals, quizzing each guest about Dad's possible whereabouts. Sympathy abounded, but solid leads did not. Considerably more time and effort was spent describing the blow by blow of the schoolhouse altercation.

"You look better than last night." Jenny stopped to scrape mud from her shoes.

"I feel better, too," said Sarah. "You do quilting?"

"Jenny joined us when she moved here to work at the health clinic," said Aunt Millie.

"Actually I'm more of a knitter." Jenny added her shoes to the pile collecting by the doorway. "I enjoy these ladies so much, I decided to expand my horizons."

Most of the women had brought along crafting projects for show and tell. They busied themselves as they chatted. Sarah felt empty-handed with all the beautiful stitchery and yarn work coming together around her. Even Jenny, the relative newcomer, had her knitting needles clicking away.

From out of nowhere, Aunt Millie produced a large wad of teal-colored yarn and a crochet hook.

"Here you go, hon'. Get yourself something going. I remember those beautiful scarves you used to make. Jane wore hers for years. I always admired that scarf."

Sarah drew out the yarn and positioned it in her hands.

Amazing. It so naturally fell into place. She chained the beginning of a scarf, slowly at first, picking up speed as rhythm set in. Softness slid across her fingers, massaging them into tranquility.

How had she had forgotten about this? The contentment, the peace of it. She stopped chaining and squeezed the fleecy skein. Some kind of wool blend. A good choice, nice and warm for icy Iowa winters.

As the room continued to fill, the women shared collective updates on flood survivors, eventually gravitating to the project they were there to plan. Sarah watched over Aunt Millie's shoulder as she wrote down names of those impacted by the flood, starring ones in the worst shape. A growing list emerged.

"This is some stack of quilts we're talking about," said Shelley. "No way we can hand stitch them. Hell'd freeze over before we ever finished. Looks like machine stitching, for sure. Not as personal, but it'll get it done."

The other women nodded or otherwise agreed, willing and eager to do whatever necessary.

"I was thinking about doing crazy quilts." Aunt Millie lifted the paper bag at her feet and held it open, exposing the oddball fabric scraps hoarded within. "We could all get started on our own with whatever we've got on hand. And that flash flood certainly was a crazy flood."

"Or we could make them by salvaging," Elspeth chimed in. "You know, things that got too damaged by the flood to repair. No sense letting things go to waste."

"Hold on, now." Shelley's booming voice rose above the twittering. "You think people who lost everything would want that? Something out of that god-awful water? Sounds pretty disgusting to me. What do you think, Sarah? You're the people expert."

The women went silent, all eyes centered on Sarah.

Her crochet hook stilled. Shelley had caught her flat-footed. It seemed bizarre, so out of place. This group of women had watched over her, disciplined her, some even changing her diapers. Now they were looking to her for a definitive read on a social issue.

Their perspective of her had changed. Could it be only hers was not keeping up?

She cleared her throat, creating time to consider the question. "It would depend a lot on the person. How about you, Sylvia? Would you want something made from salvage?"

"I suppose if it was well-laundered, it would be okay. Maybe if it was something that had been my own. But that floodwater was nasty. Those pig farms are upriver. Who knows what all was in that water? It smelled to high heaven that night." Sylvia shuddered.

"What happened?" Sarah recalled what Chet had told her. At the time, she'd been dismissive, assuming his retelling of Sylvia's evacuation was as blown out of proportion as any other story he came up with. Perhaps she'd been too hasty.

The other women looked away, or busied themselves with their crafts. Sylvia at first remained silent. Not unexpected—the experience was still fresh.

"That was real scary, all right," she finally said. "I didn't know what to do. That old house is all I got left of the life me and Charlie had. I couldn't just leave it. But the boys came by, and made me get out. They loaded up things I already had in boxes. Some of them ended up downstream anyway, after the squad car started sinking. Roy came out and helped, you see.

"I thought we'd be goners for sure—me and Jimmy were in the squad car with Roy when it got swamped. Stewy brought his Green Gertie and towed us out. He saved us. Roy says Stewy's gonna get some kind of medal for everything he did to help folks that night."

No wonder she was so subdued. Sylvia had been through the ringer. And Lil was right about Jimmy still being around. For once he'd been a good son, rescuing his mother in her time of dire need. He must have done a lot of growing up since their volatile parting all those years ago. "Thank heavens you made it out all right. I know we can't do much about the things you lost, but can you think of anything this group could make that you would like?"

"You know, you got me thinking. Those boxes of Charlie's old things. I only kept them for sentimental reasons, they're in such bad shape. But a quilt out of his old favorites—now, that would be a delight. I think he'd be downright honored if those things got put to good use again. Not just for me, but anybody else going without right now."

"That's absolutely inspired," said Jenny. "I'd love to be part of a project like that."

The other women chatted up their approval.

"You know, Sarah, I always hoped you and my Jimmy would get together again someday," said Sylvia.

"What ever happened with Jimmy? Nate tells me a little about people back home every now and then. But he hasn't said much about Jimmy."

Sylvia stared downward, stitches fumbling. She set the knitting aside. "He's still around. I don't see him much. While you were away with your schooling, he got himself into trouble, mixed up with drugs."

"You don't have to bring up that old story." The sudden emergence of Aunt Millie's protective mother hen further piqued curiosity. A story to be told, one with sensitivities.

"Sarah was family all through high school," said Sylvia. "She's still family, far as I'm concerned. Everybody else here already knows. She may as well, too."

The women were respectfully silent while Sylvia gathered her thoughts.

"Jimmy and his father had a falling out. You see, Jimmy started taking things from around the house to pay for drugs. When Charlie figured it out, he was fit to be tied. He told Jimmy he wasn't welcome home anymore. Like he completely disowned him. I couldn't do nothing for it. Charlie'd just start drinking, if I tried."

"Who'd think we'd ever have that problem in our nice little town?" Elspeth sounded truly perplexed. On one hand it was refreshing, the naivety depicted by such bewilderment over a drug problem. But it highlighted how hardened she herself had become, perhaps even jaded, since leaving Marshland. Thanks to day-to-day clinical exposures, the story of a family member with a drug habit didn't feel at all unusual or remarkable.

But this time it involved someone she'd once been close to.

"He did get his drug problem taken care of." Sylvia shot a pointed glance at Elspeth. "In fact, after Charlie passed, Jimmy came by and tried to give me some money. Something about making restitution, a program he was doing. I told him I didn't care about the money. I just wanted him in our lives again. He was so ashamed at it all. He hardly looked me in the eye."

"We're certainly all hoping he's won that battle for good," said Jenny.

"So he's still here in Marshland?" said Sarah.

"During the flood we didn't talk about what he was doing. I don't know where he's staying. Some of his old buddies' families tell me things every now and then. Last I heard, he's still doing construction, mostly further south. Wherever the work is, I guess."

"Why, yes." Elspeth came to life. "I know for a fact. He's worked on Uncle Toddy's projects. And Uncle Toddy doesn't hire drug-taking people. Not if he knows about it."

"Maybe now that he's getting his life straightened out, he'll settle down with some nice lady. Make me some grandbabies. A family of his own might change things. He'd understand the sense of staying in touch."

It was not surprising Jimmy had eventually bottomed out. He'd always been on the wild side. Probably wouldn't have completed high school if not for her encouragement. He was plenty smart, but had needed a regular kick in the pants to follow through on anything. There'd been many an occasion when his homework had more her mark on it than his.

Old disappointments—how hurt she'd been when he laughed off the idea of applying to schools. How she could never get him to consider any goal much beyond the next twenty-four hours, which for Jimmy meant mainly fooling around with monster trucks or hanging out with rowdy friends. He had pressured her to forget about school and help him carouse. When she told him she was leaving anyway, he became indignant and acted out of anger. It was the last time she ever heard from him.

If only she had known then what she knew now. What if something could have been done to derail him from that track? He might have already been using in high school. She had been so innocent back then, she wouldn't have recognized it if it stared her in the face. It certainly would have explained his lack of academic motivation.

"I'm sorry about what you've been through." It stung to think of all Sylvia had endured. Such a dear, sweet woman, having watched her son progressively lose himself to drug abuse. "And now losing so much in the flood."

"I'm not even sure yet about what was lost. Lots of folks have been helping me clear out whatever didn't get rescued. It's all pretty much ruined. Some things I didn't know where to find before the flood. Now things are even stuck up in trees. I don't know where to begin."

"Tell us what's worth looking for," said Shelley. "It might help us think up something."

"Well, there's one thing that nags at me most. Remember that gorgeous heirloom jewelry I showed y'all, those pieces Charlie's mother left for her granddaughter? When Jimmy was having his problems, Charlie was afraid he'd get hold of it and sell it for drugs. So he said he'd stash it where Jimmy couldn't never find it. I figured it was in a safe deposit box or something.

"Then Charlie had that stroke. Y'all know he was never the same. Never said much more of anything, let alone what happened to that jewelry. We looked around after he was gone. But we never found a safe deposit box, or nothing. It might've been hidden somewhere and got washed away when the flood came through. Or it's in the mud we shoveled out."

"What did you do with everything you hauled out?" Shelley asked.

"It's still there, piled up where the front lawn used to be. They say the National Guard's coming through next week to take everything away."

"That settles it," said Shelley. "If it's going to the dump anyway, let's throw ourselves a party and go through it. Hell, let's take it apart. We'll make sure that jewelry's not hidden in something out there. We'll call it a treasure hunt. Who knows what we'll find?"

"If nothing else, I bet there's change under the sofa cushions." Elspeth, well-absorbed in thoughts of a salvaging project, took no notice of the light laughter following her comment.

"And we can talk about those home furnishings of yours we all spent part of our lives with," said Aunt Millie. "We'll all give it a proper goodbye. We could bring rakes and shovels, too, in case that jewelry ended up out in the mud. I bet we could talk the men folk into donating a little brawn. Especially if we work in a promise of food."

"It could be the kick-off for the quilting project, too," said Shelley.

"I'll videotape the whole thing," Aunt Millie added. "You'll have it forever that way, digitalized."

"That's so sweet of you," said Sylvia. "All of you, doing this for me. You're bar none the best friends a gal could ever have. Yes. Let's have us a treasure hunt this weekend."

By the time Sarah was ready to leave, the fete was a fully planned event, sustenance to be provided by barbecue potluck. Everybody was going to pitch in with something. Sarah mostly listened, soaking in the warmth of their bonded tenacity.

They would make it through this mishap just fine. Together, the way they always had.

"Take this along with you." Aunt Millie stuffed the yarn and crochet hook into a small denim bag and placed it in Sarah's hands. "It'll give you something productive to do when you're sitting around by yourself in that motel room."

"Take these with you, too." She handed Sarah two photographs: the one of young Sam in his tux, and the shot of teenage Jane and Mildred in the convertible.

"Thanks Aunt Millie, for everything." Sarah hugged her. It was hard to let go, as it also appeared for Aunt Millie. "I'll make copies of these pictures and return them to you. Tell Uncle Harold goodbye for me."

"Come by again before you leave town and tell him yourself. Come to the barbecue, too. You need to stop and eat sometime."

"There's no way I'd miss it." By the time she had completed her farewells, visions of Harold's barbecued chicken were already dancing across her taste buds.

*****

"Following around that Turner gal didn't turn up nothing." Steve rolled down the window the rest of the way and took off his cap, dabbing away perspiration with his sleeve.

"Where did she go?"

"I kept an eye on that shack while I was working the warehouse. She never showed. I got off early, and went on over to city hall. That pretty little Miata was right where you said. But she wasn't around. So I found something useful to do there and just waited."

"How resourceful."

"After a while, she showed up and drove to the Lone Pine. Then she went to a house down by the river until dark. A whole bunch of women started showing up, so I skedaddled before anybody took mind of me. Later on, I drove around the block a bit. She was still there. Far as I know, she never got nowhere near that shed."

"While you were on your wild-goose chase, I took the liberty of checking her motel room."

Steve studied him. "How'd you manage that?"

"She left a window open."

Steve threw down his hat. "You climbed through a window, in broad daylight? That's crazy. Someone on the road might've seen you."

"No need to panic. I scouted it out first. Most people staying there weren't around. Probably out doing disaster crap. The maid was working the other end of the building. And the highway was clear."

"You're still taking too many damn chances."

"How 'bout I go smack Sam around a bit, and get a key that way?" He smirked. "I've got an even better idea. Let's round up Sarah, make him do a trade to get her back. Have us a good time with her."

Steve scowled instead of saying anything. He was being joked around with. But that was how it started out with the trailer abode. It started out as a joke, and then turned real. Good people didn't deserve this. "What you got to show for your break-in?"

"I didn't find it. If she has one, it must be on the key ring she carries. It wasn't a total loss, though. I did find these little honeys. Help yourself."

He removed a prescription bottle from his shirt pocket and tossed it. Steve snatched it out of the air and read the label.

"Muscle relaxant? I got no problems with my muscles." He handed it back.

"Don't be such a pussy. Maybe you wouldn't be so uptight if you'd try a little something for it. Maybe even enjoy yourself for once."

"You take these just for fun? Is that what this is all about? Money for drugs?"

"Of course not. But it don't hurt to go ahead and enjoy the perks of life. Especially when you know you'll be running into a little extra spending money. Can't forget the freebies you find along the way." He held up the prescription bottle and grinned.

CHAPTER NINE

Thursday, June 5th

"How's Junior doing?"

The Paulson standing before her today was the one she'd originally caught sight of, strolling through her childhood stomping grounds as though he didn't have a care in the world. The hair that yesterday had been slicked back had returned to a tumble of squiggles. His attire would fit in with any barnyard scene, mirroring the character of that beat up knapsack that followed him everywhere. He clearly hadn't bothered to shave.

In spite of it, he looked comfortable with himself, so different from the tense and formal vibe of the previous day's outing. It felt like they were heading out for a climb in the hills, or a float down the river, rather than getting ready to jump headlong into a disaster operation.

It was surprising, the calm she felt at the sight of his more relaxed presentation. Especially since it was exactly what had thrown her off about him in the first place. Now it only felt like Paulson being Paulson. Easy, and comfortable. Appealing, even. The very last descriptor she thought she'd ever use to describe Paulson Forbes.

"Junior is doing fine." He nosed them through the Lone Pine parking maze and out onto the highway. "All set up in her new digs. It gave me something to do last night besides think about work."

"It would be fun to see her in her new home. If you wouldn't mind showing me sometime."

"Yeah, sure."

"I had a great visit with Aunt Millie and Uncle Harold. I saw people I hadn't seen in years. They're planning this big barbecue tomorrow to help out an old friend. I promised Aunt Millie I'd show up. Why don't you come, too? They won't mind if I bring my carpool buddy."

"Uh, yeah, okay."

"Anyway, after I got back to the motel I called Nate. He's still tied up—big surprise. I told him don't worry about it. It's not critical for him to be here, other than to satisfy his own mind. He'd just sit around wheel spinning, same as me."

"Good." His eyes were glued to the road. He seemed oddly distant.

She shrugged it off. "Nate said the fire department had been in touch. The fire inspector decided the old wiring was to blame."

"Certainly got the most votes in the rumor mill."

"It's nice to know it wasn't arson, or carelessness. Still doesn't tell us anything about Dad. Nate says the police have drawn one big blank. I told him about running into Lil. So far she's been the only one with anything at all useful. It keeps making me wonder why I bother to be here."

"I can tell you exactly why you're here." He crouched over the steering wheel and assumed an Igor posture. "It's so you and I can go play disaster together, heh-heh, heh-heh."

She groaned and rolled her eyes. "Right. So I take it you're ready for another day at this. My first shot at it didn't end well. I wonder if that will affect what Lacey comes up with for us."

He didn't immediately respond. In fact, outside the effort he'd put into the Igor imitation, it was as if his higher functioning brain was still in a jar back at the lab.

"I'm not sure how much longer I'll be able to do this," he said. "My director dumped a huge administrative task into my lap. I understand why she picked me for it. It's disaster related. I know more about what's going on right now than anybody else in the local mental health system. But this looks way out of my league."

"Lacey's an information powerhouse. Bring it up with her."

"That's probably where I'll start, since I can't seem to get through to the director. To be honest, I don't have a handle on what it's for. The services it describes aren't actual treatment. It's for hiring people to do what we're already doing with volunteers. It doesn't add up."

"Does sound odd, doesn't it."

"Until I hear more from my director, my future with the operation is on hold. Unless Lacey can shed a little light."

*****

Lacey eyed her, nodding approval. "You look ready for the field today."

"I'm ready for wherever you want to send me." Sarah struck a pose, drawing exaggerated attention to her new clothes.

Paulson watched Sarah head toward the canteen, her form definitely made for well-fitting jeans.

"Mental health meeting, first up," Lacey called after her.

"How did the day off go?" she asked Paulson.

"Restful. You were right. I needed it."

"Your color's back. Sarah seems better this morning, too. Not so distracted. More engaged."

"I noticed, too. She spent time with some old friends yesterday. And I took her into Willsey to pick up a few things."

"So it's working out, then."

Paulson switched his pack to the other shoulder, thinking up how to skirt it. "It turns out she's quite the survivor. Her sense of humor is something else. Even in the middle of really tense moments."

It wasn't a complete glossing over. His teaming up with Sarah truly was better off than the day before. But he couldn't get more specific than that—no. Especially while reporting to Lacey.

"Let's see if we can keep the tense moments limited to helping troubled clients," she said.

"You've got my vote there. Before we're tied up, I'd like to pick your brain about something." He described the materials the director had sent, since he'd forgotten to stop by and pick them up from the clinic. *Talk about mental blocks.*

"Sounds like the FEMA crisis counseling program. I remember a frustrated administrator once telling me it would be more pragmatic if everybody who put in overtime on all that paperwork simply took second jobs bagging groceries, and we used those earnings to fund services instead. Wait'll you see the paperwork for the long-term program."

Typical bureaucracy. Even in disaster. "Is it worth it? If volunteers are already taking care of it, why should we bother?"

"The feds designate responsibility for this to local public health programs. Relief organizations like ours only do what the community can't do on its own. Once federal programs get going, everybody else goes home."

He mulled it over. "I suppose it's all well and good. But this psychological first aid stuff only goes so far. It's not going to take care of significant conditions—PTSD, depression, substance abuse—everything else we'll be seeing down the road because of this flood. What does this program do for them? Anything?"

"The idea is prevention. Keeping symptoms at bay."

"You and I both know that won't work for everybody. And people most affected, most at risk, almost always have the fewest resources. The poor, the disabled. Any outcast populations."

"Yes, I know resilience carries the day for most of them," he added before Lacey could interrupt. "And those who already qualified for free services will be taken care of. But what about everybody else? These days, even people with insurance have trouble coming up with co-pays. What happens with them?"

"Many areas have groups of mental health professionals who offer pro bono services during disaster. We often use them for referrals."

"There aren't any such groups in Marshland, or in the entire county for that matter. I, Paulson Forbes, am the mental health program, a half-time position at that. The waiting list is outrageous. Lots of people end up going to Willsey, paying out of pocket. But services there have their limits, too. It sounds like the citizens of Marshland are pretty much out of luck."

"I know. Yes. I know." There was a trace of something vulnerable, almost haggard in how she said it.

It was the first time any sort of chink had appeared in her armor. She'd been the unwavering bulwark of confidence, no matter how extreme, unusual, or out and out weird things became. Until now. "So what do I do with this application, other than get pissed off?"

She sighed. "It's not so bad, as far as your role. Several counties are affected. Someone at state level is probably working it out. I'll have a word with a few people this morning."

"Thanks." *And lots of luck.* The director certainly was taking her time responding to his voice message. He'd left it some time ago.

"Tell you what. Hang around for fill in and hotshot. Spend the day here. I'll find things for you to do. That way you'll be more available for your director's call. Or if I dig up anything."

"Why not." Given his nosedive in enthusiasm, it wasn't like he'd be able to concentrate on what he did, anyway. Being stuck inside administrating would fall right in step.

"It'll be a good learning experience, seeing what goes on at the leadership end. You seem to be pretty much it for disaster mental health around here. You'll be in a better position to collaborate, the next time you're waiting for the cavalry to show up."

"Right now probably isn't the best time to consider my future with disaster work. It's becoming as frustratingly outrageous as the job I left behind in Detroit."

"It's the nature of the beast. If we're going to do any good, someone's got to play dragon slayer. There will be obstacles. Sometimes the dragon wins. But in the end, we do good for those who need someone to advocate for them."

"It's times like this that I wonder how much simpler life would be if I'd settled for being a Starbucks barista." He scanned the crowded room, the administrative brew bubbling away. What would it be like, spending a day submerged in it? "I'll give it a shot. It'll be easier to blow off steam here."

"Just keep those 'tense moments' to a minimum. We do a lot of staff mental health here at headquarters. It won't help any if the DMH support always looks ready to blow a cork."

*****

Sarah returned, her satchel bulging with bottled water, handouts, and other supplies she'd gathered up along the way. Paulson and Lacey had become cloistered with the other mental health staff. She squeezed in, positioning her awkward load between her feet.

Lacey was already in full swing. Everywhere she looked, the stir of aimless disorganization had transitioned into peers gathered in small groups. Their day was about to begin.

And she was about to become a functioning part of it. A massive team, one that was truly making a difference. At least, she would her do her darnedest. It was hard to judge what would happen, with her role still a floating mystery. Or if her assignment would get her any closer to finding Dad.

"The latest monkey wrench is the weather," said Lacey. "By now, everybody's heard about the new storm. Water's still up in places from the last one, and the flood plains are saturated. For a little added excitement, this new weather system is expected to have tornado cells."

"I've never been in a tornado before," said one of the new workers. "What are we supposed to do if they say there's one coming?"

"Follow the instructions of whoever's in charge at your site."

Whatever that turned out to be. Did these out of town supervisors really know what to do during a tornado? The worker who asked about it didn't look particularly reassured.

Lacey went on with her spiel. "Meanwhile, assignments are the same as yesterday. Paulson and Sarah are back from their days off. Paulson will be here with me today. I'm still working on Sarah's assignment. Any questions? Okay, let's go make it happen."

Workers put chairs away and gathered up belongings. Lacey doled out answers and reassurances as she herded them on their way.

Sarah's urge to tap her toe against the concrete eventually won out. So this was what they meant by "hurry up and wait."

"So, what's my assignment?" she asked Lacey, once everybody else had gotten in gear.

"For starters, check in with Jenny at staff health. She needs to give you the green light."

"I feel pretty good today. Really. My back is still bothering me a little, but it's nothing I can't deal with." She didn't mention the missing prescription meds. Given how that stuff affected her, she was in no hurry to track down a refill.

"You look okay to me. Staff nurses will still want to keep an eye on you, all the same. They asked if I'd assign you to one of their all-purpose teams."

"An all-purpose team?" This she had to see.

"There's one going out today that needs a mental health worker. It's someone who hurt her ankle. They're checking on injury-related needs."

"Wouldn't she already have had medical attention by now? It's been three or four days."

"Our disaster nurses don't do usual medical treatment, the same as you don't do traditional mental health intervention. They pass out public health-type advice. They make sure survivors with injuries or other maladies aren't so wrapped up in recovery work that they put off treatment too long. They also help set up referrals and arrange to pay for certain things—disaster-related doctor visits, lost medications, and the like."

Sarah mentally reviewed what she'd read about her own function. Nothing came to mind about her role in such a scenario. "So, what about me? What am I there for?"

"Same as any other assignment. Tend to any mental health issues you run into. Do a little psychological first aid, whatever else needed. Keep in mind that those with physical injuries are at greater risk down the road for emotional problems. Take it from there. You know the drill."

"Sounds pretty straightforward. Where do I find the rest of my team?"

It felt even more like high school than the day before.

Nurse Bonnie and the caseworker, Marsha, were giggling like schoolgirls over some inside joke as Sarah approached them. In spite of the unorthodox culture spilling out around her, the team concept did have a sense of adventure to it. Several different professionals addressing a client's needs in one sitting seemed practical, almost common sense.

She climbed into the back seat to discover a small, wizened man with large burgundy-rimmed glasses, decked out in full disaster-form regalia. If it weren't for the vest swamping his elfin frame, she would be checking his shirt for a pocket protector. He greeted her with an enthusiastic handshake.

"I'm Stan. I do Public Affairs."

"Public Affairs. That's working with the media, right?"

"That's me." Pride seeped from every pore.

"I don't get it. What's that got to do with a sprained ankle?"

"I'm not here for that. A charity group financed repairs for her house. A TV crew is coming out to do a piece."

"Nice human interest story I guess. Pretty mild-mannered, though."

"All those dramatic flood scenes have lost their wallop. The media need something else to keep ratings up. They might play up the angle of builders hurrying to get the roof fixed before the next storm hits."

Marsha stopped giggling long enough to take note of their previously invisible passenger. "So what exactly do you do when you go to one of these?"

"In part, I make sure they don't overdo it for her. Protect her from invasion, if need be. Sometimes the media crew looks to me for information, or as an inroad to get to stories. I might even share my idea about the race with the storm."

"Could you do something to get me on TV?" said Marsha. "I can do 'Raindrops Keep Falling on My Head' on my kazoo."

Bonnie and Marsha dissolved into another round of laughter.

"If they want to interview us, I can brief you all on it." Stan seemed oblivious to the disaster version of gallows humor. "Not just so you do a better job, but also because disaster insignia looms large. We've got these vests on. Whatever you say or do on camera can end up being attributed to the relief organizations. We always need to look good to the public. This is all paid for by public donations."

"Does Lacey know about this?" said Sarah. "My supervisor. She didn't say anything about a TV crew being there."

"Probably not. I found out about it myself just before I hitched a ride with you guys."

"Are you sure it's okay for me to be interviewed? This is my first case assignment in disaster, ever. What do I know?"

"Say only what you know for sure. Or describe your role with the operation. If you're worried, have a word with your manager."

He quickly punched a number into his phone and handed it to her.

What, he's memorized them already?

*****

He leaned his chin into one hand, bounced the Superball against the wall with the other, and tracked the climbing progress of a small black spider that seemed extraordinarily responsive to wall vibrations. He picked up his feet and rested them on the table.

So this was what his day would be about. Sitting on the phone while his manager goes to another meeting. *Whoopee.*

Before disappearing, Lacey had assigned him the lackluster task of backtracking hours he'd worked so far so they could insert them into the records. It had taken five minutes, tops.

How stimulating. He yawned.

Most phone calls involved issues that only Lacey could resolve. Few on the other end had much interest in casual conversation. Only so much creativity could be put into filling out message slips. All in all, headquarters life was breathtakingly dull.

He checked again for messages on his cell. If only his director would call back.

Once again the mental health phone went off.

"Don't wait on me, Itsy," he told the spider. "Mental health. This is Paulson."

There was silence.

"Hello?"

"I was expecting Lacey. This is Sarah."

Now, that's more like it. "Sarah. Thanks for rescuing me. I don't know how I'll ever recover from the excitement of a day at disaster operations central."

"You've been doing it all of an hour, and already you're bored?"

"It seems a lot longer when you're watching paint dry."

"Is Lacey there? I have a question for her."

"Like everybody else. She's in a meeting. Is it something I might be able to take care of?"

"I don't know. We just found out a TV crew might show up where I'm going."

"I can write up another message for her. I don't recommend holding your breath for a return call, though. The way she darts around this place is like Junior tending her habitat. Do you think you can handle it without talking to her? I'm not supposed to pull her out of the meeting unless it's an emergency."

"The public affairs guy says he can coach us."

"I see someone at a table that says 'public affairs.' I could ask her about it. She looks as bored as me. I could even count it as a mental health contact. For myself, if nobody else."

"I guess so. It's better than nothing."

He set down the phone and crossed the room. The worker he'd spotted was sketching spectacles and a lightening bolt scar on a newspaper photo of Mayor Schwartz. Apparently to go along with the wizard's hat she'd already crafted onto his head.

"So this is how you handle the excitement."

"Sitting back and waiting for the mayor to make more promises," she said. "Playing Little Switzerland as needed. How are things in your corner?"

"Pretty dead."

"Enjoy it while you can. It'll change when the managers get back with the latest."

"Question: I've got a mental health worker on the line who says a public affairs worker came with them, in case they get interviewed."

"That would be the Frieda Martinson case. Stan drew the assignment. I got stuck here. Is there a problem?"

"The mental health worker on the team is pretty green. She's a little nervous."

"Don't worry about it. Stan will take good care of her."

She went back to her artwork. He returned to the phone.

"It's all legit. Just go along with whatever Stan tells you. That's what he's there for."

"I'll give it my best. See you later."

"Good luck with it." *Not so fast.* He scrambled for subterfuge, anything that might extend the conversation. "Wait . . . do you know if you'll be here by lunch?"

"I don't know. We might do some other referrals. It depends how long this one takes."

"Okay. Well, if you can get away, maybe Lacey will let me loose for a while. We could get a bite somewhere. Compare notes on our assignments. Yours is more interesting than mine."

"I wouldn't mind a visit to Uncle Harold's deli. I haven't been there in years."

"Sounds good. Just keep me posted." He waited, hoping for something more. "Is there anything else I can do?"

"That's it, but thanks for asking. I better get going."

"Right." He'd milked it dry. *Damn.* "Okay then. Have a nice day."

CHAPTER TEN

Lacey's meeting finally broke up. Within seconds, noise rose to a dull roar, as disaster relief managers scattered in all directions to dive into various tasks. Paulson handed Lacey the stack of phone messages.

She gave them a perfunctory glance and set them aside. "I've come up with a task for you."

Thank God.

"I'm tied up this morning with inclement weather planning. One of the managers pulled me aside about somebody. It's a worker who's here, right now, but will probably soon leave the operation. His supervisor wants us to give him a once over."

"So this guy didn't come asking for help. The higher-ups think he needs it." *Figures.*

"Yeah. He's behind me. That short guy, by himself at the canteen. Recognize him? He's listed as a local community volunteer."

Paulson looked over her shoulder and spotted a youngish man, sitting alone. Hunched over, and fiddling with his water bottle.

"I've seen him around," he said. "I don't know him. He does look down in the dumps."

"He's been working places like the warehouse and bulk distribution. He joined early on, when they weren't sticklers about sign-up. Finally someone brought him in for registration. He was almost immediately uncooperative."

"Was it the health interview? Maybe there's a condition he's afraid would come out."

"Something to keep in mind. It's hard to say more without more specifics."

At last, something he could sink his teeth into.

"His manager says he's a nice guy, and a hard worker," Lacey continued. "He'd prefer to keep him around. But rules are rules."

"It sounds like this isn't just about him, then."

"Their cadre has several days of disaster bonding under their belts. Probably exhausted, too, since most have been at it a week now. They're invested in the idea that mental health can save the day."

"I can only accomplish so much. But I'll give this one a shot." He nodded in the direction of the hangdog looking disaster responder.

"I'll intervene with others, if need be. Meanwhile, client number one is sitting right there."

It was all he could do to keep from rubbing his hands together. Finally, real work. The work he was there for. "I'll go feel him out. What's his name?"

"Steve."

*****

As a child, Sarah always thought Frieda Martinson looked like a female version of "Tiny Tim," a character on one of those reruns Mom used to watch. Even with bandaging and crutches, Frieda managed to tiptoe through the parlor as if she were on four-inch heels, her voice a labile falsetto that most would assume to be a put-on. Having known her most of her life, however, Sarah knew it was for real. And it was not at all surprising that Frieda hadn't been able to avoid becoming a casualty.

Frieda served them weak tea in chipped antique china, in spite of protestations that such niceties were unnecessary. Noisy construction workers swarming the roof brought frequent thumping and distant murmurings into the room.

"I said, how is your ankle doing?" Bonnie yelled over a sudden crescendo of hammering.

"What?" Frieda shouted back.

"Your ankle. What your insurance company didn't cover. Those crutches?"

"Oh, it's not so bad. I got the crutches last winter when I slipped on the ice. I just got them from the broom closet, and off to the emergency clinic we went."

She could probably get there blindfolded.

The pounding came to a reprieve. Stan released and flexed the fingers he kept jamming in his ears. "Is there someplace on the other side of the house where we might chat? Your parlor is absolutely lovely. But I have very sensitive hearing. It's hard for me to listen."

"I know just the place. Let's go sit out on the porch. We'll have our tea party out there."

Sarah lurched forward and grabbed the tray of china, sliding it away before Frieda could get hold of it. "How about if I carry this? You show us the way."

The porch setting was as delightful as promised, as if it had been made for the beautiful spring day. One side overlooked the colorful flowering meadows surrounding Frieda's neighborhood. To the other side were construction-related obstructions—of little matter to her compatriots, who were busy appraising options ranging from hanging swings to deck chairs.

She set the china on the patio table, which unfortunately placed them with the less alluring view. However it positioned them well away from the swings, rockers and any other potential conduits for Frieda's accident proneness. Resigned to duty, the team members dragged additional chairs to the table. While Bonnie and Marsha reorganized their paperwork, Sarah went over the material on emotional recovery after disaster.

Frieda smiled back at her, vacuous. "Thanks, but I'm fine. I've been through much worse than a sprained ankle."

Perhaps re-explaining the angle of trauma during disaster would be a good idea, as per Lacey's last-minute reminder. But then again, Frieda's life had always been one disaster after another. They never seemed to faze her. She really did seem fine, from a mental health perspective. She'd likely be fine later. *My work is done here.*

Bonnie and Marsha were busy with their part of the interview when a van plastered with gigantic GNAT lettering crept up the drive. Two grimy passenger vehicles followed.

"It's the TV crew." Marsha jumped up for a better look.

"I hate to do this to you nice folks. It looks like time for that interview I told y'all about."

"Don't worry, Frieda." Bonnie stepped up to help her out of her chair. "We'll be okay here. You go right ahead. Have yourself a good time. We'll all be rallying for you."

They watched her negotiate the porch steps, which eventually required Stan's hurried assistance. With that mishap averted, they sat back in their patio chairs and prepared to watch the show.

Stan briefly introduced himself to the interviewer then rejoined them. "Always keep in mind that whenever a TV camera's around, assume you're being filmed. Even if it's pointed in the opposite direction. Act the way you would if you were the one being interviewed. That way you can be sure they won't catch you scratching where it itches or something."

Sarah gave herself a once over, checking for anything that might not be presentable. The new fieldwork clothing seemed to be holding up well.

The camera crew scampered about in preparation. Sporadic hammering and voices of men hard at work on Frieda's roof were still within earshot. The technicians positioned the camera so the reconstruction activity could serve as the backdrop.

"This is fun." Marsha strained for a better view of the television personality, who was having a preliminary conversation with Frieda and the charity representative. "I wish they were closer so we could hear what's going on."

"I suspect they purposely chose that spot. This way, street noise and our conversation won't be a problem." Stan hushed his voice, the interview about to begin. "We'll probably have to wait until it airs to hear what they talk about."

Frieda's peculiarities would look great on TV.

Sarah let her mind wander, and waited for the interview to be over with.

Except . . . something suddenly felt wrong. Something had changed. Become off somehow. She took another look at Frieda.

No, she didn't appear to have positioned herself in a way that might risk life or limb, hers or others. The interviewer had seen to that by propping her up against a fencepost. Sarah studied the specifics of the roof repair project. They were in the process of passing materials up to an area where some reframing was going on.

But that wasn't it. Something not happening was setting off her instincts.

A worker standing on the ladder appeared mentally stalled, or somehow disengaged from the systematic regimen driving the rest of his group. His arms mainly dangled at his sides. He kept gazing in the general direction of the porch, unaware of the lumber someone below was trying to hand him. He eventually noticed and passed it to the next worker. Afterwards he turned their way and again stilled.

Was he okay? Was it some kind of seizure activity? Maybe she should say something to Nurse Bonnie.

The man clambered down the ladder and had a brief word with the foreman. Then began walking toward them.

Could it be . . .

As he distanced himself from the roofing activity, he removed his hardhat and dropped it to the ground. Then quickened to a more natural pace.

That swagger. That tilt of the chin.

Sarah stood. Stan was saying something, but she tuned it out. She proceeded off the porch and took a few uneasy steps.

Jimmy Orton.

Jimmy also stopped, leaving a couple of paces between them.

The creases and shadows lining his face suggested a rough history, consistent with what Sylvia had told her. But that familiar twinkle—it was still there. That same devil-may-care, defiant, let's-have-fun freedom that had prompted so many escapes from her adolescent preoccupation with academics.

"Sarah. I'm . . . sorry."

Sorry? She had no idea what to say, what to do. Or even what his apology specifically referred to. There'd been no preparation time, no opportunity to think it through. Her brain still occasionally rattled with commentary she wished she'd shared during their break-up. But nothing was easily at hand for responding to something like this.

"I'm sorry it ended for us the way it did," he continued. "I was an ass about it. It took a few years and a lot of hard knocks to get it figured out."

She finally found a way to unclench her teeth. "Apology accepted."

He continued to gaze at her, uncertainty ruling his appearance as much as it probably did for hers. He was taller now, more so with those thick-heeled work boots. He had filled out considerably. His exposed arms were beaded with perspiration. So tan and buff, an expectable result of many hours of heavy outdoor labor.

He was no longer a boy, that boy who'd journeyed along with her during their first serious boyfriend/girlfriend pairing. Nor the boy who had awakened her blossoming teenage sexuality. She could read those memories in his eyes. Eyes that at the same time looked distant. Yet seeking.

Without warning, he reached out and pulled her toward him, those burly arms clasping her to his chest. It was startling, so abrupt. He held her tightly, with such quiet desperation. When she raised her head to look at him, he immediately covered her mouth with his. Not as the boy she had once known, but with the maturity and experience of a man.

The passion of it was both disarming and intoxicating. Her knees gave out. Jimmy held her up, her limp body leaning backwards, her brain feeling like mush.

The construction noise stopped, replaced by enthusiastic applause. Stan's voice was still back there, too. Though now it sounded like he was barely keeping himself from becoming apoplectic.

When Jimmy finally released her, the television personality was already halfway there, microphone in hand.

"Well, what do we have here?" He was practically drooling.

They turned to face him. Jimmy kept an arm wrapped across her shoulders. He pulled her into his side.

Something's wrong about this. It did not feel like affection. His actions felt more territorial than anything else.

Her back muscle spasmed.

"We went to high school together." Jimmy was smooth as ever, as if he'd been giving interviews to celebrity personalities his entire life.

"Now it looks like we're doing disaster work together. I've been doing repairs. Sarah . . . is with a relief organization?"

"She's a real nice counseling lady, like I told you." Frieda hobbled up next to the interviewer. "She's been helping us disaster victims. She came back home just to help us out."

"And now you've found each other again. Right here on our show."

Stan finally wedged himself into the action, popping up between them and the subtly humming recording equipment.

"Could we please have a word?" Stan's nerdy overfamiliarity slowly backed the interviewer away.

"I hope I didn't get you in trouble." While Jimmy watched Stan's theatrics Sarah extricated herself from his grasp, ordering her knees to get with the program.

It didn't feel right. None of it. Not just her complaining back muscle, or finding herself in front of a television camera. Nothing about this spontaneous interchange with Jimmy felt like a genuine experience of reunion. Once again it was all Jimmy, going after what Jimmy wanted. As if she were still only a pawn to be used, just like when they'd parted all those years ago.

"I see you're still a big fan of seizing the moment." She straightened her vest.

"I'm glad to see you. You can't hardly fault me for that, can you?" His face wore that half-serious smirk, one so well remembered. And almost always succeeded in ticking her off. Which he surely hadn't forgotten.

"I suppose this really isn't the best time or place. We probably should have waited until . . ."

His face darkened. He backed away, then snatched up his hardhat. "Just when was I supposed to make a move? It took over a decade for this chance to come around."

"Jimmy, I only meant that . . . "

"I see things haven't changed much for you either, Sarah." Swagger took him back to the construction area. So familiar, yet a stranger.

"See you around town," he called over his shoulder.

*****

Paulson paused, considered how best to approach Steve.

It could be the man was angry, or feeling mistreated and singled out. Maybe he was only unhappy about needing to leave. Or perhaps it was as he'd suggested to Lacey, that he was anxious about revealing something embarrassing. Just worn out, maybe? And this was an excuse to end his involvement. It could be all of the above. Or something entirely different.

He dispensed a cup of coffee, the slow, steady trickle paralleling his mental shift into provider self. "Mind if I join you?"

"Make yourself at home. I'll be heading out soon enough, all the same."

"You're leaving?" Paulson tried a sip of coffee as he sat.

"Not that I really want to. Don't got no choice."

"There's always choices. I'm Paulson, with mental health." He offered his hand.

Steve gave it an anemic squeeze then let it go. "I thought I seen you before. That first day after the flood, wasn't it? In that neighborhood we worked in. Over by the river."

"We sure did make the rounds. What a mess down there."

"We gave them a good piece of help, we did. I did enjoy that. All those good folks, helping one another. Working so hard to get things right. It's an honor, doing this work."

"I don't think I've run into you before this happened. Where are you from?"

"I'm from nowhere right now. My folks moved out to Willsey several years back. I been staying with them a while. Between jobs, you see. It's been hard with this recession. Doing disaster work's a fine way to go, while waiting on work that pays, that is."

"What kind of work do you do?"

"Handyman, home repairs. Construction, if I can get it. I heard tell about some on line for down by the river. A resort or something, where them neighborhoods got washed away. I been hanging around, see, hoping to talk to the right person."

That story again. Another installment to fuel outcries over the proposed zoning changes. Fears they'd be muscled through, in spite of overwhelming public sentiment.

Yet Steve's strategizing sounded based on an outcome already set in stone. Did he know something more than everybody else? "So you found work, then. That's why you're leaving?"

"Well, no. It was a conflicting point of view. About what's necessary, for this job."

"Like what? If you don't mind my asking."

"They said they need everyone to do a criminal background check." His slumped form straightened, stiffening as he leaned back and folded his arms. "Now that just don't seem right. There's all sorts of good people out there who made mistakes when they was just kids. Or did wrong, then mended their ways. Why do they need to know about all that? It invades privacy."

So apparently Steve had run afoul of the law somewhere along the line and wanted to keep it under wraps. Couldn't say he blamed him.

"I might be able to clear your mind a bit on that one. Yes, relief organizations try to keep the criminal element out of the picture. You wouldn't want sex offenders, drug dealers or violent criminals around to cause harm to disaster survivors, or staff either, for that matter."

"Course not. But that's not what I'm talking about."

"My understanding is that the criminal background check covers the last several years, not a worker's entire lifetime. Things that happened when they were minors probably wouldn't be released anyway. Even if something did turn up on the background check, it would be kept private. Like anything you say to me, while we sit here talking."

"Is that right." Steve looked thoughtful. "Maybe I should look into that then." In spite of the positive resolve of his words, despondent eyes continued staring at the ground.

"You don't look encouraged."

"I don't mean to be unappreciative. It's something else."

"I'm here to lend an ear. Like I said, anything you say is between you and me. Unless, of course, I hear something that says you might hurt yourself or someone else."

Steve laughed. "I'm not thinking about doing myself in or nothing. And I wouldn't hurt nobody, not knowing it anyway."

"Is this private enough, here?"

Steve gave the headquarters hubbub a dubious glance. "How about we get some fresh air?"

"I've been waiting for such an offer all morning." He followed Steve out the back, into the city hall parking lot. Most of the rental car fleet had left. Few other people could be seen, just a couple workers taking tobacco breaks at the far end of the lot.

Steve sat on the edge of the curb. Paulson joined him.

"It's like this." Steve picked up a wayward wood chip and studied it before tossing it in with its parking strip cohorts. "I got this friend who's in a pickle."

Him again, the infamous friend with so many problems. It would be mighty interesting to meet that poor guy someday.

"My friend . . . let's call him Ted."

"Okay. What sort of problem does Ted have?"

"Back when he was a kid, he had himself a piece of trouble. You see, for a while there he fell in with a bad crowd. They were getting into people's houses and the like—taking money, or things they'd sell. Made a little spending money, for this or that. It got him trouble with the law."

Steve stopped to take a draw from his water bottle.

"That's all over and done with." He wiped his chin with his sleeve. "Then, times got tough. Moneywise. Not too long ago he met up again with someone he done highway cleanup with. This friend had ideas about breaking into homes in those evacuated areas. He said those folks would have it all made up for by FEMA and the like, anyhow. So they might as well take advantage."

Clinical tracking came to a screeching halt. Clashing agenda leaped into its place: Dora's perp. Did Steve know something about who hurt Dora?

"He also said making it hard for folks living by the river might run them off. It would move things along for construction jobs. The delay would be done with. There'd be plenty of work for folks like me. And Ted."

A dozen questions assailed him, all wanting to take command of his tongue at once.

Your professional duty. Client first, Steve's personal dilemma. Not the particulars of what you're itching to grill him over.

"Ted's been staying on the right side of the law all this time. He didn't want no part of it. Then his friend said all he wanted was to know how to get into places without causing a ruckus. He just wanted me to give him some learning, see. Help a bit with scouting things out. Easy places to get into. How to break in. Then he'd share some of what he got from it.

"Ted went along at first. But it didn't go how he was told. Now he wants out, altogether. But this friend, he's a bad one. Scary enough on a good day. Ted doesn't want any harm coming his way. Or to his family."

"Has Ted considered telling the police?"

"No way. He knows what the law'll do."

"Did Ted's friend directly threaten him?"

Steve thought about it. "I guess not. He worries about it all the same, I think."

"That's a tough one. My advice to Ted is to tell the police. Yes, he made a bad mistake. He shouldn't have gotten involved. There will probably be consequences. But my guess is, it won't be as bad as if he got caught some other way."

Paulson jotted some information on the back of a card and handed it to him.

"Ted can call this number for free legal advice. The police might be able to protect him. They'll probably be more lenient if he comes forward on his own. If this friend is as bad as you say, he'd probably sell Ted out anyway, if he got caught."

"I thought about that."

"I wish I had better answers. But this is a problem for the law, not mental health." And now here he was, stuck with fragmentary knowledge he wished he'd never seen hide nor hair of.

"Thanks all the same. It was good to talk about it with someone, knowing it won't get out or nothing. About my friend Ted, that is."

"What do you think you'll do next?"

Steve finally looked up. "I think I'll stay on a bit longer, after all. I'm feeling better about things."

"See you around, then. If there's anything else you want to talk about, you can get in touch anytime. The mental health manager knows how to find me."

As Steve left, Paulson slurped down the last of his coffee, stone cold. Competing lines of thought collided, conflict of interest rearing its ugly head every way he looked.

His own head was beginning to hurt. To top it off, this was probably one of those situations he was supposed to bring Lacey into.

Not a chance, this time. Steve had been vehement about privacy. Given the situation, he may very well need help again, from someone he trusted. It would stay with him.

He enjoyed a few last breaths of freedom and took his time getting back into the building. The work setting he'd memorized down to its last tedious detail now looked less familiar, less secure, knowing he was keeping something from Lacey. Hopefully he wouldn't come to regret it.

"Good news." Lacey was waiting for him. "Between me, your director, government liaison, and some state people, we figured out what you're supposed do with the application forms."

"That was quick. All I got to show for my efforts are these lumps from beating my head against the wall."

"It helps to have friends in high places." She was clearly savoring her victory over the system. Her satisfied grin was reminiscent of the Cheshire cat.

He, on the other hand, felt like a delinquent. Here he was, keeping key secrets from the magical mommy who had just gone the extra mile to solve a major problem for him.

"There's good news and bad news," she continued. "The good news is that there are only certain pieces of information your director needs dug up for her. Most of it's right here at headquarters. The bad news is that I've been so busy, I haven't had time to compile stats you'll need. You're welcome to do it. I was going to suggest it anyway, so you'd have the experience."

"Sure. How bad can it be?" Cooperating with her pencil-pushing agenda might help quiet the ongoing sting of guilt.

CHAPTER ELEVEN

Paulson searched his pack for acetaminophen. *This idiocy is for the birds.* Yes, lining the bottom of a birdcage. That would be quite the appropriate placement.

He stopped and stared at the indecipherable collection of forms spread out before him. The services tallied weren't for the Marshland operation alone. They were for the entire state.

He downed a couple of tablets.

Lacey returned from her latest mad dash. "Over at public affairs there's a TV going. They're airing an interview with a client we've been helping. You up for watching?"

He shoved aside the paperwork. "Gladly."

They joined other headquarters staff jockeying for a view of the flat-screen unit. The public affairs manager, Brian, stood on guard, wolfing down the last of a bologna and cheese sandwich.

"I haven't talked with Stan much about it yet." He licked a glob of mustard off his fingers. "He's on his way. He said there'd been a wrinkle to iron out. Something about a mental health worker. He said he took care of it. Do you know what that was about?"

"That would be Sarah," said Lacey. "I haven't spoken with her since this morning."

Brian hushed everyone as the GNAT GNews at GNoon lead-in music started up. The interview with the disaster survivor was part of the opening story, woven in with the latest inclement weather report. The impromptu audience appeared mesmerized.

"Hey, that's Frieda," one of the local workers called out. "Getting banged up finally got her fifteen minutes of fame."

Some of the other locals snickered or whispered similar sentiments among themselves.

"Enough, you guys." Brian turned up the volume.

The interview focused on the night of the flood. A discussion of relief services followed, with heavy emphasis on what their disaster partners were doing to fix Frieda's roof.

"Look," said a voice in the crowd. "Someone in a disaster vest, back next to the house."

"Could be Sarah," said Lacey. "One of ours."

It did look like Sarah. Talking with some jock-looking guy.

"This is Jack Flores, with GNAT GNews." It was a wrap.

As if on cue, the construction worker in the background pulled a startled-looking disaster responder in for a hot close one. The scene abruptly ended.

The broadcast transitioned into a story about boiling contaminated water. The headquarters viewers did not appear to be following it, however, still caught up in the last scene.

Was that really Sarah? It couldn't be. What had just rolled out was definitely not her MO.

"You sure train your workers well, Lacey," some joker called out. When she glared at him he held up his hands and pretended to duck. She wadded up a piece of paper and threw it at him.

Amidst the joking around, other reactions ranged from hysterical laughter to murmurs of concern. The technician replayed the clip, adding keystroke magic that let them zoom in. It didn't look any better the second time—and it was definitely Sarah. Lacey had hands over her face, yet continued to peek at the screen through her fingers.

"Stan said he took care of a wrinkle," said Brian. "If this made it on the air, I can hardly wait to hear what it was he took care of."

Paulson was doing his best not to think about it. He had succeeded in gaining mastery over the initial swell of violated possessiveness.

Concern was moving in. The whole thing didn't add up. Not for the Sarah he'd come to know. What happened there was highly unlikely to be any of her doing. The way that jock had grabbed her could have easily been a predatory violation, not a passionate or affectionate gesture. Judging it accurately from long-distance was impossible, especially without knowing what they were saying to each other.

"I'd like to hear what Stan has to say myself." Lacey looked ready to deck somebody. "What's this going to do to the credibility of mental health workers on this operation? We work so hard for staff acceptance and trust. I keep telling them—when they put on that vest, they're no longer themselves. They're DMH. They need to demonstrate solid professional demeanor. That's how people have confidence in them."

"You guys are making way too big a deal of it." Brian walked her away from the rhetoric on boiling water. Paulson followed.

"Sure, it didn't make her look like a professional," Brian continued. "But near as I could tell, she wasn't offering a professional opinion. You should be thanking her for making you look human, like one of the rest of us, instead of some kind of stuffed shirt. I'd rather share my problems with a real person than with some sterile automaton. You wouldn't find me on your doorstep if I hadn't gotten to know you first."

"I hear what you're saying," said Lacey. "But our field has its zealous types. Same as yours. For them, everything is black or white. No flexibility in consideration of culture or context. You wouldn't believe how hard it used to be for therapists working in rural areas—where everybody knows everybody, and avoiding dual relationships is impossible."

"I can vouch for that," said Paulson. "If less crazy standards hadn't come along, Marshland would still be going without mental health support. Or I'd have to commute from Willsey. It gets tricky, believe me. It beats the alternative, though."

Though he was less sure of that, now. In fact it felt downright hypocritical, considering how he was handling his latest duality issue: Steve's revelations, and his indecision over what to do with them.

Why did he keep finding himself in this kind of dilemma? Were his motives really all that pure, for anything? Self-reproach set in.

I've been around Sarah too long. Her slant toward excessive self-criticism was getting the better of him.

"Expectations regarding dual relationships are more realistic now," Lacey continued with Brian. "But disaster mental health is still getting the bugs worked out. Some workers like to talk with someone they know personally. Others want a complete stranger, cushioned within rigidly defined roles. One choice is not better than the other—individual differences, circumstances, flexibility all apply. But until there's anything definitive, we should err on the side of caution."

Brian rolled his eyes. "Whatever. As far as what the average TV viewer sees, Sarah's not even going to be noticed. They were tiny figures in the background. And mostly blocked by shrubbery. We only picked them out because we were looking for ourselves."

"I hope you're right." Lacey's preoccupied gaze dropped, her hands going to her pockets.

"Make the best of the situation. You know, turn it around somehow. It could even help with how people around here view DMH." Brian gave her shoulder a friendly squeeze and leaned in. "Don't forget, you're pretty much the champion at one-upmanship," he whispered.

Paulson accompanied her retreat in disgrace to their designated corner.

"Hey, Lacey." The logistics manager waved her down. "I like that new mental health intervention I just saw on TV. How do I sign up for that?"

"Anytime you want, Manny."

The joking around amidst his underlings turned into "whoa's" and "woo-hoo's."

"What on earth was she thinking," Lacey grumbled.

Jenny caught up with them. "I overheard the IT guys taking bets on how long it'll take before that clip shows up on YouTube. Wanna bet it's someone in IT who pans in and posts it?"

"I'm not worried about IT. For all their goofiness, they wouldn't purposely make us look like a bunch of flakes. I'm more concerned about whatever's going on with Sarah. Where's her better judgment? I had her pegged as someone whose professionalism, if anything, went overboard. Maybe she's not doing as well as I thought. Maybe I shouldn't be sending her out."

"Go easy when you catch up with her," said Jenny. "This is a bit much for someone who's trying to recover from a recent injury. Trouble seems to follow that poor woman everywhere."

Lacey looked away and shook her head.

"Send her over when you're finished with her, so I can check her out. Better yet, send her to me first."

"Want me to call her?" It wasn't an attempt to be helpful. With his initial reaction successfully tamped down, gut instinct screamed at him to get to the bottom of this. Sarah had been so fragile right after her injury. There were all those other stressors hanging over her, too: her missing father and losing her childhood home, not to mention having been thrown off the dock into a sea of clinical practice she had yet to master. It had to be even more trying for overachievers like her.

Then there was that damned video clip, grinding his nose into the reality that his interest in her was far more personal than clinical. What to do about that realization wasn't so clear. It only complicated things further.

"Find out where she is, and when they expect to get here." Lacey gave the back of her neck a series of robotic pinches, as if counting vertebrae. "She's going to need somebody neutral to unload with, by the time the rest of us get done with her. I'm not sending her anywhere until all of us have had a chance to size her up."

Paulson picked up the phone, and then set it down. The outreach team was coming up the walk.

*****

Stan was first to enter. He scurried ahead of everybody, his head scrunched into the oversized vest like a turtle evading a predator. Lacey met Sarah at the door and pointed her toward staff health. Sarah plopped into a chair at Jenny's station and waited.

The last half hour of her first ever disaster team assignment was a hundred and eighty degrees from the drama at Frieda's, other than Bonnie and Marsha regarding her with renewed interest. An attempt to follow up with a shelter resident who'd supposedly returned to his damaged home was a waste of time. The place was deserted. It had meant a lot of aimless driving around. Sarah had spent most of it staring out the window, watching the dirt roads of her youth go by.

Me and Jimmy Orton. What a joke. The same as it was panning out for this whole disaster mental health business. Dismal failure after dismal failure.

She couldn't complain about the imposed lull in activity. Her backseat placement had let her keep to herself, with Stan busily glued to the screen of his handheld. The privacy even accommodated shedding a tear or two unnoticed. Hopefully her eyes hadn't turned red or puffy.

"How was your morning?" Jenny was back. "Any problems with your injuries?"

"No. My back still bugs me every now and then, but that's it."

"You might try some ice on it when you get back to your motel room. Take the plastic bag out of the motel room waste basket, and go to the ice machine . . ."

"Been there, done that." Though it stung to hear she had not been as uniquely resourceful as she'd assumed at the time.

Jenny moved in, conspiratorial. "Fair warning. We watched the interview at that lady's house. At the end, we saw you in the background. That was, um, pretty steamy."

Sarah groaned. "Stan said he took care of all that."

"Apparently not." Jenny reconsidered. "There's more? What else happened?"

"Never mind. The less that's out, the better."

After earning Jenny's blessing to continue, she thanked her for the heads up and scanned the room for Lacey. It was anybody's guess what her superior's assessment of that hare-brained episode would be. She needed to at least give the appearance of being functional, if ever to get assigned near the action. That was where clues about Dad would be. She was sure of it.

If she'd had her ducks lined up at Frieda's, she would have asked that TV guy what he knew. Or asked him to announce something about her missing father. In fact, she could have said something herself, while she was on camera. Thanks to Jimmy, it never even crossed her mind.

Blast him, anyway.

Lacey was not at the mental health corner. Paulson sat in her place, hunched over piles of paperwork—a phenomenal change in backdrop for the man. He looked like a chimpanzee in an orchestra pit.

"Sarah." Lacey was standing just outside a conference room. "In here, please."

So she was being called into the principal's office. She stepped inside. Lacey shut the door behind them and motioned her to sit at the ridiculously long meeting table.

"Do you ever watch Monday night football?" Lacey seated herself across from her.

"All the time." Rows of empty chairs to either side underscored her aloneness in the debacle. Alone and exposed. With Lacey's eyes drilling her straight on. *Breathe.*

"I'm reminded of that segment they call 'C'Mon, Man.' Where they showcase noteworthy blunders."

"I think I know where you're going with this." *Keep cool.* As if presenting herself on TV as an easy score was just another day at the office. "Jenny warned me about the GNAT GNews at GNoon."

"The tagline might read 'Disaster Mental Health Responder Found Necking in Bushes with Construction Worker.' Catchy, isn't it?"

Sarah cringed. Words came tumbling out. "I owe you an explanation. Jimmy is an old acquaintance. We dated in high school. I hadn't seen him since. He was . . . enthusiastic about seeing me again. I got myself out of it as best I could. I guess not soon enough."

Lacey still looked chagrined. "I suppose we could always pass it off as purposely staged—something to keep staff spirits up. It certainly did supply the high point for headquarters entertainment today."

"So the interview ended with that smooch?" There was a bit of humor to be found in it, if she set aside her rattled ego long enough. Especially since Lacey didn't sound like she was about to toss her out on her ear because of this latest bungling. "It does sound staged, doesn't it."

"Be prepared to get razzed. Paulson and I have been bearing the brunt of it so far."

"Paulson saw it too?" This wouldn't do a thing for her standing in her mentor's eyes. Anything positive, that is.

"By now, everybody's seen it. It even made it to national headquarters. I'm still trying to figure out who instigated that little piece of show and tell." Lacey's accusatory glance out the boardroom window settled in the direction of the logistics manager's corner. "Is there anything else I should know about this?"

Most likely. She was still reeling from the previous outing of a failure in judgment. "Only that I wish everything I try to do in this business didn't somehow fall flat. So far nothing seems to be going the way it's supposed to. That TV interviewer even wanted to do some kind of exposé on our chance meeting, on Jimmy and me. Stan squelched that."

"It probably would have been a nice story under other circumstances." Lacey got up and slowly paced. "All in all, I think we probably don't need to worry much about it. What got on the air won't bother disaster survivors who recognized you. The majority of them watched you grow up, anyway, and everything that goes along with that. But to staff, it looks like lack of discretion. They need to see you as somebody they can trust to assist them in a time of need, or able to handle vulnerable clients they want to refer."

"I'm perfectly capable of helping people manage disaster stress." In spite of all the stumbling, she certainly knew what to do with stress reactions. That was just business as usual. If there was such a thing for disaster.

Maybe she was being too hard on herself. Lacey was acting like her failures were forgivable.

"Let them see that competence," said Lacey. "If you go along with the joking, and stick to your most sophisticated professional self from now on, it'll die a natural death."

"How long will it take?"

"Not long, if you stay low profile. New gossip will move into its place. You okay with this?"

"I grew up in a small town. I'm used to not having any secrets. Thanks for the warning about headquarters staff, though. It gives me time to think up a few comebacks."

She could live without being dished up yet another serving of humble pie. Which meant figuring out how she was going to explain herself to Paulson.

*****

Paulson positioned himself so he could watch Sarah without being too obvious. Trying to look busy had let him avoid eye-to-eye, until now. With Sarah and Lacey finally exiting the meeting room, he sneaked a series of quick glances. They seemed on good terms. Maybe even laughing about something together.

"My offer for picnic lunch still holds." He searched their faces as they approached.

"Take your time," said Lacey. "I'll hold down the fort. I'll buzz you if anything comes up. Don't go too far."

"We'll be a couple of blocks down, at Harold's," Sarah told her.

"You definitely win the prize for most interesting morning assignment." He opened the door for Sarah, only to quickly step aside for a parade of admin types filing in.

Her bland expression didn't say much about how she was taking the halfwit remark he hadn't thought through first. How might he steer onto some lighthearted inroad?

He felt lost in space about where Sarah was with anything—the incident on television, the visit with Jenny, the outcome of whatever lecture she'd received from Lacey. Or where he stood with Sarah, for that matter. Had she actually asked him out on some kind of date that morning, while he'd been obsessing about grant forms?

And, by the way, who the hell was that guy?

"Did your morning get any better?" she finally said. "Hear anything from your director?"

"Lacey got through to her somehow. It's still a headache, but not as bad as I thought."

The bell dangling on the grocery door bounced, dinging their arrival. They ordered their sandwiches. Paulson took a quick look out the side entrance. As rumored, the mud and debris were gone. The picnic tables had a fresh coat of forest green. Other headquarters staff that preferred spending lunch hour in relative serenity had already discovered them.

"I have a better idea." Sarah led him to the back of the store.

The office door was propped open. Harold was sitting at his desk, filling every square inch of a padded swivel chair. A lively game of solitaire danced across his computer monitor.

"Well, hello there, darlin'. Didn't expect to see you again so soon. Sure was nice having you over last night."

"It was great to see you and Aunt Millie, too. It made a world of difference."

"That's good to hear. Is there something I can do for you?"

"Is that old bench still out back?"

"Sure is. Y'all want to have your sandwiches there? Go right ahead, honey."

The bench turned out to be a long slider rocker, situated on a secluded porch. It made for a perfect escape, as out of the way as possible and still in the middle of town, walled off from both passing traffic and store activity. Young trees and other spring foliage burst out above the confines of the creek beds. Sounds of trickling water obscured both street noise and deli chatter.

They sat and unwrapped their sandwiches. Sarah plowed through hers as ravenously as always. How did she always make such short work of it, and at the same time seem delicate and ladylike?

"This has been an eventful morning." She wadded up her sandwich wrapping. "Like everything else going on the last few days."

She tossed the trash toward a compact dumpster. A cloud of flies took flight and quickly resettled on what smelled like overripe fruit.

"I hear that interview made it to headquarters," she continued. "That had to be interesting."

If she only knew. But this utter candidness—what was he to do with it? He'd expected to do a bunch of subtle digging. Instead, she seemed primed for a monologue about it all on her own.

"My experiences of late have brought up things. Things I haven't examined with much honesty. Beliefs, and feelings. Ones that come and go. Pretty much ever since I left home. Being here again has forced me to face certain facts."

She put the creaky rocker in motion and gazed into the leafy canopy.

"It's obvious now, how much I romanticized my past. Some of the blame goes to those TV classics I'm addicted to, the ones Mom and I watched together. Fifties and sixties shows sugarcoat real life. Good guys are always the good guys. Bad guys are always the bad guys. There's not much in between. Families and relationships looked like how everybody wished they were, not what they really are. It perpetuated an urban myth—you honorably pursue the carrot at the end of the stick and everything comes together. Very simplistic and agreeable. Great escapes from reality. Especially for a generation recovering from World War II. And the Depression."

"Those shows do have the charm factor going." Her analysis of early TV programming pretty much said it all. But where was she going with it? He settled his free arm over the back of the rocker, bracing for the unpredictable.

"There was this boyfriend of mine when I was a teenager. That's who that was at Frieda's. Those first years away at school, I'd fantasize about it. Except it was a revisionist version, escapes into romantic memories of the supposedly terrific guy I left behind. True to the tenets of melodrama, we couldn't be together. Like Romeo and Juliet. We belonged to two completely different worlds.

"Relationships I've had since haven't gotten anywhere. Something always cropped up to show that the latest 'Mr. Wonderful' had traits that didn't fit in with the stereotypical romantic male lead. The miles between me and Jimmy spared him from that kind of scrutiny.

"As he demonstrated for the greater TV viewing audience, he was glad to see me again. I wish I could say the same. I can't, in spite of my old fantasies. Or perhaps, because of them. With Jimmy being Jimmy, it took less than five minutes for his usual self to show up. The guy hasn't changed a bit. He's still the self-absorbed jerk he was in high school. Back then, I couldn't acknowledge it because I was too much 'in love'."

Paulson gave up on the last of the sandwich. It wasn't settling well.

"So much of where I've ended up—" She paused. "There was Dad. He became the 'bad guy,' since he didn't like Jimmy. He talked like he didn't want me to have a career, either. Though I must admit, he was right about Jimmy."

"There's nothing like the advantage of life experience," said Paulson. "But just try pointing that out to a teenager."

"After Mom died, I didn't come back here any more than I had to. It wasn't only trouble getting along with Dad. I felt somehow . . . left out. Mom kept her disease to herself. When we finally found out what was going on, all we could do was sit around and watch her wither away. But through it all, I committed the greater crime; I tossed to the wind everything connecting me to my roots."

"It had to be a very sad time. You can't fault yourself for where that rollercoaster left you."

"I thought I'd found my way by pouring myself into a groove after my training. A very narrow one. Like it was the totality of who I was. Yes, I became successful. But what did I miss out on, while zeroed in on the prize? Personally, and professionally.

"This disaster mental health business, for example. It looks like more healing takes place because of support systems than traditional techniques or interventions. Like Aunt Millie's quilting group. I could see emotional recovery taking place right before my eyes. Then there's the preventive work, like that talk you gave at the town meeting. And the psychoeducational materials I gave Frieda about what to expect, and what to do if it happens."

"It's new," said Paulson. "Many mental health professionals haven't heard much about it."

"It's embarrassing, in a way. I've been stuck. Maybe even arrogant. I thought I had it all sewn up. That I was a finely polished specimen, a spectacular success as a human being, thanks to my professional accomplishments. That it was enough to go around playing the 'big expert' at conferences. To stand in front of whatever adoring throng I could find to present myself to."

"You were doing a service for your colleagues. You helped them get their CE."

"There is that. But looking back, my motivations were more about me, not about helping conference participants. What Mom would have called an 'ego trip.' I'm wondering if my choice to practice this is only a stand-in for dealing with my own grief issues."

"You're being awfully hard on yourself. And looking at way too much at once." In fact it was getting hard to keep up.

"Circumstances chose it, the timing. Perhaps this is the only way I'd hear the wake-up call."

The rocker picked up speed. Paulson tightened his sweaty grip. True confessions like this were nothing new. But in this context, coming from Sarah . . . where was she heading?

"Living through a disaster. Being here in Marshland again. It changed things. It's obvious how shallow my thinking has been. I can't push it onto the back burner any more. When I'm Aunt Millie's age, I want what she has: a close circle of lifelong friends, a dedicated life partner. To be part of a community, not just signed onto duty with fellow professionals.

Grandchildren showing up on weekends. Frivolous pastimes, too, to just let loose.

"But I want to be able to look back on my career with pride, too. That my legacy, my footprint, leaves the world a better place. Not just dust collecting on some celluloid credit roll, or a copyright grant with my name on it."

There was a break in her soliloquy. Was he supposed to say something?

Probably not. She seemed to be talking more to herself than to him. Just being there was beginning to feel voyeuristic.

She started up again. "My career in disaster mental health has been, well, a disaster. Pretty much every new thing I've tried has gone south. That makes it an ideal place to start. There's nowhere to go but up. This work is more personal, more connected with the real world than anything else I've done to date."

He gave up. It was impossible to wrap his brain around so many loose threads. How did she do it? His sensibilities were shouting "tilt" with each new revelation.

Cut to the chase. "Is there something I can do?"

The steady squeaking ceased. Sarah dropped her hands to her knees and stared at them. Contrite, like a little girl getting ready to confess to sneaking treats from the cookie jar. "At times I've treated you unfairly. I'm sorry about that."

"No need to apologize. I saw something was eating at you. I just didn't know what it was."

"The reason I'm telling you all this . . . can we start over?" She looked up, expectant. Every bit the little girl with the curl in the middle of her forehead.

You bet. Wait. Start over with what, exactly?

Harold strolled onto the porch. "I brought you two the last of the brownies." He handed them each a cello-wrapped square. "These were always a special favorite of Sarah's."

"Thanks, Uncle Harold." An easy show of delight lit up a face from an earlier era, a little girl beaming up at someone she loved and trusted without question. Such pristine transparency. Almost a completely different person.

"You bet, honey. You take all the time you want back here."

"Thanks, but we need to get going." Sarah got up from the bench. "We're supposed to take referrals this afternoon."

"Sounds like you're having a good time with this here disaster."

"We do what we can," said Paulson.

Harold guffawed. "Y'all come do lunch here anytime you want."

She walked alongside him at a leisurely pace, conversation monopolized by her concerns about a hyper mass care worker she'd met at headquarters. An inroad to pick up where they'd left off had not yet opened up.

It was just as well. He had yet to digest it all, so much to sift through and absorb. Especially that last comment about starting over. With disaster mentoring? With their collegial relationship? Their personal relationship? Do they even have a personal relationship?

And why couldn't he just man up and ask a few simple questions.

Upon arriving at headquarters they followed Lacey to the canteen. They watched and waited while she refilled her dented-up travel mug.

"I have an assignment for you two. We need you to pay a visit to sites that don't have ongoing mental health staff. Just say hello, check how they're doing. Lend an ear if needed. A list of site addresses is back on our table."

"Got it." Sarah went to look for it.

"All clear?" Lacey asked Paulson. "If you think it would be better for her to sit this one out, you could probably handle it on your own."

Good question. "We talked during lunch. She seems to be coming through everything okay."

Sarah rejoined them, scanning the list she carried. "Any priorities? Special problems?"

"That local chapter for the relief organization. They sound pretty burnt out already. Go there first. Also, I don't think DMH has been to the warehouse since the night of the fire. Weren't you on site during that, Paulson?"

"All evening. Until most of the crowd left."

"Then you're already familiar with the situation. You up to it, Sarah?"

"Of course. Going by the warehouse will also give me a chance to take a look at what's left of Dad's shop."

CHAPTER TWELVE

The chapter personnel did indeed seem burnt out. Sarah agreed with Paulson's observation that they needed to split up if they were to make it to everybody. Identifying which ones were interested in taking advantage of their services didn't take long.

Paulson was almost immediately sequestered in the director's office. Given his client's wan and bleary-eyed appearance, Sarah guessed Paulson would be in there for the long haul.

The string of consultations became redundant as Sarah chipped away at repercussions of what staff had experienced over the past week. But the redundancy served well for getting practice, as well as finally building up a little confidence over how she could help people.

Until now, she hadn't given much thought to what went on in the days preceding the storm. Listening to staff describe it was an education in itself. As personal stories piled up, it was little wonder people were burning out. Preparations had begun a full two days before the flood hit. They'd been tasked with setting up seven shelters, even though only three of them turned out to be needed. They had also supported the early sandbagging efforts and feeding operations.

Staff seemed accustomed to the unpredictability and extreme time commitment of the work, at least on the surface. Wear and tear played itself out, regardless. Especially since the flash flood had caught them off guard. There'd been a lot of frantic last-minute adjustments. And now, with another storm coming, they would soon endure another round. It meant putting in more twelve-hour days, or possibly even longer. It didn't sound like any of them had had a day off.

Her afternoon continued on as a counseling marathon, one client after another. Most were already familiar with disaster self-care, some even more so than she. Making themselves follow through on standard recommendations, however, was another story. That turned out to be the real work of the job—helping them find ways to take time to pay attention to their own well-being amid the chaos.

Time passed quickly. The work felt energizing, rather than draining. She was accomplishing something: reassuring workers who acted like they needed some kind of permission to take care of themselves. How would they apply what she shared? What would their ultimate choices be? She'd probably never know. But for the first time, she felt certain she'd done everything that was professionally possible. At last, one for the success column.

Late in the afternoon she was still at it. Paulson continued with whatever he was doing with the director. If they made it to the warehouse at all before day's end, it would be dark. She would again need to put off checking out Dad's shop if they hung around much longer.

Satisfied that the critical cases were tended to, she went ahead and packed up her supplies. She sat at a vacant desk and waited for Paulson.

"Do you know what they're doing in there?" Sarah asked a nearby office assistant. "We need to hit the road."

"Probably the same as you did with us," she said. "The director has been taking phone calls all the while he's been in there. It's probably slowing things a bit. By the way, did you get a chance to talk to Ollie?"

"Which one's Ollie?"

"He's a volunteer who helps out with reception. He's not doing so good. He just finished refurbishing his house when the flood hit. He's been working on that place for as long as I've known him. Now it's probably in worse shape than when he started. Nobody's been allowed to go back and look around in that neighborhood yet, either. Last I heard, the whole area might end up condemned."

"How's he holding up?" Sarah asked.

"Just moping around, not getting much done. I'm pretty sure he's still here, somewhere. I haven't seen him for a while."

"Last I saw, he was headed for the cellar," said another worker.

"Ollie?"

The gloomy enclosure would not be suitable for much other than storage. She negotiated the concrete steps and passed through the main area. Both sides were crammed with erector set shelving and supplies stacked all the way to the exposed plumbing. The overflow of deliveries had been dumped on the floor, creating a second layer.

"I'm back here." A gentle voice drifted in from the next room.

Sarah continued beyond the flickering illumination of a bare light bulb. Pushing open a second door, she found herself in a sparsely filled cubby, much of it taken up by an ancient water heater. Light streamed into the overflow area from a narrow window a few feet overhead. Ollie was directly below it, seated on a stool and leaning against the dark concrete wall. She squinted into the sunlight and tried to make out his features.

"I'm Sarah, with disaster mental health." She began to extend a hand then stopped, her eyes adjusted well enough to see that the hands flopped in his lap showed no signs of motion.

"Someone told us you were coming," he said.

She transitioned her hands to her pockets and scanned the surroundings. One wall consisted of relatively empty shelving. "Looks like you really got cleaned out. Back here, anyway."

"This is where we keep handouts. And forms." He slowly rose from his perch. "We need to restock."

He moved into the minimal lighting. He was unbelievably short and round, easily fitting the classification of morbidly obese. His shaved head seemed as a miniaturized version of the human globe upon which it sat. Small glasses posed on his bulbous nose further accentuated the impression of a poster child for banning the existence of fast food.

"Interesting," she said, though it wasn't. "Is this where mental health handouts came from?"

"Probably. Some things came from the regional office. Want to help? You could tell me what we've still got here for DMH."

"I'll see what I can do." She had no idea which forms and handouts were used exclusively by DMH. But if taking on a warehouse task would help her get in sync with someone who looked as glum as Ollie, she was game.

She located and pulled together pamphlets and forms that looked familiar. While she worked, the sound of thumps and thuds started up in the next room, boxes and shelving on the move. Ollie was up and active.

Good.

Several minutes later he reentered.

"I put all the DMH forms I recognize on this one shelf. I'm not sure if . . ."

Ollie closed the door and leaned against it. He looked horrible, thoroughly exhausted. He slowly slid downward, finally plopping on the floor in a sitting position.

This was her cue. "Is there something you wanted to talk about?"

"It's nothing talking will change."

His arranging for privacy suggested otherwise. "I heard about your house. I'm sorry."

"It was a part of me—that project. Been fixing it up eight years now. Eight years."

"That's a long time."

"Have you ever done feather-duster painting? When you're done, it looks like that really fancy wallpaper. My Cousin Albert didn't believe it. He looked for seams every time he came over. Then told me it must be some kind of seamless wallpaper."

He laughed softly and adjusted his glasses.

"I put glitter in that paint. It was a pale rosy color. When the morning sun came in, the whole wall came to life. It just about did a tango."

"It must have been beautiful," said Sarah. "I imagine you'll redo it the same way, then?"

"I did all that back when I was still a slim Jim." He looked down, his chin resting on the pudginess beneath it. "I can't do much of anything now, without tuckering out. I've got a whole house to start over with."

"You can take it a bit at a time. FEMA can help you, too. And you'll get a chance to show your cousin how feather duster painting is done. Maybe he'll even help."

"It's not the same. A couple years ago I had a hard time. My doctor gave me pills. These." He pulled a prescription bottle from his shirt pocket. He held it in front of his flushed face, rotating it slowly in his fingers.

"They worked real fine. But I put on weight like a son of a gun. Now look at me."

Actually, he was beginning to look rather woozy.

Her inner alarm clanged, the one warning her of that disagreeable possibility among the depressed. Every therapist hated to consider it. Yet doing so was critical.

"Sorry to put you in this position." He closed his eyes, appearing at peace. "You're such a nice lady. All the folks here. Real nice people."

The pill bottle rolled from his hand into the trapezoid of sunshine lighting the floor. The container was empty.

"Ollie." She kneeled next to him. "Did you take all these?"

She squinted at the label. It was one of the newer antipsychotic medications. Deadly in large doses.

"We've got to get you out of here. You need help. I'll help you."

"You can't." He smiled, as if luxuriating in a pleasant dream. "You can't get by. I'm just too damn big. The other door's blocked, too. They'll never get in. Not for a long time."

Her thoughts raced, thinking about Paulson's recent accounting of a client suicide. How it had affected him. Her own professional failures over the last few days . . .

No. Not this time. No way. Nobody had ever tried to end their life on her watch. She was not about to let it happen there, imprisoned in the chapter cellar of all places. She had to get Ollie to the hospital. ASAP.

"This isn't what you want." She assembled an argument. Calm and soothing was the way to go. Her heart was racing. "You just want the pain and sadness to end. There are other ways to make it better. Think about people who care about you. Think about your cousin Albert."

"I knew I had to do it now, when they said y'all were coming." He took the empty container from her hand and turned it from side to side, watching it glisten in the sunlight. "I'd lose my nerve if I waited." His head rolled to one side. He sighed, surrendering to a bizarre state of contentment.

"Stop it, Ollie." She grabbed him by the shoulders and tried to shake him.

His bulk barely moved. His eyes closed. He was silent, unresponsive.

She tried to push him away from the door. He wouldn't budge. Her shoulder kept coming against spongy roundness. It was too hard to pull him one way or the other.

She pressed a speed-dial on her cell phone and waited.

No ringing. She looked at the display screen. The "No Service" message jumped out at her.

Options were now mortally limited.

Think. She surveyed the walls of their vault-like environment. Nobody would hear if she cried out. But there was that narrow overhead window . . .

She strained for a better view of the window's particulars. It was too high to see if it was one that could be opened, or if she would need to break the glass. If that were even possible. Nothing in the room looked heavy enough to do the job, and even with adrenaline overload, her cloaked fist probably wouldn't have enough brawn behind it to punch through that industrial-strength glass.

She stacked a couple of unwieldy cardboard boxes and climbed on top of them. Her line of vision just breeched the windowsill's crest. A rusty handle, just out of reach, came into view. Relieved, she again scanned the room, considering what else was sturdy enough to stand on. She got down and snatched up Ollie's stool. She added its meager height to the top of the boxes.

Ollie still looked peaceful. She did a hasty check—he was still breathing, steady and easy, but otherwise, deathly still.

She eased her way up the wobbly makeshift ladder. At first opportunity she grabbed the window handle and steadied her footing.

The handle twisted with ease. *Thank heavens.* She gave the window a determined shove.

Then another. It didn't give. In all likelihood, it hadn't been opened in decades.

After several determined jolts she was rewarded with a sudden chilling screech. She forced the window open as far as it would go and peeked out at the area below.

Hopes were immediately dashed. There was nothing below but a steady downward expanse of concrete foundation. A few feet out from its base was the edge of a cliff, with about a thirty-foot drop-off down to the river. The mere glimpse of it was dizzying.

Across the river, the only signs of civilization were an overgrown hayfield, the remains of old fencing, and a barn in a state of collapse. No sign of people anywhere. Even if there were, the rush of water below and the whistling gusty wind would drown out any calling for help.

She tried again for a cell phone signal, without success.

A sloping ledge jutted out from beneath, just under the window. It looked like a continuation of the façade décor out front. Flashes of old adventure shows danced in her head, heroes inching their way along ledges to escape the bad guys, or rescue damsels in distress. She shuddered.

Not for this kid. But surely she could get out far enough to coax up a few bars of phone service.

She dragged herself further up, the metal window frame cutting into her fingers. When her knee caught purchase on the windowsill she maneuvered higher and leaned out. The view of the chasm loomed below. She stopped, light-headedness halting her progress.

There was no need to fear, however. Her hips were securely jammed, wedged in the narrow opening. She couldn't move further out if she wanted to.

Her lower foot suddenly flew out from under, accompanied by sounds of tearing cardboard and a stool bouncing on concrete. She was stuck, half in and half out, pinched as if by a pair of pliers. The heat of the ledge burned into her elbows. The drop to the river below . . .

Focus. There was no choice but to ignore the hell of it. It would be curtains for Ollie, if she didn't.

Then again, how long would she be able to dangle there, crushed at the hips, and her front end frying like a hush puppy?

She fumbled around at her waist, grabbing at where she remembered pocketing her phone. It felt lower than expected, partially wedged between her hips and the window frame. With considerable prying and prodding, she yanked it out. It immediately slipped from her sweaty hand. Clattering, it slid down the ledge.

Her arm shot out and trapped it, inches from dropping into the gulch below. She slowly scooped it toward her. She laid her face against it. *Slow down.*

One at a time, she wiped damp palms against her grimy-smelling shirt. She took careful hold of the phone. Squinting in brightness, she tipped the screen to multiple angles. She couldn't make out a thing. Was there service? Glare obscured all.

She punched in numbers anyway and listened. Her jaw clenched as she waited.

Please, let me hear it. The pounding in her ears produced even more interference than the rumbles of river and wind.

Was that faint ringing? Or just the wind, or maybe tinnitus.

A confident voice answered. "What is your emergency?"

*****

"I could have lived without the humiliation of those rescue workers having to pry me out." Sarah scratched at tape on the dressing someone had insisted on applying to her elbow. "What's Lacey going to say this time? This is hardly staying low profile."

"She said she was proud of you." Paulson steered out onto the main highway. "You did what had to be done."

Sarah still looked wired. He himself continued to be stunned. More like amazed. She had shown such unexpected tenacity, keeping a clear head through an extraordinarily nerve-wracking situation. She'd been put to the test. And passed it, with flying colors.

The interview with the chapter director had been intense. He hadn't known what was going on with Ollie and Sarah until leaving the director's office. By then, emergency personnel were overrunning the place. The next thing he knew, an EMT was walking Sarah up from the frigid bowels of the building, introducing the question of how she'd managed to become so disheveled and overheated. It had taken some explaining.

"I was so relieved when I heard that dispatcher's voice," said Sarah. "She stayed on the line until the first responders got there, the poor woman. I spent the whole time complaining about that window. She kept telling me not to crawl out further. I assured her not to worry. The sound

154

of those doors finally getting battered down—that was music to my ears."

"I suppose few people can claim to have been held captive in a storage room by a post-it note blockade." This could be it, his chance. An opportunity to get back to her thoughts about the two of them. She'd found her way through something considerably more harrowing, and did look disheveled. But her eyes were bright, her mood energized. There was no sign of being overwhelmed.

Sarah turned down the visor and looked in the mirror. She grimaced and began fussing with her hair.

"You kept your head," Paulson continued. "You thought outside the box, just the way you're supposed to. A lot of disaster mental health is like that. In situations both large and small."

"It was like what Lacey said about crisis, too." She set down her comb. "I never considered flailing around and screaming, like people do on TV. I kept thinking about the next step, what I needed to do. What might happen to Ollie if I didn't."

"It worked, what you did. The EMT seems to think he'll be okay."

She unwrapped a sani-wipe and dabbed at smudges on her shirt. "How did it go with the director?"

"He didn't want to let the reins loose. He's new. It's his first major disaster. I think he felt overwhelmed by the responsibility. He wants to make sure he does everything he's supposed to."

"Understandable."

"He figured on using local staff for the new storm, even though they're already doing almost everything. I tried to talk him into giving them a day off. Especially now, while there's still visiting staff to fill in. I'm not sure what he decided. How did it go for you? Other than Ollie."

"I kept reminding myself I wasn't there to do therapy. It wasn't always easy. Those guys sure like to overdo it."

"It's hard for them to step back. They see so much need."

"Something to keep in mind." She returned the comb to her satchel.

"Is this helpful?" He glanced at her. "For starting over, like you said you wanted. Reviewing what we've done after an assignment?"

"Very much so. What will happen next?"

Not the answer he'd hoped for. His preferred agenda was far more personal. But if this was what it was, well, it was what it was. He swallowed back the swell of disappointment.

Move on. "Sandbagging will start up again. The shelters will reopen or get revamped."

She nodded, her gaze of concentration lost in the passing scenery.

It continued to gnaw. So it was only their mentoring relationship she wanted to start over. It fit. He'd certainly seen evidence of it. She hadn't looked primed to throw herself into the comforting arms of a significant other after her ordeal on the ledge. At least, not with him.

I get it. Go with it. For now.

By the time they made it back to Marshland the shelter's suppertime shift was probably well under way. When they reached the warehouse they first stopped to orient themselves at the site of the fire. Faint whiffs of smoke and damp charcoal lingered. Yellow warning tape encircled the structure, a serendipitous reminder of where outer walls had once stood.

The storage room was still intact. Damaged areas of the former shop looked sifted through, probably by the fire investigators. Other than that, not much had changed since Sunday night. Except the relative calm. During the fire, numerous bystanders had stood around and fidgeted—watching, sharing worries about how far it would spread. It had been a busy evening of trying to reassure people that all would be okay when the final outcome was still anybody's guess.

Sarah was picking her way through it, encircling the taped off area. Occasionally she stopped to examine charred and twisted car parts that were intermingled with blackened wood and drifts of ash.

"Someone in the warehouse noticed the fire first. That's who called it in." Paulson worked his way toward where she was examining what was left of the back wall. "The workers had already cleared out. Mostly out into the street with the other spectators. By the time I got here, the front end was fully engulfed. The firefighters concentrated on this area, back here. They did a good job of keeping it from spreading to other buildings."

"Do you know who called it in? Whoever stumbled on it first . . ."

"Sarah, Paulson. Fancy meeting y'all here." A forklift rumbled out of the warehouse. Chet bobbed in its seat and waved his hat, much like a five-year-old trying to catch his parents' attention from a carnival ride. He parked it off to one side.

"How do you like my new ride? Sure don't measure up to yours though, huh, Sarah?" His carefree laughter joined his clumsy maneuvering of the heavy equipment.

"We're just checking in," Paulson called out from a safe distance. "Making sure you guys are doing okay."

"These guys are great. Best bunch of guys I could ever work with."

"We were wondering specifically about the fire the other night," said Sarah.

"Nothing fazes these boys. We keep too busy for that. We . . ." A querulous look disrupted the testimonial. "Now that I think on it, there were some others around that were mighty upset. A lot of folks were down here that night."

"I'm sure I must have missed a few things. What do you remember? Does anyone in particular come to mind?"

"There was that new guy, the one who's dark colored. You know, the shelter manager. I saw him out here, later on. He was pacing all over, nervous like. Sure is nice of him to be so worried about us folks. He don't even live here."

"Let's get supper at the shelter, if they're still serving." Sarah jotted down some notes. "The mental health worker assigned there might tell us more about how the manager is doing."

"Anyone else you can think of?" Paulson said to Chet.

"Everyone got excited that night. Me, too, even. Me and Sam had good times here, you know. But what's gone is gone."

"What about the storage room?" Sarah reached around a blackened stud to pull at the padlock arrangement. "Do you know what Dad keeps in here?"

"Back when we were working the shop, that's where he put the fancy equipment. And poisons, and the like. Mostly because of you kids being around. Don't know what he's got in there now. I haven't seen that padlock in years. It's a good thing it's there, though. If it wasn't, anybody could get at it, especially now that the building's gone."

157

Paulson considered the security aspect. "Have you seen anyone bother it?"

"Nah, I'm around here all day. No one's been near it. Just folks coming and going to the warehouse. We'd see it if anybody tried to mess with it. They couldn't break in if they wanted to, no how. Me and Sam did right by that room. You wouldn't believe all the nails we used. That was a great project, what me and Sam . . . "

"I wonder if we should check inside," said Sarah. "Since Dad and Nate aren't here. There might be water or smoke damage that should be tended to. Except I have no idea where the key is. For all I know, it's washed downriver, along with the house."

"I bet I know exactly where it is." Chet strutted up to the surviving structures. "Used to keep the spare right handy. I bet it's there, same as always. Unless it got burnt up or something."

He ducked under the tape and tramped through the drifted ash. He reached up and ran his hand along some high molding. He lifted a loose chunk of trim. From out of nowhere came an old brass key.

"See? What'd I tell you. I bet you want to hang onto this. Until Sam gets back. He's always got his own key for this. He don't need this one."

He handed it to Sarah. She stared at the piece of metal resting in her palm, most likely last used by her father. When she looked up at him, the little girl was back. "Is there time for me to check this out now?"

How could he say no to that?

"Tell you what. I'll meet with the warehouse supervisor and take care of whatever. You go ahead. If I need you, I'll come looking."

CHAPTER THIRTEEN

"Here, I'll do that." Chet performed a practiced ritual of unlocking the padlock, sliding it and the chain from the fixtures, then hanging the whole wad over a soot-smudged coat hook.

"That's how we always did it." He paused at each step of the demonstration, taking fullest possible advantage of the opportunity to show off. "Just like that."

He left to tend to his forklift.

Sarah stepped inside the darkened enclosure. The generic clutter was not immediately identifiable. Without the advantage of windows or electricity, the only lighting was whatever made it in through the open door. Not much, with the sun so low.

She got the flashlight out and swept the beam over the room's contents.

It was packed. Cardboard boxes and Rubbermaid tubs were stacked everywhere. Plastic bags filled to the brim were crammed in every spare corner. Fortunately, she didn't have to brush any dusty cobwebs out of her face. In fact, everything looked fresh and well cared for, as if recently cleaned or reorganized. She squeezed and scooted between containers and assessed what was there.

Ouch. She grabbed at her thigh. It had hit against a corner of camouflaged furniture jutting out from under a stack of boxes. She massaged what would surely become a colorful bruise as she leaned further for a closer look.

What's this doing in here? It was the antique secretary Mom had been so fond of. When they were little, she and Nate threw blankets over it and played campout. The last time she'd seen it was after Mom's memorial service, sitting in her parents' front room.

Why would Dad put such a lovely piece in storage?

It finally caught up. Tears welled. She could kick herself for not thinking of it earlier.

This was where Dad put everything. The family treasures. Anything he didn't want to risk losing, if the house got flooded.

She scrutinized the clutter anew, spurred on by the joy of discovery. In the far corner stood the old filing cabinet, the one that always stored important paperwork. Familiar waterproof containers stacked to one side probably still held photographs. Beneath them sat that fancy microwave Mom had been so proud of. Other electronics and shop machinery were scattered here and there.

A faded orange and green depiction of citrus fruit peeked out from beneath a folded quilt. On a rush, she shoved things out of the way and jerked out the bulky cardboard crate, struggling to turn it lengthwise in cramped space.

There it was. "Sarah," in bold felt marker. She ran a loving hand over the sagging lid.

The box containing her childhood.

The collection had come into being after she and Nate moved out. Dad wanted to remodel. Her room still contained a lot of castoffs. He asked her to go through them. The box sitting in her lap was the product of that effort, the early treasures she did not wish to part with.

And she'd figured them gone forever. Dad, God bless him, had rescued them. Here they were, safe and sound.

Or were they? She tore at multiple rounds of duct tape and yanked off the lid.

She sighed relief. It was still there, the well-loved compilation of keepsakes, small toys, and books. Fellow sojourners of childhood.

Wait a minute. Some items were unfamiliar. They certainly weren't anything she remembered putting in there.

She fingered the fresh-looking manila folder sitting on top and opened it. Inside was a collection of immature drawings. She smiled, remembering where she'd last seen them. They'd been on the refrigerator door forever, much to her chagrin as a teenager. Beneath the folder was her baby book, complete with stamped newborn footprints. And a tiny set of pink booties, ones she so often had begged to be allowed to use on her dolls. Eventually doing so in secrecy.

Tucked along one side of the box was an oversized envelope. She lifted the flap and peered inside. It was packed with old report cards, evidence of a scholar in the making.

Mom did this. Mom added these things, during her final days.

Sarah's throat tightened. She struggled, unable to hold it back, the sudden heave of her chest. A swell of pain, fighting its way out from the depths of her soul.

It could not be contained. Tears blurred her vision and soon poured out without restraint. She could no longer fight it. Grief was having its say.

She wept freely. Time and place disappeared as she was overtaken by snippets of a relationship long gone: Mom, guiding her through childhood trials and tribulations; Mom with her friends and with Dad; Mom's spontaneity, her quirks, her *Star Trek* fetish. Everything that made her so unique and dear came flooding back.

As the pain lessened, tears slowed.

Reality knocked. Paulson would soon return.

She brushed away her tears and reassessed her surroundings, her gaze eventually settling on the box before her. There was so much to go through in that one box, alone. Exploring further would be better with more light, more space. Someplace she could take her time. Better yet, with a glass of wine, sitting by a crackling fire. A chance to reminisce about things forgotten.

She reluctantly slipped on the lid and secured it.

*****

"Sarah. You still in there?" Paulson rounded the corner and peeked through the open door.

Sarah was sitting on the floor. Telltale tracks streaked her cheeks. She was leaning back against an old quilt and cradling some beat-up cardboard box.

"Are you okay?"

"I'm home," she said.

He opened then closed his mouth. *What?*

"Just me and my Mom in here." She rested her chin on top of the box and smiled up at him.

*****

The three of them stood side by side, surveying the room's contents.

Chet broke the silence. "Well, I'll be. Sam's the smartest man I know. Can you believe it? He figured it right out that his house would flood. And, he was right. The whole darn house got washed away. But everything important is right here in this room."

"Dad might not want it left this way," said Sarah. "I mean, this door was never meant to be external, exposed to the open. What's going to happen when it starts raining again?"

"You could put those things in my basement," said Chet. "There's plenty of room there."

"Your basement flooded last weekend," Paulson reminded him. "Another storm's on the way. I imagine you won't even leave your own things there this time around."

"Paulson, you're the second most smartest man I know. You're absolutely right."

"How about my garage?" said Paulson. "It's private. I don't use it for much. Mainly for my bike, during bad weather. There's plenty of space. It's secure."

"I can help move it," said Chet. "Can't be more than a couple loads, especially if we use my truck. We could do it right now."

"I think Dad would approve." The solution made sense. Paulson seemed sufficiently familiar with particulars of Dad's life to suggest Dad would trust him to stand guard over his belongings. "If you're sure it's not an imposition."

Paulson and Chet both reassured her.

"I'll check with Nate, too. After supper. We've still got business at the shelter."

"Wait a minute," said Paulson. "If Sam comes back before we can let him know what we did, he'll be upset to find everything missing."

"You know, I got a fix for that, too." Chet puffed up, again beaming in his element. "We left notes all the time back when we worked the shop. We just put them in an envelope, and stuck them up somewhere. Couldn't text or nothing, with Sam not doing cell phones and all."

*****

"Chet was right about his warehouse buddies." Paulson toyed with the teriyaki chicken. There was greater enjoyment to be had by simply sitting and gazing across the table.

Sarah looked more loosened up than he'd ever seen her. Happy, even.

"You'd never know there'd been a fire," he continued. "They were taking a breather when I came in. Playing some practical joke on their supervisor."

"What about the person who called it in?" Sarah's plate was already most of the way scraped clean. "How was he doing?"

"Nobody knows who it was. Just that the call came from the warehouse."

"Too bad. I'd like to thank him. I'll bet Dad would, too."

Concentrating on the business at hand was taking concerted effort. In addition to the distraction of Sarah's new approachability, the busy day had drained him to boot level. A moving operation after dinner was going to make his day even longer.

If only Sarah would slow down, take time to enjoy a little easy companionship.

"What does the shelter manager look like?" Her professional self was right on cue, zeroing in on the day's remaining chore. "I've never met him. Is he here?"

"That's him over by the kitchen, talking with Shelley."

"I should say hello to Shelley anyway." She picked up her tray of used eating utensils and was gone before he could come up with a ploy for delaying her.

"Nice work with chapter staff." Lacey moved in with a plate of food, positioning herself where Sarah had been.

"The credit goes mainly to Sarah."

"She does keep things exciting, doesn't she?"

"We touched bases with pretty much everybody." He leaned to one side, straining for a better view of the spirited exchange between Sarah and Shelley. "Whoever was there, anyway. I think I got the director to ease up a bit. Oh, yeah. And we looked around at the warehouse, too."

"You can't help yourself, can you?" Lacey slowly bit into a roll. Her eyes twinkled.

"What?"

"You've had the look of a Labrador puppy ever since I caught sight of you in here."

He blushed. "I . . . don't know what you're talking about." Like Lacey wasn't going to see right through that lie.

"You look at her like you can't let her out of your sight."

"Well, I am supposed to be supervising her."

"Not that closely. The jig is up, Paulson. You can't fool Mother Lacey."

"It's that obvious?" He abandoned the botched effort at poker face.

"You realize, I assume, that this complicates your ability to work together."

"I'm just looking out after her. I'm not bugging her for anything more. She wants to learn how to do this. She has a lot of good skills already. Sarah's complex, and unique. So spirited, and strong, and still . . . I don't know, somehow delicate."

"I don't know about 'delicate.' That's one tough cookie over there."

"Perhaps."

"Food for thought. Did you see *The Bucket List*?"

"That movie about two guys who make friends during cancer treatment."

"As far as I know, the story's completely fictional. The piece of human nature it portrays, however—that's for real. Those two men were complete opposites. You wouldn't expect them to ever cross paths, let alone have anything to do with each other if they did. Yet their personal disasters drew them together. They bonded in ways that were otherwise highly unlikely."

Paulson pretended to listen while keeping an eye out for Sarah, who had succeeded in starting up a conversation with the shelter manager. "Yes, a very touching film."

"I bring it up because it relates to a review article I saw a while back. It was on anxious arousal and interpersonal attraction. People who go through crises together tend to bond. You've probably seen evidence of it over and over with this flood—strangers helping strangers, new friendships arising. 'Disaster bonding,' it's often called. You probably saw it with ER staff. Same thing. It can happen with any type of emergency responder."

"I remember it all right." He watched Sarah pull out a stress pamphlet. "Some days I felt like I needed a scorecard."

"Then you're probably already well aware that people who share crises can make for strange bedfellows. One day they wake up and it hits them they know very little about one another. In some scenarios, this can be downright dangerous."

The bedfellows comment snapped his full attention to the other side of the table. "What are you saying, Lacey?"

"You and Sarah have known each other briefly, as far as relationships go. Yet you're so conspicuous about your attraction to her, it's already getting back to me through the rumor mill."

"Half of what comes out of the rumor mill is myth anyway." He fidgeted with his fork. Had he been that obvious? "Everybody knows that. What's your point?"

"It's always possible you've stumbled onto the woman of your dreams. Who am I to say? But it could just as easily be purely situational. My point is that you might want to consider cooling your jets. Take things with a bit more caution. That way, nobody gets hurt."

The suggestion, that she would dare even offer it, was downright offensive. Who did Lacey think she was? He felt his eyes narrow. "I would never do anything to hurt Sarah."

"In this business, I size up people in a hurry. I'm not so worried about Sarah. From what I've seen, she could stand toe to toe with just about any adversity and bludgeon her way through it. She's a natural. A keeper, if we can talk her into it.

"However." She reached across the table and placed a hand to his arm. "This is Mother Lacey here. I'm concerned about you."

"Me?" It took a few seconds to understand her implication; a few more to formulate a response civil enough to share. "I'm a big boy, Lacey. Maybe you've been around the block a few more times. But I've got a good five or ten years' life experience over Sarah. Not to mention fifteen years of social work. I can certainly look out for myself."

"And you also wear your heart on your sleeve, where it bruises a lot more easily."

There wasn't much he could safely say to that. Everything coming to mind would only have his defensiveness prove her point for her.

What was she expecting of him, anyway? This was none of her business. And she was getting pretty damned over-controlling. Even for an administrator.

"Your sensitivity is one of your greatest assets," she continued. "During disaster, it can set you up for downfalls because emotions run so high. I'm only suggesting you look out for yourself."

"I hear you, and I thank you for your concern." He glanced across the room, where Sarah was still entrenched in her consultation. "But the way I see it, this is between me and Sarah."

"Then, enough said. As long as it doesn't interfere with relief effort functioning. I have a mental health operation to run here." She took a few quick bites of supper. "Shall we take a look at how things are shaping up for tomorrow?"

He had expected more pushback. The quick transition left him tongue-tied. "Uh . . . okay."

"The next storm is moving in. Rain should be here by tomorrow evening. This time it'll be even worse. Many are still reeling from the last flood. Many residents will be all the more vulnerable, from a mental health perspective. Especially during the waiting and wondering."

"What's the plan?"

"People tend to gather around sandbagging operations, even when there isn't much work left to be done. It's a good opportunity for outreach. We need DMH workers to follow the vehicles that are taking food and beverages."

"I take it you mean me and Sarah."

"I think you'll like it. Report to the feeding kitchen, bright and early. Six a.m. at the latest. Pass this on to Sarah when she's done over there. I assume you'll still be here."

"I have no intent of moving from this spot."

Lacey smiled and shook her head.

"Hey, Paulson." Chet dropped into the chair next to him. "Truck's ready. First time I've seen the bottom of that bed since, I don't know. Sometime last year, I reckon. My buddies at the warehouse helped. Didn't take any time at all."

Chet waved at a gathering of warehouse workers. A couple of them waved back. Steve was among them, still looking as though he was carrying the weight of the world on his shoulders.

What else does that guy know? Perhaps he'd been in touch with the authorities by now. There had to be some way of finding out. If he got lucky maybe he'd run into Dave or Roy, and be able to check the status of that one.

"Ready to load her up?" Chet's bright-eyed enthusiasm stared back, rearing and ready.

"I don't know if Sarah's talked to Nate yet."

"I'm back." Sarah reached under the table and grabbed her satchel. "No. Nate didn't pick up. I left him a message. Let's just do it."

Between Chet's pickup and the additional space offered by the rental car they succeeded in loading most of the storage room's contents. Sarah gave Chet the note she'd prepared. He stuck it in an envelope and wrote "Sam" across it in big block letters.

"No way he can miss this." Chet attached it to a couple of small rusty nails just inside the door. "He'll read it, right off. Just like old times."

"How did it go with the shelter manager?" The relative privacy of the rental car presented opportunity to mentor.

"He talked about the new storm, and sheltering needs. I don't think he was any more on edge than anybody else. When I mentioned the fire, he looked embarrassed. Really, very sweet. He said he'd been worried about the supplies stored in the warehouse, if the fire would spread there. They'd just gotten it all delivered that afternoon. Apparently the first night at the shelter was a real fiasco. The flash flood made for a lot more evacuees than they'd anticipated. They were only able to do supper by cleaning out Uncle Harold's deli. It's understandable he'd be worried. But near as I can tell, it's old news."

"A lot has happened since then. Like this new storm he has to think about." Paulson veered into the alleyway fronting the apartment complex. He checked the rearview mirror, making sure Chet's truck made the turn. "That reminds me. I was supposed to tell you about tomorrow. Lacey wants us to follow the feeding trucks that will be heading toward the sandbagging."

"That fits well with the barbecue. It'll put us close to Sylvia's."

Sylvia's?

A chance to go with Sarah to a social event certainly had a place on his priority list. Doing it at the home of the mother of Sarah's old flame—that was knotty. What if her callous-looking ex showed up? Would he be gracious? Or would he constantly fight off the urge to deck him?

I've been out of circulation too long.

A half hour later, the contents of the two vehicles sat on his garage floor.

"I can move the last of it for you later." Chet slammed the gate to the truck bed.

"Then here, hang on to this. You'll need it." Sarah gave Chet the key to the padlock.

"Sure thing. Another big day tomorrow. Lots more stuff coming to the warehouse."

"Is this a good time to take a quick peek at Junior?" Sarah nodded in the direction of his front door. "I know it's getting late."

"Sure! I mean . . . sure." Paulson glanced down, noting ash-covered footwear. "How about we hose these off a little and leave them out here. Not that it's the Taj Majal or anything in there."

*****

Sarah scanned the small front room as she stepped onto a faded area rug that had seen better days. Some patches were so worn, the gleam of polished wood peeked through bare weave. What remained, however, felt exceptionally soft. It was welcoming and cushiony to the soles of her tired feet.

The sofa had early-American garage sale written all over it; an oversized plaid throw covered most of whatever had once passed for upholstery. The flimsy-looking end table and heavy lamp holding it down also looked worse for wear. At least they appeared clean and well dusted. Though the haphazard cache of paperback novels made need for dusting difficult to judge.

Opposite the sofa, where one would expect to find an entertainment unit, stood an elaborate aquarium, conspicuous in its extravagance. Junior apparently served as resident entertainer. She wafted about, exploring coral and other whimsical accessories.

Sarah knelt in front of the glass for a better view. The fish approached, bumping its nose against the glass. "Look—she's looking at me. Do you think she remembers me?"

"How could she forget. Remember how entertaining we were at the mall?"

"This habitat you've created is beautiful. I could sit here and stare at it all evening."

"Take your time. I've got books on tropical fish if you're interested. I used to dive. This tank here is my Midwestern edition of scuba diving."

"That's a sport I've always wondered about. It sounds so exotic. Like exploring a faraway distant world."

"It is. Distant, relatively unseen. Peaceful."

"It'll be some time before I'm in a position to try out something like that. But I'd love to take a look at your books."

*****

"None of this would've happened if you hadn't thrown it in the disaster vehicle. I told you right off, that car could end up with somebody else. It was you that said it'd be fine and dandy to stick it in there. Far as that goes, if I hadn't called that fire in, everything'd be burnt up now anyhow."

"According to you, they were coming to get that car right then and there. Where else do you think you could have hidden it?"

"I don't rightly know. But it shouldn't have been there in the first place."

"You're the one that blew our chance to be done with it. I can't believe you just stood and watched while they opened it up. Twice. Then let them walk off with everything."

"What was I supposed to do?" Steve flapped his hands in frustration. "That Chet was always right around the corner. There wasn't anything to do, with him always there helping out."

"You could have offered to help, yourself. Then when the duffle turned up, all you'd have to do is haul it off when they weren't looking."

"That'd be a stretch, pulling that off."

"So how badly do you want it, anyway? We could have just raided where Sam's squatting, got what we needed, and been done by now. But oh, no. You vetoed that, like everything else."

Steve glared at him. "I told you, I don't want no part of anything that might hurt folks."

"Spare me, please."

"All I want now is to make sure the authorities don't get hold of it. They still got our prints in the system, you know. Otherwise I'd be telling you to have at it however you want."

"I see two pair of shoes. She's hanging around for the night?"

"I expect so."

The porch light came on and the screen door swung open. Paulson and Sarah stepped out. She stooped down and picked up one set of shoes, balancing a stack of books in her other arm. She laughed after Paulson said something.

"Now isn't this cozy."

"That Paulson's a good sort. I don't want no part of messing with his abode."

"He might be back. Better not try anything tonight. You can be the one who keeps him busy tomorrow. And come up with a few bright ideas about how I might get into this garage."

CHAPTER FOURTEEN

Friday, June 6ᵗʰ

"The operation will cover two routes, one truck apiece. Visit as many sites listed in your handout as there's time for. Be sure to stay on top of weather updates. By noon, emergency management will be telling everyone to get out. Our leaving encourages people to follow suit. So be prompt about it. This time around, DMH is following."

Paulson obliged the supervisor by waving from where they stood; Sarah waved as well.

"Let them know if you come across anyone you think might benefit. Review your PFA handout so you know what to refer. Questions?"

The group shuffled and fidgeted, no doubt more focused on what they had left to do before they could hit the road.

"Okay," said the supervisor. "Let's go."

They scampered into the loading area like rabbits turned loose into a cabbage patch.

The previous evening had been seventh heaven—once Paulson got himself to relax, that is. It had turned into an opportunity to talk about diving and other conversational topics for which he hadn't had an interested audience in some time. Fortification with the red wine of questionable maturity they'd found stashed in the back of his refrigerator made it all the more enjoyable. Thankfully it had been neither so stale nor plentiful that a hangover would spoil his day.

He walked Sarah to the parking lot. "Have a nice morning."

"You, too. Let's meet up here afterwards. We can talk about it. Sylvia's should be in full swing by then, too."

"I wonder what the treasure hunters turned up." Hopefully not Sylvia's son.

"I'd also like a closer look at Dad's things, if we're not too tired. Something else of mine might be in there. And it might help Dad if I took inventory. We wrecked whatever system he had for knowing what was what when we moved everything. Not much was labeled."

"Fine by me," he called after her. She was already darting off after her team.

At the loading area, workers were busy stocking the red and white feeding truck he'd most likely stare at the back of for much of the day. They snapped him up and put him to work. Hot meals were already prepared and waiting. He helped load a procession of unwieldy Cambros, individually packaged foods, canned water, and serving supplies. By the time all was in place, his muscles howled in agony. Watching those dainty-looking seniors heft them around made it all the more humiliating. He had to get in better shape.

The overcast sky began to darken, hinting of the coming deluge. This was earlier than predicted. Whether feeding operations would have time to complete their routes before having to turn back was beginning to look doubtful.

The first stop was the site where the flash flood had emptied into town. A mound of sand had been dumped in the now-vacant lot bordering the breech. The towering concrete levee was positioned upstream, looking like some kind of road to nowhere. Or a half-finished overpass, abandoned for no apparent reason.

People of about every size, shape, age, gender, and socioeconomic group rambled around on site. Most were pitching in to shovel sand, hold bags, or transport them in wheelbarrows. Several men were laboring at the overflow area, positioning filled bags, tarps, lumber, and concrete blocks into a formidable-looking structure.

"That over there could be tightened up a bit." Stooped over his cane was Victor Biddle, proprietor of Vic's Antiques and Collectables. Also apparently a self-designated overseer.

"This is one fantastic job, Vic."

"A sight to behold, ain't it? Folks from every walk of life, coming down and pitching in. I've never been so proud of our community."

"Do they expect another flash flood?"

"Hard to say. Last time around, it was because of logs and debris getting tangled. Dammed up its own little reservoir. When the water got to be too much, it gave way. That's why it came through fast, the way it did. It was right here, where we're building this wall."

"So what are chances of the exact same thing happening again?"

"Not much. Fact is, they say they'll get it worse south of here this time. It don't matter none. Building our own dam is how we fight back. With the river, and with city hall. If Mayor Schwartz isn't gonna protect us, we'll take care of it ourselves. Besides, if there's flooding of any sort, it's no mystery that this here bank needs shoring up. So it's worth it."

"In more ways than one, so it seems."

"That storm's looking to be obliging enough to get itself over with before poker night, too. I'm looking forward to that. Business as usual, for a change. Cards, beer, popcorn, a few camping lanterns just in case, and good buddies all around. What more could you ask for?"

"Too bad Sam's not here. I know he's a big fan of Saturday night cards."

"Last I saw him, he said he was coming. Did he tell you otherwise?"

"When?" Paulson tensed. "When did you see Sam?"

"Just the other day. He had something he'd found after the flood. Washed up right there in his backyard. He wanted to know what it was. Maybe get it back to whoever it belonged to."

"His daughter's here. She's been looking all over for him. She's worried sick."

"I heard Sarah was back. I thought she was just helping out with the flood. I didn't expect Sam wasn't in touch with her."

"What day did you see him?"

"It was at least Monday or Tuesday. Long after flood night. But he told me he'd be there for poker, come hell or high water." Vic let out a hoot. "Now don't that beat all. He did have himself a little of both, didn't he."

"What did he have to say about the shop fire?"

Vic looked thoughtful. "You know, he didn't say a word. You'd never figure he just lost the place he'd done business in for so long. I kind of wondered about it at the time. What's he doing researching some marginal antique when he's got that burnt-up shop to contend with? Maybe just getting away from it awhile, was what I figured. I didn't say nothing about it. He was in such good spirits, in spite of it all. Why rock the boat? I figured, good for him."

Or did Sam simply not know. "I'll pass on to Sarah what you told me. We can at least say for certain that Sam wasn't a victim in that fire then."

"Great gobs of goose grease. Yes, let her know her daddy was alive and kicking last I saw him."

"Did he say where he was staying?"

"No. I figure someplace nearby, since he brought that thing in to me instead of to those smarty pants fellers in Willsey."

Another disaster relief van pulled into the lot. Workers poured out, unloading supplementary items. Steve was among them. Mechanical motions set out gloves, masks. Steve was dragging.

"Thanks for your help, Vic." Paulson sat in the car and got hold of Sarah.

He relayed Vic's story. Silence followed. "Sarah? You still there?"

There were a few quiet sniffles. "Thanks, Paulson. This is wonderful news. What a relief. I should have thought to check again with Victor myself. I'm going to call Nate right this minute. Then Chet. I'll let Nate update the authorities. Now all we need to do is figure out where Dad's staying."

"Since it's highly likely he'll turn up at poker night, we can always catch up with him there. Do you know who's hosting? I didn't ask."

"Chet will know." Her voice was still halting.

"Are you okay?"

"I'm fine, you worrywart. I'll see you around noon."

So he would be sharing her with Sam over the weekend. It lifted a substantial burden. It was a really good day.

He pocketed his phone and scanned the area for Steve. He spotted him hovering over his stockpile, still a gloomy Gus.

Looks like a job for mental health.

"I see you're still with us." Paulson made a show of examining the supplies. "They're putting you to good use, too."

"I reckon so."

Paulson repositioned himself to be less likely overheard. "You okay? You look worn out."

"Just lots of things to think about. With all that's happening."

"Something you want to talk about?"

Steve looked down, kicking loose dirt with the toe of his boot. "Maybe. How about later, without all these folks around."

"When would be a good time?"

"End of shift is good. I'll be at the warehouse about then. Around six, I suppose."

He would be looking for something to do then anyway, with Sarah tied up in her father's stash. "I can arrange it."

The first raindrops were splattering by the time the feeding operations returned to the kitchen. Paulson and Sarah helped with the unloading and cleaning and said their goodbyes.

"I can hardly wait to tell Lacey." She looked it, practically bouncing in her seat as she buckled in. "I've been bugging her about leads for an eternity."

The discovery energized him as well. He'd finally done it, found something concrete to ease Sarah's worries. Raise her spirits.

She looked like she was actually enjoying his company for a change, too. Until now, most conversation initiated by Sarah had been the question and answer kind, usually some piece of trivia about how or why something was done. At the moment she was being spontaneously personal, even more so than during their impromptu happy hour.

The real Sarah.

By the time they reached headquarters, steady and determined rainfall blurred all with translucent grayness. Occasional gusty winds intensified the drenching for those so unfortunate to be caught in it. Yet inner warmth lingered, residue of having made a big difference in the life of a disaster survivor. It was all the more gratifying that it was Sarah. Such intense appreciation lit up her eyes. A hint of possibility, perhaps, to be able to see him as something more than a mentor?

They sprinted across the parking lot and into city hall, hesitating at the entry to shake out the marginally effective raingear. Headquarters seemed eerily quiet, insulated from the weather mayhem. It was also oddly deserted.

Lacey was still at her station, the phone glued to her head—looking more and more like an extra natural appendage. While waiting for her to free herself, they wandered toward the canteen. The spread of comfort food beckoned, his gut rumbling. Foraging was in order.

Sarah stopped him. "Don't spoil your appetite. Save it for barbecue. You won't regret it."

"Who will be there?" He restricted himself to a large pretzel. His appetite probably would be a moot point anyway, if her ex turned up.

"It started out as just the quilters and their husbands. Yesterday, Shelley told me other friends and family are coming. It should be quite a crowd."

Not what he wanted to hear. *Sylvia's kid* . . .

Lacey finished her call and motioned them over. "Tell me about the sandbagging." She continued to scribble on her notepad.

"It was a fantastic morning," said Sarah. "Everybody was so focused and energetic. There was anxiety, of course. But they put it to good use working on flood barriers. I ran into people I hadn't seen since high school. Even my old social science teacher. When I told him about my career, he looked proud enough to bust.

"But Paulson had the best news of the day." She smiled up at him.

Paulson told Lacey what he'd heard about Sam.

"I'm really happy for you, Sarah," said Lacey. "That must be a huge load off."

"What more do we have going for the afternoon?" said Paulson. "I've got an appointment with a worker after his shift. And Sarah and I still need lunch."

"Here's where we stand. Areas saturated from the last rainstorm are expected to have problems. Right now we're under a flood watch, probably upgraded to flood warning before long. Tornado warnings aren't out of the question.

"Some of last weekend's shelters have reopened. The one here in Marshland is beefing up. The visiting mental health staff is either supporting the shelters, or sheltering in place. Other client services are standing down until the storm passes. Once it's over, we'll regroup."

"Does this mean Sarah and I have hotshot duty?"

"Back up a bit. You guys are the locals. You'll be dealing with this for some time. Take it easy while you have the chance."

"Are you sure?" said Sarah. "I'm finally beginning to feel like I know what I'm doing."

"I appreciate your enthusiasm. But I can take care of any hotshot issues. Look around you." She gestured at the minimal skeleton crew loitering at their desks. "There's not much going on here. So go have fun. Or take a nap. Whatever suits you. Seek appropriate shelter if things start looking dicey. You know the drill. I'll see you in the morning."

"Don't need to tell me twice." Paulson winked at Lacey as he led Sarah away by the elbow. Lacey rolled her eyes. At least she'd stopped harassing him about it.

And now, he was on his way to a social diversion with Sarah. It had even been Sarah's idea. It didn't get any better.

*****

By the time they'd negotiated the detours in Sylvia's neighborhood, heavy-duty gutter wash paralleled their journey. Anything not grassy, paved over or graveled looked like a muddy bog.

Salvaged wooden planks were set out as footpaths along the soggy puddling at Sylvia's ravaged lot. They wound their way down, over the muck and around debris piles, until the planking delivered them to the remains of Sylvia's front walk. Large blue tarps were strung up along one side of the house, sheltering what was left of the deck below. Wafts of smoke curled out from under a jerrybuilt awning.

"Ah, the smell." Sarah inhaled the ecstasy of it as they hurried off the planks and sought cover. "Barbecue in a rainstorm. I haven't been to a barbecue of any sort in ages."

Harold was first to greet them, nobly strutting in a well-worn apron and chef's hat, tongs in hand. "A man's gotta believe in something . . .

177

and I believe I'll have another" was spread across the bib of his apron, further accented with soot smudges and barbecue sauce spatter.

"We're having us a flood party." He toasted them with the Coors Light in his other hand.

"Looks like my kind of party," said Paulson. "Which way to the brewskies?"

"Help yourself, over in that cooler. There's sodas and other things, too. Millie stuck some Two Buck Chuck in there if you're so inclined. Food's laid out in the kitchen."

Paulson dug around in the ice for microbrews.

Most of the merrymaking had moved inside. The interior of Sylvia's looked similar to Aunt Millie's basement—water-stained walls, boarded up windows, baseboard stripped of carpeting. In sharp contrast to the dreariness, an attentively decorated table was positioned in the middle of the room, decked out in lace and candles. It was the first greet all who entered, like some sort of shrine. Spread out on the table was what had to be the booty pillaged from the mud and debris piles earlier in the day.

"Look at everything we found." Elspeth stood watch over the display. "Some of it isn't even Sylvia's. No telling who it all belongs to. We did find a few knickknacks and other things that were hers, though."

"Where is she? And Aunt Millie, and Shelley?"

"Sylvia and Mildred are in the kitchen. Shelley's gone back to the shelter already. She's overseeing things for the dinner crowd. She says she'll make sure those out of town people don't mess up the local cuisine. I'm going there soon, too. It's my job to get tonight's newcomers registered. You have no idea . . ."

While one ear attended to Elspeth's prattling, she glanced around at other partygoers. Friends and acquaintances she hadn't seen in over a decade were gathered, talking and laughing together. Making the best of things, enjoying each other in spite of the weather insanity. While sipping her microbrew she caught a glimpse of Paulson, talking up a storm with a couple of Sylvia's neighbors. He stepped into some unidentifiable impersonation as he emphasized a point.

What a clown. This is the life.

Elspeth interrupted the existential meandering. "Look here, here's Uncle Toddy."

The large form of Todd Goode loomed up alongside.

"See? It's Sarah. After all these years, she's back again. Helping with the flood."

"It's been some time, hasn't it?" said Todd. "I hear you're done with school, and in business for yourself. Good for you. You're helping us give Marshland a good name. We're moving this community up in the world with people like you to show us off."

The sappy commendations practically dripped. *What's he after?* "Hello, Mr. Goode. I don't remember when we last crossed paths, either. I was probably still in high school."

"Just 'Todd' will do now, honey. You've joined the grown-up world. As a fine young woman, at that. We're all so proud of you. Say, I was sorry to hear about your old neighborhood. Do you know what your daddy's plans are?"

"Not really. I assume he'll rebuild." She congratulated herself for successfully squelching the urge to point out the obvious contradiction— condescending drivel amidst a claim that he didn't see her as a child.

"You know, those retirement neighborhoods are pretty nice these days. Lots of services for folks when they start needing a little assistance, or medical care, and the like."

Next he would probably tell her just the place for Dad to move to. Something Todd had a finger into. "I've never known Dad to be at a loss for figuring out what he wants. But I'll take that under advisement."

"Being in the business you're in, I imagine you've got a better idea than the rest of us about the changes and needs he'll have down the line. With you and your brother so far away, I bet it'd be a comfort knowing he was someplace where others can keep an eye on him."

He had a point there. But a sell job is a sell job, and that's precisely what he was dishing out.

Todd handed her a business card. "Now, if your daddy has any thoughts of selling out, you give me a call. I'll fix him up with something real nice. I'd pay top dollar for that land of his, too. What a burden, for a man his age. Contending with a mess like that, and having to start all over again."

Patience was wearing thin. He truly believed he could convince her to sell off and pave over the plot of land she'd grown up on. How empty-headed did he think she was? *Boss Hogg lives.*

Paulson passed nearby, making his way toward the kitchen.

179

"Thanks, uh, 'Todd'." She pocketed the card. "Excuse me."

"Ready for some food?" Paulson asked, as she came up alongside him. "Watching plates go by has been torture."

The counter was laden with a potluck buffet. Aunt Millie and Sylvia were replenishing serving bowls. Or at least Aunt Millie was. Sylvia was holding onto an opened Tupperware container, lost in a vacant stare.

"We made it," said Sarah. "I see you found a few things. That plunger was a nice touch."

Aunt Millie and Sylvia looked at each other. They giggled, then burst out laughing. Seeing Sylvia come to life was a relief. Capacity for humor was there—at least for the moment. There was hope yet.

"The plunger was Elspeth's find," said Aunt Millie. "One of the few things out there that was actually Sylvia's. Elspeth was so proud, we just had to stick it in the display."

"I'm glad you could be here." Sylvia set down the container and gave her a motherly hug. "You too, Paulson. It's nice y'all could come work together the way you're doing, too."

"The first thing we've got to do is get some food in you." Aunt Millie took each of them by the elbow and led them to the head of the buffet line. "I bet you two have been hard at work. I know you, Sarah. Your appetite's surely calling you this way."

"Thanks, Mildred," said Paulson. "I've been drooling ever since the aroma hit at curbside."

"Dish up." Aunt Millie gave his bicep a playful pinch. "We need a little more meat on these bones."

While they filled their plates Aunt Millie lowered her voice. "I hope you two get a chance to talk with Sylvia. She's been nervous as a cat ever since the rain started up. She had quite an adventure during the last storm."

"I know. Roy's here," said Paulson. "The deputy that helped her get out. I just now heard some of the finer details. That was one harrowing experience. For all of them."

"I've been staying with her as much as I can. Not much that I do seems to make a difference. You see, I heard about that man, out at the disaster office." Aunt Millie paused, struggling for words. "I guess what I'm trying to say is . . ." Her eyes drifted in the direction of Sylvia.

"Could be the storm will have to pass before she gets out of hyper-arousal," said Sarah. "But your being with her helps. Even if it isn't showing. I can't think of anyone I would want more to be with her right now than you."

"Thanks, hon'. I'll do what I can."

They returned to the card table where Sylvia was sitting. Sarah joined her. "I assume you didn't find the heirlooms. I didn't see them in the display."

"It's a darn shame. If only Charlie'd told me what he done with them."

"It's still possible they're in a safe deposit box somewhere." While doing justice to the potato salad, Sarah brainstormed other optimistic possibilities. "Or maybe he gave them to someone for safekeeping. Someone who hasn't come forward with them yet."

"If that's the case, shame on him." Aunt Millie bit into a homemade donut. "Or her."

"Perhaps it's just been forgotten." Paulson leaned against the kitchen wall and dug into his lunch. "How often do people get around to looking at what's in their safe deposit boxes? It could turn up any time. Even if it's not for years. What a great surprise to look forward to."

"I'm going to hold onto that thought, and . . . Oh!" Sylvia jumped, as a gang of teenagers banged through the kitchen door.

Sarah recognized some of them—she had last seen them during the scuffle at the school auditorium.

"Wipe off your shoes first, dear," said Sylvia.

"Give it a rest, Ma. There's no way you're going to keep all that mud outta here."

The boys grabbed up donuts and cookies and left as rambunctiously as they had entered.

"That boy could use a good tongue-lashing." Mildred shot a steady ray of mother-eye in the direction of the retreating teens. "Adolescence defines rudeness, but he's getting a little old for this. That was uncalled for."

"That's Jimmy's little brother?" It was hard to fathom, seeing him now even taller than she was. "He was barely in elementary school the last time I saw him."

"It's hardest on him, not having his daddy around no more. Jimmy don't do nothing much to help. Or be a man for him to look up to, with the problems of his own. I'm afraid he'll end up even worse off than Jimmy. Those kids he brings around are always stirring up trouble."

Aunt Millie wrapped an arm across Sylvia's shoulders and gave her a squeeze. "He'll come around, Syl', just like Jimmy."

"But what'll happen between now and then? It hangs on me so much." The empty stare reclaimed Sylvia. She slowly leaned into her friend.

"How about some really good news?" In all the excitement, the best part of the day had yet to be shared. "Victor saw Dad at the junk store."

Paulson summarized his conversation with Victor.

"Why in the world isn't he getting in touch with anybody, then?" said Aunt Millie. "It's like he's purposely hiding out."

"I'll find out soon enough," said Sarah. "I'm going to crash his poker game. Do you know who's hosting it this week?"

"First Saturday of the month was always Stewy's; at least that was the order back when Charlie played," said Sylvia. "The game usually got started around eight."

"Yup." Chet lumbered into the increasingly crowded kitchen. "Eight o'clock at Stewy's. I'm going, too."

"I'm glad I ran into you again, Chet. I was hoping I could tag along, when you go. It would feel less . . . intrusive that way."

"I wouldn't mind being there either." Paulson looked back and forth at her and Chet.

"Sure thing," said Chet. "I sure do lots these days. Tonight I got to go back and help at the warehouse again. There's a forklift job coming up, a whole new load of supplies to move around." Chet stopped scooping up food long enough to strike a pose of importance. "That won't take me long. I already got my basement cleared out. Even set out some of them sandbags. I'll go fetch those last things of Sam's, too, and take them to Paulson's. Or maybe Sam will have someplace else he wants it to go to by then."

"I'm sure going to be interested to hear where he's been all this time," said Sarah. "And why he's keeping us in the dark."

CHAPTER FIFTEEN

"Listen up, everybody." Roy, who until now comfortably fit the stereotype of police officers and donuts, sheathed his phone as the room quieted. "There's flood warnings and tornado warnings. Water's coming up. Funnel clouds have been spotted to the west, maybe headed this way. No mandatory evacuations yet. But everybody's advised to go home. Stay inside and stay tuned for updates. Or go where you usually shelter for these things. Sorry, folks. Looks like the party's over."

Disappointed groans mixed with other commentary. The women began gathering up remains of the potluck while the men folded chairs, tables, and other extras brought in for the event. Sarah helped Aunt Millie prepare portions of leftovers for doggy bags.

"You're coming home with us," Aunt Millie informed Sylvia. "We're not putting you through another ordeal like the last one."

Sylvia was still and silent, liquid eyes staring at the floor. The standoff ended when she offered a barely discernable nod.

"Thank you, honey." Todd accepted a sizable foil-wrapped plate from Sarah. "Don't you forget what I told you about your daddy and his property."

"You're welcome." She left it at that. It was the only way to make sure something unsocialized didn't find its way out.

The teenager Todd had in tow was eyeing the plate of leftovers already.

Todd Goode's son—one of the rabble-rousers in the auditorium lobby. *Surprise, surprise.*

"Come on." Paulson had retrieved their coats. "I'll drop you off and you can get started on your inventory. It'll give me enough time to make my six o'clock."

"Give me a hand with these coolers, would you?" Harold stood at the kitchen door. "This old back of mine just ain't what it used to be."

Paulson tossed the keys to Sarah. "Go start it up. I'll be right with you."

The rain hadn't let up at all. If anything, it looked even more determined that Marshland would live up to its name. Sarah cloaked herself with her raincoat and picked her way along the planks leading to the road. She almost ran headlong into someone similarly preoccupied.

"Well, well. Fancy meeting you here." Jimmy. Again.

She searched for a way to walk around him. There was none, other than over the forbiddingly swampy bog. She was trapped, and forced to deal with him, one way or the other. And on top of that, out on a mud plain, in the middle of a heavy rainstorm. *How fitting.* "So you decided to grace Sylvia with your presence?"

"I've been keeping track of the weather situation. Thought I'd see if Ma needed any help."

"How thoughtful of you. Can I get by?"

"I hear we made it on TV yesterday, if you look hard enough."

"I heard it was . . . charming. I'm trying to get to my car, please."

"The one you share with your buddy, there. I hear you only hang with mental health people these days. That's good. Maybe it'll help."

A smirk snaked out from the depths of his raingear. The guy had no intention of budging. Instead, here he'd stay, taunting her. Doing whatever he could to bait her into an argument. Just like old times.

What had she ever seen in him? It was embarrassing.

The tremor of footfalls on planking approached from behind.

"Thanks for your professional opinion, Dr. Orton. Can we get by now?"

"And here's the man of the hour."

She looked behind her. Paulson's gaze was zeroed in on Jimmy. Even through the rain she picked up the sharpened intensity in those eyes, a sort that was difficult to interpret. Maybe she'd rather not.

"Is there a problem?" Paulson raised his voice, well heard over rain pelting on planks and flood debris.

"Depends who you ask." Jimmy continued to look down at her, chin tilted to frame his condescending stare.

Paulson's tone turned steely. "Would you like us to stand aside for you?"

Jimmy smiled. He stepped to the edge of the walkway and made a grandiose gesture for them to pass. As they attempted it, he pressed down on the edge of a plank. Both of them stumbled. Paulson landed in the muck, seat first. Sarah caught herself on his shoulders.

"Tsk, tsk." Jimmy turned to walk away.

Paulson prepared to stand, throwing a leg forward. His foot caught Jimmy's boot. Jimmy teetered, then slipped, tumbling headlong into a pile of debris.

Just then Roy stepped out on the deck, his beady-eyed cop look scrutinizing the scene. "Everybody okay out here?"

Jimmy tried to get up, but slipped again.

"We're fine." Paulson scooted further down the plank and accepted Sarah's hand, his glare all the while locked with Jimmy's. "Be sure to warn everybody to watch their step. It's getting dicey out here."

Roy stepped down and helped Jimmy get his footing. He kept firm hold of his elbow through Jimmy's failed attempt to jerk it away.

"See you around town," Sarah called to Jimmy over her shoulder. She gave the lagging Paulson a tug toward the car. "You didn't hurt yourself, did you?"

"Just my pride." At roadside he wiped off what mud he could, his eyes still focused on Jimmy's progress toward his mother's house. "How about you?"

"I'm sorry you ended up in the middle of this." She buckled herself into the passenger seat. "With Jimmy, I mean. Why can't he let it go? It's like there's some kind of edict, that he has to harass me over our past."

"Oh, come on. You know a hardened character when you see one. It's no big shock he's like this. Especially with what I've heard about him lately. It would be a nice surprise if he really had cleaned up his act."

When the car's engine started up, she started as well. She was more wired than she'd realized.

She wrapped her arms around herself. "It's like finding myself in the middle of some kind of bizarre culture shock. The last few years, my social life has been almost entirely made up of people in health professions. Basically reasonable people. They'd get weeded out during training if they were as interpersonally inept as Jimmy. These days I'm only around that type of behavior when I treat it, not as part of my personal life."

"Stick with me, kid." He went into Bogart mode. "It's an interesting world out here."

*****

Some roads looked more like shallow rivers. They travelled them in relative silence, other than occasional spray rasping the car's underside. Paulson navigated through detours, vigilant for whatever else had changed the last few hours. One newly flooded route forced them to wait in a prolonged backup. Sarah used it as opportunity to lean her seat back and close her eyes.

The silence in the car invited brooding. He was not inclined toward violence. Had never been. Though inadvertently tripping Jimmy could certainly qualify.

Who am I kidding? Fat chance that was accidental. He had become so protective of Sarah, and so quickly.

Then there was that other time and place when he'd lost it, back at headquarters. When Lacey forced him to take a day off. He'd taken that break. Yet here he was, once again acting too challenged to reel himself in when it was called for. *What's with me?*

After dealing with a few more back roads he ferreted out the freedom of the main highway—still open, thankfully. Rain splattered across blacktop in watery sheets. He took it easy on the accelerator. "Need to stop at the motel?"

"No, let's go straight to your place." Sarah stretched, and looked around. "You're awfully quiet."

"Just tired, like you. Another long day."

"This whole thing is going by so quickly. A couple more days, and I'll probably be on my way home. So much has happened, in so little time. I don't even feel like I'm the same person any more."

*****

The overhead garage door squawked as Paulson heaved. He stepped under cover and waved; Sarah rushed in to join him. He tightened up his raingear and went out to inspect the drainage situation, though the thundering along the downspouts suggested it was moving along just fine. From the refuge of the stuffy garage she watched him make the rounds in the unmerciful torrent. Wind gusts occasionally sent it sideways.

Weather in her hometown seemed to have changed from what she remembered.

Paulson shook water from his raincoat then hung it on a hook. She had already done so, the heat and humidity of the garage interior almost stifling. He unlocked the connecting door to his apartment. "Will you be okay with the garage door up? It's pretty nasty out there."

"It's fine. I prefer fresh air, and it's beginning to take care of the stuffiness. It'll do something for the smoke smell, too. These things reek. I can close the door myself, if the wind direction changes or something."

"Take your time. I need to go clean up for my six o'clock."

The scatter of bags and boxes yielded no clue of how best to tackle the job. The lateness of the hour when they'd dumped them there had generated little enthusiasm for considering order or organization. Some of the boxes looked heavy.

What did I get myself into. She fanned herself with the notepad retrieved from her satchel. Lacey had been absolutely right about the small spiral type being sufficient for whatever writing needed to happen. At the time, the suggestion seemed counterintuitive. Now it made perfect sense. Fieldwork was more about taking immediate action and moving on to the next person while you have the chance. Not standing around and taking elaborate notes.

Flipping through the pages, it told a spotty story of how she'd spent the last few days. Most of what she'd written consisted of information like directions and contact numbers.

She stroked the wire binding, smiling at the memories. She had grown, had advanced, during the history of these scribblings. And tonight the notepad would serve the purpose of recording whatever was in all these bags and other nondescript containers Dad had saved. Perhaps the notepad itself would become a keepsake for her childhood belongings, a last leg of childhood she could finally leave behind.

Time marches on. She tended to duty.

The first box to stand out was the one with her name on it. It would have been more fun to drag it into Paulson's apartment and continue sorting through it. Drift back into old memories. Bask in the delight of what hadn't been lost, after all.

But there was a job to do. She sighed.

While they were unloading the night before, she had noted at least four good-sized containers labeled "Nate." Also several larger items she recognized as his, now leaning in a corner next to Paulson's furnace.

So Nate had hung on to darn near everything. Leave it to Nate to avoid any kind of definitive decision-making.

She separated out big brother's boxes, lined them up, and opened them. She was still assessing them when Paulson returned, looking considerably less bedraggled.

"How's it coming?" He ran a comb through damp hair.

"I'm beginning by separating out Nate's things." The freshness of the shower he brought back with him left her envious. She could only imagine what she must smell like by now. "Since they can't be stored at Dad's any more, he may want to take them home. Or maybe he'll finally weed through it all. I can't believe Dad actually took time to rescue some of this junk. Talk about hyper-responsible. That's Dad, I guess."

"Happy cataloging. Try not to fall in." He pocketed the comb and did a sloppy runway spin. "Did I get all the mud off?"

"You look fine."

"Seriously, though. Are you sure you're okay doing this by yourself? Some of these things are hard to move around. It's kind of dark in here, too, isn't it." He flicked on an overhead light. "Do you have a flashlight? You might need one if the electricity goes out."

"I have a flashlight." She nodded to where she'd dropped her satchel.

"That plastic tub by the door is a disaster kit, if you need a lantern or something."

"I'll keep that in mind."

"If the tornado siren goes off, the safest place to go is my bathroom. The landlord has a storm cellar, too, if there's time . . ."

"Stop worrying. Go see your client, before he thinks he's been abandoned. And be careful out there."

"It's all here. It looks like Dad saved every broken toy and stray Lego. You name it. I'll email you a list. You're going to love hearing what's in here."

"I'd forgotten Dad still had that stuff," said Nate. "Even my old tin of Lego's?"

"If I recall, they're mine now. You were supposed to have outgrown them."

"Consider it payback for the time you shaved Donkey Boy."

"You told me we were even on that score. As long as I didn't tell your friends you were still in love with that thing."

"Okay. So the tin of Lego's is yours. But when Dad gets home, I'm telling."

Interest in playful bantering evaporated at mention of Dad. "I hope Vic wasn't mistaken about when it was he saw him. Is there any chance you can be here for when he's supposed to turn up? It's a Saturday, after all."

"I don't know if I can get a flight on such short notice. Maybe standby. I'll check. Who knows, maybe by tomorrow night we'll be camping out at Stewy's together."

Promises, promises. Nothing if not consistent.

After ending the call, the collection of items loomed larger, highlighting the enormity of the task in front of her. At the time it had felt like a good peace offering for Dad. The process itself, however, was quickly losing its appeal.

How long Paulson would be tied up with his client was hard to say. His returning would be the best excuse to quit for the day.

Her eyelids felt droopy. She sighed and let her hands rest on the pile of Nate's castoffs. Should she continue sorting, or go relax with Junior? Maybe she should throw together a late snack for when Paulson got back. Though if his kitchen was anything like a typical bachelor's, he probably didn't have much on hand to work with. She should have agreed to take some of the potluck leftovers.

But, she had this project to get over with. Better to forge ahead, make at least a little more headway before giving up. It wouldn't take much effort to catalog furniture, and other larger pieces.

"Well, well. What's this? Moving in? You sure are a fast worker." Jimmy stepped under the overhang, taking advantage of shelter from the downpour.

How annoying. "So you've taken up stalking now?"

"Don't flatter yourself." He looked around at the bags and boxes. "What's all this stuff?"

"It's Dad's. Paulson is letting us store things here until Dad figures out what he wants done with it." She moved away and stepped behind a stack of boxes. She raised a lid, feigning interest in its contents. "What's your excuse for being here? I thought you were helping your Ma."

"Ma didn't need help. Half of Marshland's there. I was going by and saw you up here."

He dropped a drenched poncho at the garage entry and began poking around in Nate's things. He picked up a worn and faded football. "Some of this looks familiar. Here, catch."

She ignored the ball sailing by and pretended to sort through the boxes positioned between them. If she were lucky, he would hurry up with whatever snide remarks he still had stored up and be on his way.

He crossed over to retrieve the ball. He stopped next to her and held it in front of her.

"Can you believe this? It looks like that same ball we used to steal out of Nate's room. We'd throw it around, just to irritate him." He tossed it back into one of the boxes. "I really did miss you, you know. It's too bad we're always on the bad end of things."

"It's done, Jimmy." She continued to snatch up items and pretend to examine them. "We're in different worlds now."

"You haven't changed so much. I could tell, yesterday."

He was uncomfortably close. She moved aside to the next stack of boxes, attempting to seem dispassionate, in spite of what her blood pressure reading had to be. The last thing she wanted was to let him know he'd gotten to her again. Or do anything else that might encourage his increasingly dubious behavior.

He continued to move in, regardless.

"You liked it." He ran a finger along her shoulder. "Back at Frieda's. I could tell. I remember what you like. We could have some fun while your boyfriend is out saving the world."

"Back off, Jimmy. And he's not my boyfriend. He's a coworker. A mentor. This is getting over the top, even for you." She gave up the pretense of disinterest and turned, locking eyes with him.

The notebook fell from her hand. It was not Jimmy. Not the Jimmy she knew. She was face to face with the wide-eyed glaze of substance abuse.

Jimmy was no longer clean.

What was he like when in this state? She didn't know in the slightest. He might get out of hand. Exactly how under the influence was he at the moment?

He moved in closer. The wall came up against her from behind.

"I said back off." It came out higher, louder than intended.

Jimmy laughed and set out an arm above her, his hand planting against the wall that was now pressing into her back.

"You don't really mean that, do you?" He sounded like he truly believed what he was saying.

His overheated scent was suffocating. She abruptly squirted herself out of confinement and tried to create distance. The effort came to a halt when he caught her from behind. On adrenaline and pure instinct, she threw up her arms and dropped. She slid from his grasp and rolled a couple times. When she came to a stop she looked up, reassessed.

Blast it all. She was even further back in the garage than she'd started.

"Now that was damn clever." Jimmy laughed as he watched her pick herself up. "I wouldn't mind seeing that again."

She searched for an escape route, looked to the parking area for possible assistance. Of course not, in this. Just pounding rain drawing that steady gray barrier between her and freedom.

The door into the apartment was to her left, several feet away. She made a quick move for it, a last-ditch effort.

Jimmy was quicker. He grabbed her arm and spun her around. He pushed her up against the door, hard.

"Jimmy, I can't hardly breathe like this." She reached down behind her, groping at the doorknob, trying to remember if the door opened in or out.

"How's about this, then." He teased her shirt with a few little tugs.

"Stop it!" She tried to scream, her arms pinned in place between them.

An aroused male body continued to press against her.

A large pudgy hand and arm shot across her field of vision. It nailed Jimmy at his neck and slammed him into the wall.

"What the heck do you think you're doing?" Chet roared.

She broke away, gasping for breath. Chet was red in the face, in a state of rage. Jimmy struggled impotently against the wall as Chet restrained him.

"Don't hurt him!" She gave Chet's arm several fruitless tugs. "Please. You'll just cause trouble for yourself, trouble for us all. Let him go. He's not himself right now."

She grabbed the satchel and dug around for her phone. Contents fell, rattling as they hit concrete. Including the clatter of scattering phone parts.

Double blast. She dropped the satchel and scrambled to pick up pieces. She may as well have had on heavy gloves, her attempts to reassemble it so clumsy. Any dexterity seemed to have been erased by the fear of needing to get two large, out-of-control men in check.

At last the pieces clicked into place. Powering up moved at a snail's pace. She retried it. It wasn't cooperating the way it should.

Broken? She fought to clear her head, consider other options. Should she go find one of Paulson's neighbors? She looked down the walk toward the landlord's office. The light was on.

When she looked back at the scuffle, Chet had eased up. He was getting a hold on himself. *Thank God.* Eventually he loosened his grasp, and Jimmy pulled free.

"Don't you never come near her again." Chet's measured monotone was blood-chilling.

Jimmy looked around, as if not sure where he was. Finally he stormed off without a word. The screech of sudden acceleration soon followed.

Sarah realized she was trembling.

"He didn't hurt you, did he?" Chet sounded like an innocent again, looking down at her with his gentle questioning gaze.

"I'm . . . okay. Just a little shook up. Chet, listen. Jimmy's using again. He would never have done this before, ever. I should have noticed it. Something was wrong when he first walked in. I can see that, now. I should have been paying more attention."

Chet frowned. "He don't have any business pushing you around that way, drugs or no drugs."

"He shouldn't be driving. He's a mess. Someone could get hurt. Especially with road conditions the way they are. We need to tell the sheriff."

"I'm calling Paulson." He reached into his shirt pocket. "He knows about things like this. I'll follow Jimmy, just in case."

God only knew what might happen if Chet caught up with him. "Let the sheriff take care of it, Chet."

He continued to his truck regardless, phone to his ear.

*****

"I sure do appreciate you coming out like this. Making a special trip and all."

Trying to get somewhere with Steve had evolved into a long string of miscues. At first he assumed cultural deprivation was the likely culprit. Steve wasn't someone who under normal circumstances would have much involvement with counselors. He might not even have a particularly accurate understanding of what counselors did. But no matter how much Paulson simplified his questioning, the false starts of the consultation kept piling up.

"Disaster stirs up all sorts of things for people," said Paulson. "It's best to deal with it when you're ready—no sooner, no later."

"I expect all that's true enough."

The surge of rain pelting against tin echoed through the warehouse. They waited while the noise passed.

"I'm just having a hard time of it." Steve looked around, scratched his head. "I guess that's about it."

"Was it something in particular that happened, that's still bothering you?"

Steve furrowed his brow until he was practically cross-eyed. "Just bothered, is all."

"How about something that happened during the flood?" Silence. "Or maybe there's something that hadn't been that big a deal before, and it seems harder now."

Steve sat there, motionless, still at a loss for words.

What was he to make of it? It was like working with recalcitrant adolescents. Or when people went into therapy because their family members insisted on it. Maybe that was it. "Did someone else tell you that you should talk to a counselor?"

"Not that I recall, no." He stared at the floor, his body rigid. Hands in his lap, tightly clasped. Consternation best described his facial contortions.

"Does this have something to do with Ted?"

Steve looked up, puzzled. "Who?"

"Your friend, Ted. The other day we talked about him, the problem he was having. Did something happen with Ted?"

"Oh, Ted. No, not that I know about."

Paulson was stumped. Steve hadn't had such a hard time articulating his concerns other times they'd talked.

Paulson glanced toward the back of the warehouse. It was uncharacteristically empty. Perhaps the gang in logistics had set this up as some kind of joke. And any moment now, they would all burst out of the back room and deliver some outrageous punch line.

Back to basics. "Well, what symptoms are you having? Exactly what was it that made you decide talking with me would help?"

"Symptoms?"

"Like, how you feel right now. Are you feeling sad? Angry? Stressed?"

"That's it!" Steve jumped up, as animated and excited as if he had just scratched a winning lotto ticket. "Stress! I've got stress."

The cell phone in his pocket vibrated. At last, a diversion. *Any diversion.*

The chance to step away might be just what they needed. Then see if he could find a way to hit the reset button. Maybe jumpstart what felt more and more like being trapped in the middle of a Monty Python skit. "Could you excuse me for a moment, Steve? I need to take this."

"I'll be sitting right here." He visibly relaxed.

Paulson shook his head and walked away, responding to the call.

It was Chet's booming voice, amidst heavy breathing. "We got a big problem here. That Jimmy Orton. You know, Sylvia's boy? He's taking drugs again. He stopped by your place. He was real strange. Got into it with Sarah, too. She's worried he's driving the way he is."

"Is Sarah all right?"

"Shook up a bit, is all. Mostly she's talking about Jimmy and how he's not supposed to be driving. She told me to call the sheriff. I told her I'd let you take care of all that."

Chet's pickup could be heard in the background, downshifting. "Where are you now?"

"I'm following Jimmy. Well, catching up with him anyway. On Main Street, by the high school. He's driving like he's crazy. Guess he is crazy, being on drugs and all."

"I'll get the sheriff. Let Jimmy be and let Dave do his job."

He made a quick call to the dispatcher as he hurried back to his failed consultation. Noting his approach, Steve immediately returned to a state of agitated nerves.

"I'm really sorry about this. Something urgent came up. Maybe we can continue this later. How about if I drop by tomorrow? I'll bring some information on how to cope with stress."

"Sure thing." Steve looked relieved. "We can talk tomorrow."

CHAPTER SIXTEEN

Paulson joined the stream of vehicles in time to spot Chet's pickup veering onto River Road. Storm water created rivulets along the gutters of Main Street, puddling almost to the centerline.

Marshland's one traffic light chose that moment to turn yellow, then red. *Damn.* Should he run it?

No. He slammed on the brakes and slid to a stop. The rain blasting the windshield limited his vision; it presented too much risk. Waiting it out was the only reasonable choice. Especially since Lacey would go ballistic if he totaled the rental car. For an activity she'd call "extracurricular."

He rushed through twists and clicks, attempting to readjust the unfamiliar windshield wiper controls. An interminable line of cars proceeded by, most of them slow and cautious.

What was everybody doing out in the middle of this storm? Maybe the tornado warnings had been ramped up. People might have been told to head for safety. The sky did seem a lot darker.

He gave up on the wipers and drummed his fingers against the steering wheel, scanning the increasingly claustrophobic car interior for a distraction. His phone still lay where he'd tossed it, on the passenger seat.

He tried calling Chet. No answer. On a whim, he punched in Sarah's number.

She answered immediately. "Did Chet get hold of you?"

"Yes. His truck just went by. I'm following. Any idea where they're going?"

"No. I tried to call the sheriff, but my phone can't seem to make outgoing calls. What are you doing? Where are you?"

"If I can, I'm going to make sure Chet doesn't get himself into trouble."

The light turned green.

"I'll get back to you." Acceleration fishtailed him through the intersection. He strained to see further ahead. If he got lucky, a glimpse of Chet's small white truck would show up in one of the open expanses between copses of alders. But as the intersection at River Road approached, it still hadn't come into view. There were multiple turnoffs to consider.

Jimmy Orton. *Where would that asshole go?* He slowed for every side road, straining to spot distant taillights or other hints of activity.

About a half-mile down Johnson Creek Way, flashing red and blue caught his eye. He turned. As he drew nearer a squad car materialized beneath the lights, positioned diagonally and blocking passage. Chet's truck was parked to one side.

Beyond them, the Johnson Creek bridge and spillway was impassable. Water rushed effortlessly over what remained of it, as if such an impediment had never existed in the twists and turns that emptied all into Green River.

Chet was pacing along the creek bank, peering downstream, searching for something. He began side stepping down the bank, his massive form achieving a faltering slip and slide.

The sheriff was out setting up orange cones.

Paulson stopped and rolled down his window. "Dave. Got my message?"

"That's Jimmy's car down there. Backup's coming."

Paulson looked over the bank to where Chet was headed. A small beige sedan was almost completely underwater. Only the roof and part of the trunk was visible. A fortuitously placed log prevented it from being swept away all together. The car heaved and shimmied, the status of its future precarious. Jimmy was nowhere to be seen.

"Is he still in there?" Paulson scanned the water churning against the partially submerged vehicle.

"Chet says no. Says Jimmy tried to pull himself out a window. Then the car lurched or something. He hasn't seen him since."

"Chet tends to be overoptimistic. It's hard to say what he really saw."

"I know." Dave made a pointless effort to wipe away water, the heavy wind gusts sending a steady stream into his face. "If he's still in there, he's a goner—there's not much we can do now. It's too dangerous. I rousted some deputies. Roy's taking them downstream to watch for him. Shouldn't take long to get to Green River, if it's a body we're looking for."

"Could he have gotten hung up? Or climbed out somewhere between here and there?"

"We're preparing a search party for . . . if he doesn't turn up soon."

Paulson parked the car behind Chet's pickup and fastened up his raingear. Cursing the downpour, he got out and hurried to the edge of the bank. Sporadic leaf spills from the tree canopy plopped onto him.

"You're getting soaked out here." He yelled to be heard over the rushing water. "Want to come sit in the car?"

"Can you believe this, Paulson? Never seen this river like this before. Not ever."

Rising water was eating away at banked dirt and rock, chunks of it falling away. "It's dangerous down there, Chet. Be careful."

"Just trying to figure out what all happened to Jimmy. I'm sure he got out. He has to be 'round here somewhere."

The river's edge continued moving ever closer to Chet's descending bulk. Chet seemed oblivious.

"Come on! You need to get back. Get away from the water."

It was too late. The hefty clump of soil beneath Chet gave out. He splashed into the muddy water, arms flailing.

Dave was suddenly at Paulson's side. The two of them stumbled down what remained of the bank. Chet hadn't drifted far, still close to the shoreline, foundering like a hooked catfish. Paulson began to reach for him, moving further onto the disintegrating embankment.

"No, wait." Dave threw an arm in front of him, blocking his progress. "Chet! Listen. Stand up. Just stand up."

Chet looked like he heard them and stopped his flailing. He planted wobbly-looking legs beneath himself and stood, slowly gaining balance.

The water wasn't much more than knee high.

Paulson gave him a hand up as he stepped out of the water. "You okay?"

"Yeah, I'm okay. Just pretty wet."

The three of them helped each other climb the muddy bank, leaving the torrents behind.

"I'm gonna go home." Chet slowly nodded as he studied the ground. "That Jimmy Orton. One piece of work. If anybody survived that creek, it'd be him. Keeps turning up, that one. Like a bad penny."

More like stepping into a pile of something you can't scrape off your shoe.

A sudden surge rippled the whitewater. The ground Chet was staring at, that they'd stood upon only moments earlier, abruptly vanished. Only a jagged drop-off remained at their feet.

Out in the water, the sedan broke free of its constraints. It ping-ponged downstream several yards, then sank from view.

The rain was beginning to let up by the time he made it back to the apartment complex. The porch light burned bright. Just the sight of it felt warming. It was like a welcoming beacon, victorious over the blackness that had concluded the search for Jimmy.

The garage door was down. His front door locked.

When he last spoke with Sarah, she'd said she would still be there. That was quite a while ago. By now, she may very well have hitched a ride back to the motel.

He tapped on the door a couple of times before unlocking it. He slowly pushed it open.

She was sitting cross-legged on the sofa, wrapped up in the throw. His radio was turned down low, tuned in to the local station. She didn't look up. She appeared mesmerized by Junior's antics, watching the fish glide about in its liquid tranquility.

"Any sign of him?" she said.

"No." He sprinkled a few fish flakes in the tank before sitting at the other end of the sofa, the only seating option available in the miniscule room.

"Did they get his car out?"

"They can't, until the water goes down. Too unsafe for rescue or recovery."

"How's Chet?"

"He left early. He had no interest in joining the search party. Otherwise, he seemed okay."

Neither spoke for several minutes. Radio commentary droned on, joined by the occasional surge of rain thundering against the roof. It was mainly weather-related news, interspersed with local ads and political spiels—drab. Easy to tune out while he attempted to transition.

Finally getting off his feet was sublime. He waited for Sarah to get to whatever so vigorously occupied her thoughts. As the clock behind them ticked, her disconnect continued. No sign of reengaging, or moving on.

What's this about? He made a show of relaxing, though it in no way reflected the alarm ramping up within.

Persistent replays of the last few hours refused to leave him: chasing after Chet, the submerged car, soggy trekking through pine duff and brambles, the ultimate fruitlessness of their efforts. More disturbing yet, the reemergence of those very non-humanitarian fantasies. In particular, a preference to come across a body, rather than a living, breathing Jimmy.

And now Sarah seemed to have existentially vanished. Should he say something, or continue to wait it out?

The programming shifted into breaking news on the weather situation. The tornado cell had finished passing over. A few strikes here and there had come of it, the extent of the damage still being assessed. No reports of tornadoes touching down in Marshland proper. The rain was supposed to give up pretty soon. In spite of four new inches, the only flooding casualties reported in their vicinity were a few homes near Johnson Creek.

Outside, the rain pounded on. But overall, it looked like Marshland would dodge the bullet with this one. Not counting Jimmy.

Sarah finally spoke. "I wish I could have done something." She gathered the edge of the throw against her. "This is going to destroy Sylvia."

"Sad, yes. But not so unusual in the grand scheme of things—substance abusers falling off the wagon during disaster, I mean." Paulson cursed the verbal bungling. His experiences were affecting him more than he'd realized.

He paused to fiddle with the far corner of the throw while he re-gathered his thoughts. "They get separated from their twelve-step groups, or their methadone. Whatever they do to stay clean. Or the stress overwhelms what had been working for them, up until then."

"As long as you don't tell me it's common and expectable." She shifted in her seat, though not looking any more comfortable for it. At least she was coming to life.

"I suppose it's not exactly common, but it does happen."

"It was part of the DMH training. That we're supposed to advise people with ongoing conditions to check in with their providers." She finally looked him in the eye. "It never occurred to me, with Jimmy. As far as that goes, I didn't even notice he was high until it was too late to do anything. And here he was standing there, right in front of me."

"Do you really think Jimmy would listen to anything you had to say about it?"

"Maybe not. But I could have said something to Sylvia, too, if I'd been thinking straight."

"He'd listen to his mother?"

She closed her eyes, rubbing her palms into them. "It just seems so pointless, losing someone this way. Such a waste. Surely there's a way to prevent something like this."

"You can't save 'em all." The tired cliché was all he had. It was too close to home to offer more. Especially since while tromping through undergrowth, thoughts of a death in the offing had triggered snippets of memory from his own past—that client suicide. At the time, the responsibility of it had felt enormous. Ultimately it was a game changer.

He had come to terms with it eventually. In all likelihood, Sarah would for hers, too. Patience was in order.

But how bizarre, even paradoxical. Everything had come full circle. Here he was, having ridden off into the sunset to escape grief issues, only to find himself coaching a grief specialist through her own feelings about a loss.

"What I should have been thinking about didn't even occur to me." Sarah's self-criticisms continued mounting, in spite of his assurances. "The tip-offs were all there. Jimmy was struggling to find work. In the middle of recession recovery, no less. He's on the outs with his family. His father died not all that long ago. Then his community has a major flood, and his childhood home is practically washed downriver. From the looks of it, it may end up being bulldozed anyway.

"Then there are all the run-ins with me. With us. I can't imagine his other relationships work out any better. By now, his social support is probably nonexistent. With all this going on, anyone with vulnerabilities would be pushed over the edge. It's a no-brainer."

"Ripe for relapse. Yes."

"I didn't think it through, though. I didn't remember what was important when it mattered most." She sighed. "Maybe I'm not cut out for this."

"All you've run into is why we avoid treating people we're close to. We're human beings. Feelings, attachments—they get in the way."

"I don't know." She pulled off the throw and straightened. "We ought to be able to rise above it, somehow. When it's this important."

"Maybe not. Think a minute. You remember your reaction when Sylvia told you about his drug history? Your thoughts, feelings?"

"I felt bad for him." She got up and wandered over to the aquarium. She placed a hand on each side of the tank and watched Junior from above. "I worried about how he was doing. If he was okay. I hoped maybe he really had gotten his life turned around, like Sylvia said."

"You see? You reacted with caring and compassion. Because at one time, he played an important role in your life. All this means is that you're normal."

She abandoned the fish tank and turned to face him. "We're supposed to be better than normal. We're mental health professionals. People depend on us, on our informed and sound judgment."

"Which you show everybody hands down, when personal feelings aren't in the way." He smiled at the irony. "Step back and take a look at yourself, what you're doing right now."

She looked confused. "What do you mean?"

"What's your current specialty area?"

She twisted a finger-full of hair. "Grief reactions, loss."

"Let's say one of your clients was going on like this, piling up guilt feelings after a loss. What would you do? What would you tell the client?"

She said nothing, slowly wrapping her arms around herself. Her brow knitted.

"You would see the 'if only's' as perfectly normal."

Sarah's empty stare shifted away.

"You would point this out, wouldn't you? Because knowing they're not responsible, but feeling like they are, is normal. Knowing this would help them move forward, right?"

"That's what I'd probably do." In spite of the concession, her delivery of it was stone cold.

"Can you do that for yourself? Give yourself the same caring and compassion you have for your clients?"

"You've given me something to think about, Paulson." Her tone was terse. Tense. No evidence that anything he'd said had been received as intended. The chip on her shoulder was back, much as it had been at their original encounter in a flood-ravaged neighborhood. When she'd looked like she couldn't get away from him fast enough.

She'd somehow become raw. Too raw to objectively talk about her own vulnerabilities.

I moved too fast. What had he missed? She'd been going along about Jimmy as if it was little more than an unsuccessful go at providing a therapeutic intervention. Exactly what about the loss was so personal, or meaningful? Did her attachment to Jimmy linger, still?

No. He would have sensed that before now.

But how had he misjudged this so badly? "Look, I'm sorry. I shouldn't have pressed you on it. You've been through a lot tonight already. I just wanted you to feel better."

She stuck an arm into her sweater. "It's late. I shouldn't be keeping you up. I'd have left already, if I had my car. We've got a busy day tomorrow."

"You're not going in tomorrow. Unless you need to."

Her confused look came back.

"I heard from Lacey while I was out on the search. She found out what was going on at the spillway. I let her know we were having a late night. I won't be going into headquarters until later in the day, to finish with that grant application. She suggested you use tomorrow for personal business. Especially since you're planning to leave Sunday."

"Good. I'll have time to finish with Dad's things before I see him. It'll also give me a chance to see Lil."

The "I" rather than "we" felt like a slap in the face. "Lacey said you should come in at some point and out-process."

She looked so lost. So alone.

He got up from the couch and placed cautious hands at her shoulders. They were as rigid as rigor mortis. "Unless you think you'll come back later on."

"Still undecided. Sorry." She'd shut down.

Superficial remarks littered the uneasy journey to the Lone Pine.

What the hell had he done wrong? It could be that how she coped at the moment was a good thing, if there was something about the loss that was harder on her than he'd suspected. But why all the trauma? It just didn't slip into any secure place in the wheelhouse. Was it overload of some sort? This new situation, piled on top of everything else that had gone on the last several days? Maybe it was the straw that broke the camel's back.

"Are you okay?" He took his eyes from the road long enough to glance at her.

"I will be." She remained turned away, staring out the side window.

"Do you want me to pick you up and take you to headquarters tomorrow?"

"I can get myself there."

"How about the garage project. Is there something I can do to help? Before you come back and finish."

"If you unstack those big heavy boxes, that would help. They'll be easier to go through that way." Eye contact continued to evade him— blatant rejection of anything intimate, even as she accepted his offer of assistance.

It twisted his gut. Would this be the last time he ever saw her? "Absolutely. As soon as I get back, I'll take care of it."

The Lone Pine loomed ahead, all too soon.

"Thanks. Would it be possible to leave a key somewhere?"

"Here, take this one." While waiting at an intersection he wrenched a key off the ring and handed it to her. "I have a spare at home. The landlord will let me in when I get back."

When they rolled to a final stop she immediately opened the car door.

"Sarah." He reached over and touched her arm. "I don't know what I said, or did."

Her eyes met his. "It's not you. Goodnight."

*****

"It didn't seem to me I asked for anything that complicated. I may as well have tried to sneak into Grand Central Station at rush hour."

"It wasn't my fault." Indignation temporarily stole his attention from the road. Steve overcorrected and recorrected through the hydroplaning. "I did my part. I kept him busy a good piece of time. Let me tell you what, it wasn't no easy job of it, neither."

"So, plan B then. Did you get a feel for the weekend? If we wait around much longer, it might get moved again. Or they'll get a chance to look at things more closely."

"He left before we were done. We're meeting up again tomorrow."

"Apparently that's going to have to do. Or I think up something myself. I'm finished with this goddamn town."

*****

Saturday, June 7th

"I'm about ready to start using this thing as a doorstop." Lacey once again rebooted the temperamental PC. "Go get the IT guy, will you?"

An excuse to set aside his latest attempt to make sense of endless tallies and calculations was welcome. The "IT guy" with Coke-bottle glasses saw him coming. He waved acknowledgment that he was on again. Paulson continued on toward the canteen, hoping another shot of caffeine would do the trick.

He was at headquarters earlier than intended. Sleep had been fitful. He'd eventually given up, dragged himself out of bed and stumbled into the living room. The throw was still sitting in a heap, right where Sarah had left it. When he picked it up, it sent off a wave of her scent. It obliterated anything left of his sensibilities. It was the last he could stomach. He warned Junior not to throw any wild parties and left.

He returned to the mental health table with a liberal serving of headquarters' interpretation of coffee. The computer nerd was already there, hunched over their unit and talking to himself. Lacey was thumbing through Paulson's handiwork.

"Still struggling, I see." She restacked the papers. "Time for a breather."

They stepped out front. Rays of sunshine were breaking through, their vibrancy dissolving the last of the weather system.

"That tornado strike—we've got the preliminary information. It wiped out a neighborhood development out toward Willsey. It could mean more stats for your application form. In all likelihood, administration will collapse the two incidents. You should get in touch with your director again and find out what she wants you to do."

"Like that'll get me anywhere." He kicked at a pebble; it skittered out of their path.

Lacey eyed him. "Sounds like you're talking about more than disaster aftermath. Actually, you look exhausted. Why aren't you at home, sleeping it off?"

"It's nothing. I'll get over it."

"It doesn't look like nothing. Trouble in paradise?" Her eyes showed sincere concern, not the usual neutrality or harassment. *Mother Lacey.*

"Still waiting for a paradise to have trouble in." He let her take the lead as they strolled along the side of the building. "What was it you saw? It's as if you knew ahead of time I was going to get my heart stomped on."

"She's a professional survivor, first class. When things get tough, she circles the wagons and rides it out. It means at times, others can't help but find themselves shoved to the outer rim. This is how she survives. It's how she moves forward. It's probably one of the reasons she succeeds so admirably in her field. She quickly makes a niche for herself—figures out what needs to happen, sets it up, and makes it so. It wasn't hard to guess that somewhere along the line, you'd get caught in the crossfire."

"So what do I do now?"

"Accept her for who she is."

"As if I had any choice in the matter."

"When she resolves whatever it is she's resolving, you try again."

"In other words, I sit here and do nothing."

"Find a way to keep busy. Surely there's something else you could be doing."

"I've fallen behind at the office. But I'd just screw that up, too, the same as those stats."

"I can finish compiling the stats. If you're interested, a bulk distribution team's headed for the tornado damage. Want to go along? Do a little fieldwork. Get back into something you like. You're good at fieldwork. Feel up to it?"

"Sure. Why not."

She looked dubious. "Your enthusiasm is underwhelming."

CHAPTER SEVENTEEN

"Come see the baby's room." Lil whisked her off the front porch and literally dragged her to the back of the house, chattering about ins and outs of nursery décor. They arrived at a small bedroom crammed with wallpapering supplies, paint buckets, fabric samples and plastic sheeting. Sizing up the mess provided no clue of which décor Lil was settling on. Hopefully nobody would expect her to know.

"We got the crib last weekend, but it's out in the garage. Still in the box. Sean says he'll put it together in here, after I'm done decorating."

"Are you sure it's okay to be around paint fumes?" She tried to make sense of multicolored patches of paint haphazardly slapped onto the walls.

"I've got windows open when the paint's out, silly." Lil broke into a lightening-strike smile and gave her an electric hug. "Gosh, it's good to see you. Still a champion at over-thinking every speck of dirt. I swear, you could even analyze the kneecap right off that grasshopper."

Sarah looked down and flinched. A confused insect was crawling up her pant leg. She quickly brushed it off. When Lil stomped on it, she jumped a second time.

"Got the jitters today, don't you." Lil scooped up grasshopper remains for a final voyage, via the commode. "I heard from Mom this morning. About Jimmy. Did they find him yet?"

"No. Aunt Millie's with Sylvia. She said she'd call if there's word."

Actually, Aunt Millie had been in touch first thing that morning. She wanted Sarah there, with them, while they awaited news. Even over the phone her second mother had been able to ferret out her state of mind. And, of course, made no bones about pointing it out. According to Aunt Millie she'd be best off there, with her and Sylvia, where they could console one another.

She couldn't. Not with Sylvia. Not to spend the day expected to comfort the mother of a man who'd been within seconds of sexually assaulting her. How could she possibly get through it, and not have Aunt Millie figure her out? Not to mention how much worse off she'd be after spending an entire day with Sylvia, forcing herself to listen to small talk about Jimmy. She'd also have a time of it trying to resist Aunt Millie's prodding. Then keeping the whole works from spilling out, in front of Sylvia. Sylvia had it hard enough as it was.

"Earth to Sarah. Are you still there?"

"Sorry, Lil. You said . . ."

"Let's go sit in the kitchen. I'll make us herbal tea. Just like old times."

Lil's kitchen was warm and welcoming, brightly illuminated by windows that encircled the nook. Sarah sat in a warm patch of sunlight, drawn to the semblance of good cheer. While Lil puttered through the motions of brewing tea, Sarah peered out the window, up at the sky. Cloud cover was finally breaking up. Perhaps it would help the search party. Had Paulson rejoined it?

"You haven't heard a word I've said, have you?" Lil had been talking to her again.

Sarah opened her mouth, but no words followed. Tears began to spill, soon taking off by themselves.

"Oh, hon'." Lil drew Sarah's head against her swollen belly. "There, there. Just let it all out. Tell me what's bugging you so bad. Is it about Jimmy?"

"Not in the way you think." How humiliating. She should be shaking it off, getting control of herself. This was pathetic.

How much did she really want Lil to know, anyway? Could she justify dragging her into it, at all? It had been eons since they'd confided in one another.

"Well, what then?" said Lil. "Is it that new boyfriend? Mom said he looks mighty stuck on you. That he was staring at you the whole time you were talking with her last night. Did y'all get into a fight or something?"

"It's not like that. He's not my boyfriend. He's helping me learn this line of work."

"Could have fooled Mom."

"It's . . . it's something else that happened with Jimmy. Before the accident." She propped her head on her hand and gazed up at her old schoolmate.

Amazing. After all this time, Lil still radiated that aura of comfort, a mainstay of support. She had once been her best, most trusted friend.

"He was going to rape me, Lil. He probably would have, if Chet hadn't come along."

Lil sat slowly, staring in horror while Sarah fought to choke out the details.

"I'm stupefied. You poor girl. That doesn't sound at all like Jimmy. I mean, you two were always going at it about something. But nobody ever got rough or nothing."

"He's changed. He isn't the person we used to know. Whatever chemicals he's using are calling the shots."

"What did Paulson do? From what Mom said, I bet he raised holy hell. Sean'd be hunting him down and beating the crap out of him, if anybody tried that with me."

"He doesn't know. Nobody does, except you. I don't think Chet understood what was really going on, either. He acted like he thought he walked in on an argument getting out of hand."

"What do you figure on doing, then? Keep it a secret forever? Fat chance of that."

"I'm stuck. I've got two choices, poles apart. Do I keep it to myself? Just be brave, so I protect the feelings of everyone who might get hurt? It's not like he'll still be around to cause more problems. Or is that the coward's way out? Inconsiderate of those who don't understand, and . . . want to help. I have no idea how long this gutted feeling will go on. Do I hide out indefinitely?"

"Won't Paulson see something's wrong? I figured it out it myself, and I'm no counselor. As far as that goes, aren't you hanging out all day with a whole roving band of counselors? How do you keep it secret from them?"

"Paulson did notice. He doesn't understand, of course. Then I went and jumped all over him when he poked around in it. But . . . I have misgivings. What Paulson might do, if I told him. I've only known this man a few days. I've seen him look at Jimmy with such vitriol. What if he turns out to be as loosely wrapped as Jimmy?"

"He couldn't hurt Jimmy now, could he?"

"I know it doesn't make sense. Maybe I just need time to settle. To get over this feeling of being violated."

"From what Mom's been telling me, everybody thinks Paulson is a real cupcake. Wouldn't hurt a fly. Why not dump on him about what all happened? At the diner, Mom said she hears many a gal yakking about how they wouldn't mind being 'in therapy' with him."

"Maybe I'm overreacting."

"Of course you're not overreacting." Lil's balled hands landed on her hips. "That was a real world nightmare. You know what you gotta do, girl. Better than anybody. Get at it. If not with Paulson then somebody else."

"Knowing what to do and actually doing it—they're two entirely different things. Besides, I'm supposed to be the strong one, not the one who needs support. All these feelings about what happened with Jimmy—they don't make sense. Neither does how I've been treating Paulson."

"What do you mean? How have you been treating that poor guy?"

"He's only trying to help. Not just personal issues. He's teaching me how to do this type of practice. But no matter how hard I try, it gets messed up somehow. I always end up missing the boat. The whole thing puts me on edge."

"There you go, trying to be Miss Perfect again." Lil smiled. "Of course you aren't always getting it right. You've never done it before. That's why you need someone to show you. Like Paulson. It doesn't hurt none that he likes you, too. Just talk it out with him."

"I don't know. With everything that's going on, I'm . . ." Sarah's throat tightened. "Scared."

"You, scared?" Lil burst out laughing. "Sorry, I couldn't help it. Look at you. You were only eighteen when you bailed for parts unknown, all by yourself, getting by on whatever scholarships you could dig up. Then got yourself into a life that . . . well, I'm clueless about it. And here you are now, helping everybody with all kinds of hair-raising catastrophes. How could you be scared of a little one on one with some sweetheart of a guy? Who sounds like he's probably dying to help?"

"Is it really right for me to involve him? It's all so complicated."

"Paulson can decide for himself what he wants to get into. He's a grown man. He wants to help. He sees what everybody else sees, what a great gal you are. And so smart, and strong, too. You can do this, Sarah. You'll get through it fine."

"I don't know. I need time to think about it." She sampled the fragrant tea that had appeared in front of her. "But, thanks. I don't know who else I could have talked to."

"Well, what are best friends for? Now get out that fancy phone of yours and give him a call."

Her attempt went into voice messaging.

*****

"How's it they always know just what to bring?" Steve dragged a screeching bouquet of shovels. "It's last weekend again. Everything people might ask for right there, waiting."

"These are standard items the relief organization keeps on hand. I know what you're saying, though. It's amazing how quick they restock. Ready again, only a week later."

Steve appeared no more eager to get back to the previous day's ill-fated session than was he. It was as if it never happened. Paulson went along with it. Working together in bulk distribution might be more effective for connecting, anyway, considering the complete washout of the tried and true. He could always offer Steve the stress handouts at the end of the day, if it seemed right.

"Then they buy up the other things," Paulson continued. "Whatever's needed for the particular situation."

"You mean like, when we're talking with folks? Seeing what they're trying to get done."

"Exactly. In addition to giving out supplies, we're the eyes and ears. The information we gather helps the higher-ups figure out what comes next."

"Well, I'll be. I had no idea."

"You've seen a lot. You've been at it a week now. What might these folks need that they're not already getting?"

Steve thought it over. "Better doohickeys for finding stuff."

"Doohickey?"

"Right. Something they can scrape through the mud with, and find what's missing. Instead of trying to do it with shovels. Or get their hands all beat-up."

"Rakes would do that."

"The rakes we got here are for raking up leaves. Don't do no good out in that heavy mud. There were a few garden-type rakes last time around. Good strong metal ones. But they got used up, right off. Haven't seen any more since."

"Did you pass that on to your supervisor?"

"Well, no. It'd be out of line for me to tell folks how to go about their business."

"They actually like that kind of feedback. Could be the local suppliers ran dry. All the same, it wouldn't hurt to send word up the food chain."

"You think so?"

"The sooner they know, the more quickly they'll get at it."

"There's a walkie-talkie in the truck. Maybe my driver can pass this along." Steve left in search of his team leader.

Steve's exit was a good excuse for a break. Paulson stepped away from the truck and wandered to the crest of the hill, surveying neighborhoods below. Devastation on all sides, as if a bomb went off. Or multiple bombs. It was mysteriously uneven—a house leveled here, one over there completely untouched. Huge trees had snapped over like toothpicks. Some gardened areas, even a couple of lawns, looked scoured to bare earth.

Incredulous residents were still returning in trickles, exploring, salvaging whatever was left. An outreach team circulated as well. He recognized a few mental health workers in their midst.

Good. Lacey's been on the ball. The additional firepower freed him to stay put, and tend to those who came to the station. And tend to Steve.

Steve returned, wearing a satisfied grin. "You were positively right." Thumbs in his belt, he strutted his stuff like he'd just raked in first prize at the county fair. "They were right grateful, after we done told them. It fell through the cracks, they say. They're getting right on it."

"You see? You're one of us now. An old hand."

They set out the rest of the supplies. While waiting for clients to venture near, Paulson caught sight of the bulge in his vest pocket. He'd forgotten about it—the sandwich Lacey had dumped there on his way out the door. A bit mangled, but still edible. He unwrapped it and took a few bites. As he chewed, a faint high-pitched whine interrupted the stillness. Somewhere behind him, like a slow leak from a tire.

He turned to find a disheveled Irish setter cross sitting at attention. Homed in on his sandwich, and drooling.

"Well hello, buddy." Paulson reached down to scratch his ears. The dog flinched. Paulson pulled back, then tried again, taking it easy, slow movements and light strokes. Eventually the dog warmed to the attention.

Trauma—an equal opportunity storm. Both man and beast.

"Where did you come from?" He examined the dog's collar. The only identification was a generic rabies tag from a veterinary clinic in Willsey. Chances were, the dog was chipped.

"You get lost in this storm, guy?" He threw the dog a few pieces of lunchmeat.

Now you see it, now you don't. The dog eventually ended up with most of the sandwich.

"Will you look at this." Steve was down on his knees, loving up the dog as if he were a long lost soul mate. "What we got here?"

"He must be lost. There's no nametag. What do we call him, while we're waiting for the owners to come looking?"

"This here's a red dog. Something red." He deliberated. "How about Elmo?"

Paulson laughed. "Elmo works for me. How about you, Elmo?"

The dog panted and wagged his tail. Then sniffed at Paulson's pocket for another sandwich.

"Sorry, Elmo, that was it. How about some water?"

He opened a can of water and poured it into a small clean-up bucket. Elmo eagerly lapped it up. While the dog was caught up in enthusiasm,

Paulson pulled around the rabies tag and jotted down contact information.

"Tell you what." Paulson handed the number to Steve. "How about you go find a signal and call this clinic? Elmo looks well cared for. Somebody's missing this dog."

"You bet." Steve climbed up the hill, studying his cell phone display.

Paulson was handing out cleanup kits when an exquisite Lincoln Continental turned into the cul-de-sac. It stopped near the aid station.

Who brings a car like that to an aid station? Speculation ended as the driver stepped out.

Todd Goode. After a few moments of aimless looking around, he approached the supply area. Surveillance of tornado damage continued to slow his progress.

So even Todd Goode had a reality check threshold.

"It's all pretty unbelievable, isn't it?" Paulson approached him.

"Hardly ever see something like this," said Todd.

"You live out this way?"

"No, but I got a townhouse project going. Took quite a hit."

"Sorry to hear it."

"It's not a good time. Not a good time at all, for this."

Paulson walked him away from the aid station, anticipating need for privacy. "Other things going on?"

"Business. I've got quite a bit tied up in one thing or another. Still waiting for them to pan out for me."

"That's got to be tough. Especially in the middle of all this."

"I have yet to hear what insurance folks and the like have to say. What, if anything, they can do for me. Then I'll know whether last night's tornado was a curse or a blessing." Todd tucked his hands in his pockets, staring out beyond the damage. "This recession recovery, too. A real thorn in the side, for the building business. Trying to come up with jobs for folks. But if not enough people are buying around here . . . well, then."

"You have a plan for what you'll do next?"

"I've got calls to make, people to consult with. It'll all come out, one way or the other. The waiting gets rough, though. It's hard on the family. Especially the youngsters, not having what they're used to having."

Increased tension among the teenagers in town had been an issue for some time: fights, truancy, minor vandalism, increased substance abuse activity. Much of it in reaction to circumstances similar to whatever was going on in the Goode household. What mischief, what nonsense might not be perpetrated, if not for so many bored or frustrated adolescents? Some of that post-disaster looting could very well be their doing.

He continued to engage Todd, probing at telltale signs of stress. Sizing up what he was doing with it.

He gave Todd a handout. "There's not much I can do to help you with your investment predicament. But there are ways to manage the stress. If you see anything in this you want to talk about, feel free to get in touch. Any time."

Todd thanked him. He excused himself with a nod, still dragging as he retreated.

One more casualty. The storms had taken a swipe at damn near everyone—from mongrels to moguls.

Himself included, so it seemed. Particularly in regard to how his attraction to that one especially fascinating colleague seemed to turn south at every juncture. After Sarah's rocky start, she'd seemed to adjust well to disaster work. In fact she was barely missing a beat. Until last night.

What the hell was that about?

He yawned. Missed sleep was catching up. The cognitive overload would no doubt take care of itself after he squeezed in some quality rest. It wasn't going to hurt, either, to step back while healing had its way with Sarah. Simple passage of time would expose a game plan. Provided she didn't completely disappear into the sunset.

By end of day Steve looked more laid-back than he had all week. Between helping residents haul supplies and providing a listening ear, Paulson had found plenty to keep Steve busy. Paulson made good use of whatever impromptu opportunities arose—they served well to bolster Steve's waffling confidence. Steve fell right in with the flow of it, eventually becoming eager to hear Paulson's latest suggestion. It made his earlier struggle with expressing himself all the more perplexing.

The logistics crew was true to its word. A pile of rakes turned up, to the delight of those thinking about salvaging below the surface of their scattered tornado remains. All in all, it had been a good day.

He had to admit Lacey'd made a good call, sending him here.

"Roger, Roger. Mommy, there's Roger!" A little girl, about four, ran up to where Steve was playing with Elmo. The dog spotted her. He yipped and galloped toward her. The two fell into a whirling dervish of hugs and sloppy kisses, human and canine.

The mother looked on, holding back tears. "Thanks so much for calling the vet. We looked everywhere for him."

"We been calling him Elmo. 'Cause he's red," Steve told the girl, who was sniffling. Then Steve was teary-eyed as well.

The dog, on the other hand, was circling and jumping, tossing around a squeaker toy the girl had gifted him.

"That's not Elmo," she giggled. "That's Roger Dodger."

"We sure had fun making friends with Roger," said Paulson. "I even shared my lunch with him. But I'll bet he's ready for some real dog food."

"I'll feed him, Mommy. Let me feed him." Dog and child bounded toward the SUV.

"That there was real nice." Steve rose, wiping a damp cheek with the back of his sleeve.

"Yes. Times like this make it worth all the hassle. However. Now that Roger's taken care of, it's time I got on my way." He began to pack up.

Steve cornered him. "I was hoping we could talk some. Maybe you could get a bite with the rest of us, after we close this down. I know lots of good places, being so close to Willsey. Especially since Elmo got most of your lunch."

"Thanks for the offer. But Sarah's at my place about now. She's got a project she's working on. I wanted to be there to . . . just be there, you know?"

Steve's light-heartedness evaporated. Something dire was rattling around in there. Perhaps whatever had been bugging him the day before.

"You think maybe you and me could talk a bit first?" said Steve.

"I guess Sarah can wait a while longer."

They walked uphill, out of sight of the aid station. The recovery scene below opened up before them, displaying signs of progress. Cars were now parked in front of many of the homes, with some residents loading up whatever they'd salvaged. The more fortunate appeared to be moving back in. Adjusting to change. Moving towards normalcy.

And Steve was finally ready to spill it. Things were coming together.

Steve leaned against a tree. "It's that friend of mine I told you about. Ted."

"Yes, Ted. I remember."

"Well, he didn't want no more of that acquaintance."

Paulson struggled to drum up patience. He forced himself to wait it out, and tried to focus on the details of Steve's story for anything he could possibly have missed. Most of it he could recite for himself, having mentally hashed it over numerous times in hopes of digging up some clue about Dora's attacker.

Steve coaxed the story into the present. "Today he did it. Ted told his friend that he was out of it."

"You said before that Ted was worried how he'd take it. How did it go?"

"That part went fine. He didn't care. He was ready to load up and leave." Steve's agitation continued, in spite of his claim that he'd successfully avoided what he feared.

"There's something more?"

It was a return to yesterday's madness. Steve grappled for words, getting nowhere. He stepped away from the tree and began pacing.

How long do I wait? Paulson busied his mind with thoughts of highway traffic. Could be this lost cause would delay him so long he'd be competing with commuters. Maybe he could find another way home. If the back roads weren't flooded out.

He looked again at Steve. His weather-worn features had transitioned into a look of resolution. "It got all messed up, what happened with that property. They collected it all together, you see. Then they had to stash it in a hurry. Someone would find it, where it was. This old building wasn't locked or nothing. They hid it in there, just temporary. Then someone locked it up tight. They couldn't find no way to break in. So they held tight until it got opened up again."

Like Sam's building.

Couldn't be. Too much of a coincidence.

"Then the proprietor come open it up. They took everything that was in there and moved it somewhere else."

He froze. He could no longer deny what he was hearing. It couldn't be coincidence, not this level of detail. It was surreal. Steve was talking about Sam's shop, his belongings, all of which currently sat in his own garage.

"The loot got moved by good people, and Ted didn't want no part of breaking into the new place to get it. And he said as much."

Breaking in?

"So Ted says, it's all the same to him what happens to those things. He's out of it. Then he got told . . ."

Steve locked eyes with him, cementing a meeting of the minds.

"Then he's told, this afternoon, that his friend will go take care of things by himself."

Sarah.

Paulson bolted down the hill, full throttle. He dove into the rental car.

As it started up, Steve jumped in the passenger side and slammed the door. "I'm coming."

"I'm not taking time to debate it." The car peeled out of the cul-de-sac.

"You keep this up, the law will be on us."

"Suits me fine. They'll follow us there." They swerved as Paulson took out his phone and checked for a signal. No coverage, of course. There never was on this stretch of road. If he'd been thinking straight, he would have called her while they were up on that hill.

"How about you let me hang onto that?" Steve held out his hand. "I'll do any phoning you want. You keep your eyes on this here road."

He tossed the useless phone in Steve's lap and continued to accelerate. Lacey's earlier comments about crisis situations and strange bedfellows ricocheted amidst thoughts of increasingly scattered possibilities. "Who is it? Who are we coming up against?"

Steve didn't answer right away. "If he's there, it'll be known soon enough. If not, I think I'll let it be."

Paulson tried to remember exactly what Sarah had said about coming to his apartment. He had been so busy wallowing in feelings of rejection he hadn't listened that carefully. His general impression was that she was thinking about later in the day, rather than earlier. Hopefully he was wrong. Or her plans changed.

He fought off recurring memories of Dora, limp and bleeding. His brow beaded up with sweat.

"We got a signal now." Steve looked up from the phone. "What number do I call?"

"Here." Paulson snatched the phone and punched redial. It went into voice mail.

"Damn it." He tossed it back in Steve's direction. "She always picks up, no matter who it is. What if he's done something already?"

"Could be she's out of range, same as us. Maybe that's good news, looking at it that way. We'd be reaching her, if she was in town."

They came onto Marshland's main drag, squealing at corners as they neared the complex.

"If the B&E is happening, coming up quiet would be the way to go." Steve's strained voice rippled. "Wouldn't want him to panic and hurt someone in there."

"Or maybe it'd scare him off. He'll run."

"Not without being seen, he couldn't scare off."

Paulson skated to a stop on shoulder gravel, near where she'd likely find parking. He searched the line-up of neighborhood vehicles for the small red convertible. It wasn't there. Parked around back, maybe?

He wasn't about to waste precious time circling the complex. "It looks normal up there." He got out of the car.

"Don't mean nothing." Steve followed him up to his front door.

"Give me the phone." Paulson snatched it out of Steve's hands and punched numbers. "Betty? Paulson. We need Dave here. Now. My place. Yes, it's an emergency."

He hung up to avoid the dispatcher's predictable protests. He wasn't going to stand around and wait for Dave or Roy, or whoever. Flood responsibilities had scattered the local first responders all over the county. There was no telling how long it would take help to arrive.

"You got the law coming?"

"Yes." Paulson reached for the door handle.

"Don't know that I'd best hang around, then."

"Do what you need to."

CHAPTER EIGHTEEN

The screen door produced the usual screech. He winced, forcing himself to take it slowly. He unlocked and cracked open the front door.

Anxiety spiked anew. *What now?* He hadn't thought up a plan for getting past this point.

He looked back, in the direction of Steve's retreat. He seemed to have a good handle on what goes on in these sorts of situations. But he'd been quick to disappear.

At least the front door was still locked. A good sign.

He crept through the living room, the kitchen. When he arrived at the connecting door to the garage he listened against it. Nothing. He slowly turned the knob and gave it a gentle shove, getting barely an eyeball's width of vision.

The garage was dark. None of the lights were on. No sight or sound of an intruder, or Sarah. He swung the door the rest of the way open and reached for the light switch.

The blow caught him just as he registered a movement. He tumbled sideways, smacking onto the garage floor, the sound of his head hitting concrete more sickening than the sudden surge of wooziness. Sparkles, clear blank space imploded.

Don't lose consciousness. The floor beneath him disappeared. Was he still there? Such an odd sense, being both weighed down and floating at the same time.

Everything smelled black. Death—so this was what it was like. There was a faint spray of tinkling, like tiny bells. *The bells of heaven.*

Brightness passed. Snippets of stories flickered, recollections of those brought back from the brink of death. They always saw a bright light. Sometimes at the end of a long dark tunnel. Was this his own near-death experience? Or was he gone already? The light passed again.

No. That was a flashlight beam.

There was a crash, more tinkling. Glass, breaking and scattering.

At least he knew he was alive. Though still unable to move, even if he wanted to.

Activity continued in the background, more things tossed around. Items hitting the floor. Things dumped over.

"What the hell did they do with it?" An angry voice. He'd heard it, before. Couldn't place it. It was off. Something different about it. Or about his hearing.

The concrete began to feel cold, then loomed up uncomfortably hard against his throbbing head. He tried to wiggle his fingers. They cooperated.

He assessed what he could from where he laid. Squinting the eye closest to the floor let in a blurred image of a good-sized individual, turning over boxes and pawing around. Occasionally he stopped and illuminated his efforts with the flashlight.

Play possum.

The screen door screeched.

Dave wouldn't do that, come in without knocking or calling out or something first. Was it Sarah? *Don't let it be Sarah.*

"What the hell are you doing here?"

"Thought you might use some help, is all." Steve's voice. "I seen the vehicle I lent you, back there down the road. Figured you were here."

If Steve saw him lying there, he wasn't letting on. Perhaps he was hidden by shadows.

"There's no sign of that duffle. Anywhere!"

A crash, something thrown against a wall.

The distraction was opportunity to risk fully opening his eyes. Get a handle on the scene. Identify a plan. A potential weapon.

Blurriness competed, and he was unable to make anything out of it. Nothing suitable for defending himself was directly in front of him, or within easy reach. At least his head felt like it was coming on line. *Think.*

Nate's cache of old playthings, those items propped up in the corner behind him. He was pretty sure there'd been a baseball bat.

"Ain't got no answer for that," said Steve.

"All I know is whatever you've been telling me." The tone changed, turning accusatory. "I haven't seen any of it for several days."

"When I last seen it, it was in that same little room where all this got hauled from."

"You know what? I think you've had it all along."

"If so, I'd be gone already."

"I know when I'm being played for a fool."

There was a thud and a whoosh. Steve was probably getting slammed against a wall, getting the wind knocked out of him. Paulson tried to raise himself. He immediately dropped, dizzy and unstable. Reopened eyes met blackness.

Was it from lack of lighting, or the hit on the head? *Damn it.*

Turning his head slightly, he made out chaotic movement. A struggle, most of it obscured by the door still hanging open. But the view was better on that side of the garage, thanks to light from the doorway. Images sharpened as his eyes adjusted. The view of the kitchen interior came into focus.

"Paulson?" Standing in the doorway was a silhouette of Sarah.

*****

Before leaving Lil's she tried Paulson's number again, but without success. She rarely had this trouble back in the city. She'd gotten spoiled.

"Don't you worry about it, hon'." Lil dumped most of the muffins they'd baked into a paper bag. "The man gave you a key. Just show up. He'll be on cloud nine." She shoved the bag into her hands. "Now remember. All that's true about the way to a man's heart. After he tries one of these, he'll forget all about how you've been picking on him."

"I'm still nervous. What should I say to him? I don't want to mess things up even more."

"That's going to take care of itself. Wait'll you find out about make-up sex."

Sarah rolled her eyes. "It's not like that with us."

"Mind my words, that'll change. I place my money on how Mom sized it up. You're going to have to come back more than once a decade so I can gloat on it."

The rental car was not where Paulson usually parked. She spotted it about half a block away, up against the curb. That was odd.

As she came up the walk, she heard muffled voices. They sounded like they were coming from the garage, male voices. Her father? Was Dad finally back?

The front door was unlocked. She let herself in and circled to the pass through to the garage. The door was half open; they had to be in there. Weird, that they'd stand around in the dark.

"Paulson?" She reached inside and flicked on the light.

"Sarah, no!"

The door suddenly propelled toward her, bumping her. The scuffling of angry combatants once again rammed the other side. Barely visible through the cracked door was a glimpse of Paulson, sprawled out on the concrete. He made an attempt to get to his feet, unsuccessful.

Only significant injury would account for it.

"Are you hurt?" She pushed on the door as hard as she could. The door gave up little of its resistance. But it sounded like the men on the other side might have stumbled because of it.

She dropped her satchel into the gap and kept the door from closing altogether. There was a round of vulgar rhetoric, then slamming against the door again. She pushed back at it, finding only unwavering resistance.

"Sarah, wait."

The minimal view was enough to make out Paulson. He was reaching behind himself. He latched onto something long and narrow, hard to tell exactly what. Those intense eyes locked onto hers with a conspiratorial look. An "on the count of three" understanding passed.

If looks could kill.

When he nodded, she first pulled the door toward herself. Calling up all she could muster, she threw herself at the door. She plowed into it shoulder first, her back injury crying out. Paulson swung his weapon from where he sat.

There was the sound of people thudding against concrete. Along with a prolonged clatter, and the snap and crackle of shattering plastic.

She threw open the door. Paulson was still trying to get up. The two other men were now on the floor, facing away. A small wiry-looking character sat on top of somebody flat on his face, his arms twisted and pinned behind him.

She ignored them and hurried to where Paulson lay. "What happened to you?"

"Hit on the head."

"Stay put." She took stock of his condition, running a hand through his hair and examining his scalp. "I don't see any blood."

"They say third's a charm."

She continued to touch him here, there. To be absolutely sure he was still in one piece. Or something. She didn't know what she was looking for. Reassuring herself, probably.

His eyes closed. He went silent, as if exiting to a faraway place.

"Am I hurting you? Are you in pain?"

"More like meditative bliss."

From inside the house, the sheriff called out. He worked his way toward the garage.

"In here, Dave."

"Paulson? That you down there?" Dave stepped through the door, scanning the mess and scatter of people. "Holy crap. You going to tell me what the heck all this is supposed to be?"

"The one on the bottom over there is who you're here for." Paulson slowly pulled himself up to a sitting position.

Dave made a quick check on the progress of backup. He took out cuffs and slapped them onto the alleged perpetrator.

"Thanks, buddy," he said to the small man, who hopped up and scooted off. It was someone she'd seen before. Yes—that guy at the aid station, back on day one. What was he doing here?

"You can get up, too. Now." Dave gave his man in custody a nudge. No cooperation followed. He bent over and grabbed hold of his collar, lifting. He stopped partway and leaned over, taking a long look at the man's face.

"For the love of Pete. Look what we got here. We been looking far and wide. And here you are, hiding out in a garage, of all places."

Sarah gasped. It was Jimmy.

The ER physician ordered bed rest for Paulson. Paulson nonetheless insisted they first stop in at the poker game. He was far from a hundred percent. But he sounded worried about Dad's status, too. And even though he didn't come out and say it, she suspected he wanted to be with her in the event that Dad did not show up. That was his way.

"This little beauty sure does move out." He was giving the interior of the Miata a once over, running a hand across the dash.

"You ain't seen nothing yet." *Now. Tell him now.* "Before we get there . . ." *Just get it over with.* "About last night."

She went over the full details of her encounter with Jimmy. A series of sideways glances watched Paulson's expression grow increasingly darker.

"I'll kill him," he seethed under his breath.

"You already had a shot at that. You're going to have to settle for the broken ankle we left him with. And whatever scarring he gets on the ear Steve almost bit off."

"Did you tell Dave about this?"

"I gave him my version of everything while you were with the EMT."

"You're going to press charges." It wasn't a question.

"Maybe. What we did tonight—it feels like enough, for now. At least I don't feel so unraveled. I suppose additional charges would keep him off the streets a while longer. Maybe keep him in mandatory treatment."

"His mother doesn't deserve this," said Paulson.

"Oh my God." She hadn't thought about Sylvia. "She's probably heard by now. I hope Aunt Millie was still with her."

They continued down the highway in silence, accepting the soothing calm offered by the softness of dusk and passive greetings of fellow travelers' headlights. The bats were out, soaring among the trees, typical

226

for the time of year. The brightness of stars twinkling into service was another reminder of the season. They were fully visible, now that the storm clouds had moved on.

"By the way." Paulson touched her arm. "Steve wanted you to know. He wouldn't have let Jimmy hurt Sam, if he'd returned to the shed. He said he was keeping an eye on the situation. I hope we get a chance to thank him for all he's done."

"I suppose he's back in the system now. He's got a few good character witnesses if he needs them. Which reminds me. Back there at the garage, I had a hard time seeing exactly what was going on before they hit the ground."

"I was trying to get Nate's baseball bat. I figured on hitting Jimmy in the knee. Instead I ended up with this long plastic thing. After my rather lame swing, it got tangled up in their legs. Then one end got caught between some boxes. That's when it tripped them up. It's completely trashed, whatever it was. I suppose I owe Nate an apology. It looked like one of his old toys."

She smiled, certain of what it was. "That wasn't Nate's. Though he did play with it a lot. Technically, it was my mother's."

"I'm sorry, Sarah."

"I don't think she'd mind, given the circumstances." Her throat tightened. "Makes me feel like she's up there looking down, watching over us."

"So what was it?"

"If I remember right, it's called a lirpa."

"A lirpa? What's that?"

"An ancient Vulcan combat weapon. *Star Trek.*"

*****

The cards were about to be dealt when the old familiar pickup pulled up.

Sarah was first out the door. She threw herself into her startled father's arms.

Paulson kept a respectful distance.

"Sarah. Honey." Sam pulled away and looked at his daughter. "What's all this?"

"We were so worried about you," she said through tears. "Where on earth have you been?"

"I'm camped out, over at the Peterson shack."

"Where?" Sarah looked confused.

"That cabin. The one your mother and I went to every now and then, before you kids came along. It's a wreck. Nobody's stayed out there in years. No electricity. But there wasn't any at the shop, either."

"What in the world are you doing out there?" said Sarah.

"Thinking about what comes next, after all that's happened. And a little fishing. A little reading."

Stewy turned on the yard lights. He and the other men came out and joined them.

"Why didn't you tell us?" Sarah looked more hurt than angry. The little girl with the curl was back.

"All you had to do is ask Chet. I told him right plain I'd be at Peterson's."

Chet wore a vacant stare, as if a row of question marks had been stamped across his forehead. "I don't remember you saying nothing about Peterson shack. I thought that old place got tore down years ago."

"Sure enough did tell you. It was right there, in that note I left. At the shop."

A smattering of furtive glances passed among them. Sam had not yet heard about the shop's fate.

Before anybody could be involuntarily drafted to share the bad news, Chet chimed in. "That poor old building went up in smoke, Sam. When the electricity came back. All we could save was what you put in that storage room. We moved it all out to Paulson's. His place is high and dry. But that note—why, it must have gone up in smoke, too."

Sam took the news in stride. But he sighed, seemingly from the depths of his being. "That's a darn shame. Things just don't stop changing, it's true enough."

"You could always rebuild the shop," said Sarah.

"I'll miss that old place. That's a fact. But I've got no use for a place of business anymore. I've got enough to think about as it is. Like what to do about building a place to live in, back in the neighborhood. On our property, where you and Nate grew up."

"I'm glad you're going to keep it," said Sarah. "As bad off as it is now, it's still home."

"I had plenty of time to think it over, out there in the woods. That Peterson place isn't any kind of long-term solution. Fine for summer, but it's out in the middle of nowhere. Now then, building a house. That's not something I expected to do again. Not at this stage of the game."

"You know I'll help you, whatever you want to do," said Chet.

The other men murmured agreement with Chet's sentiments.

"That reminds me." Sarah did a pocket search, eventually pulling out a semi-crumpled business card. "Guess who I ran into? He thinks Nate and I ought to stick you in some kind of old folks' home."

Sam glared in disgust at the card. He held it up in front of his poker buddies and tore it into tiny pieces. They laughed, cheering him on.

"This is what I think about Todd Goode and his ideas," said Sam. "Rebuilding suits me fine. To get his goat, if nothing else. And show that no-account mayor a thing or two, while I'm at it."

"Your new place could have a shop right there by your house," Paulson came up next to Sarah. His medication haze failed to reel in the urge to reach toward her until it was too late. His arm almost found its way across her shoulders. He stopped mid-air, lowering his arm. But not quickly enough for Sam to miss it. Paulson remained as he was, there at her side.

"You always were the one for bright ideas, Paulson." Some of the twinkle returned to those gray-blue eyes. Identical to Sarah's.

"Are we going to play some cards or what?" said Stewy.

They moved inside. Paulson joined in with the weekly bonding ritual that had carried this group of men through the last few decades. Sarah stayed and watched, accepted among them this one time as an honorary observer.

"I'll just sit back here with you," Chet told her. "Don't never work out for me to play this game. These guys are too good at it. Somehow everyone always knows if I got a good hand or not. I come anyways, for all this great company."

It didn't take long for the topic of Jimmy's arrest to find its way to the table, this time for Sam's benefit. Sarah and Paulson took turns describing what they'd already told the others.

"I don't get it." Stewy examined the cards Victor had dealt. "These guys seemed to think their loot was in with Sam's things. So why wasn't it there?"

"That's the unanswered question," said Paulson. "I don't remember ever seeing a duffle bag. And near as I can tell, Jimmy went through everything with a fine-tooth comb."

"Always knew that kid was no darn good," Sam grumbled. He gestured at Victor for another card.

Chet went into his distinctive gaze of confusion.

"What is it, Chet?" asked Sarah.

"You know, I think I know what happened."

The game came to a halt. All eyes centered on Chet.

"Remember when I came by, and you and Jimmy were arguing? Well, I had those last things from the shop in my truck. You know, what didn't fit the first trip. I was supposed to drop it off. With everything that happened, I plumb forgot."

The mass exodus tripped over itself as everybody hurried out to Chet's truck. Chet opened the gate. They scrunched together, all trying to see into the cab at once without being conspicuous.

There amidst the remaining items was a pale green canvas duffle. They stood and stared in silence, curiosity eating everyone alive.

"I can tell you for a fact, that duffle isn't mine," said Sam.

"Shake and bake and take the cake," Vic finally said. "That there is stolen property. We should be getting Dave out here."

They hung around long enough to see the sheriff confiscate the recovered loot. By then Paulson was significantly dragging. He was exhausted, and his head hurt. The cigar smoke was getting to him. And it had been quite the tongue-lashing from Dave about hanging around at a poker game instead of going home and resting. But there was no way he could tear himself away from observing Sarah, happily reunited with her Dad. As well as how she lapped up the honor of being included in his long-standing Saturday night tradition.

"Can I get you a beer or something?" Chet asked her.

"It's getting late," she said. "We really should be on our way."

She gave her Dad a hug goodbye. Then moved one player over and gave Victor a squeeze, followed by a quick kiss to the top of his shiny bald head. "Thanks for hooking us up."

"It was nothing." A pink flush climbed all the way up to Vic's earlobes. "Just passing on some information. That reminds me, Sam. What in the world did you decide to do with that contraption? The one you brought to the store."

"Still don't know for sure. Especially since you can't tell me what it is."

"I did too tell you what it is. It's several things put all together."

"That doesn't help much."

Sarah whispered to Chet. "What are they talking about?"

"It's that gadget he dug up, after the flood. He's been asking all over, trying to figure out what it is."

"I still got it," said Sam. "It's out there in the Ford right now."

"Can I see it?" asked Sarah.

Chet left to find it.

"I tried tinkering with the moving parts to see if I could get it to make sense somehow," said Sam. "But it may as well be from outer space."

"I identified parts of it," said Victor. "Looked like it started out as an old-fashioned apple peeler. Then some other things got welded on."

Chet brought in the object in question. He set it in the middle of the card table.

"I could have told you what that is." Stewy picked it up, turning it from side to side in admiration. "I'm the one who put it all together."

"So what is it?" said Sarah. "I can't tell what it is, either."

"It was a project I did for Charlie several years back. He said he wanted to make artwork out of some of that old junk he always collected. A lot of it looked like your rejects, Vic."

"Charlie always was quite the collector." Victor chewed at the end of his unlit cigar.

"He gave me the parts, and showed me what he wanted welded together," Stewy continued. "It was going to be his 'folk art,' like on *Antiques Roadshow*. He said some of those things turned out to be worth hundreds of dollars. His folk art ended up in his garage, I think."

"Why would Charlie want artwork to decorate a garage?" said Sam. "That's the most darn fool thing I ever heard of."

Sarah inspected the odd contraption. "On the other hand, I can't imagine Sylvia letting him display something like this in the house."

"Wait, there's more to the story," said Stewy. "You know how ol' Charlie liked to have himself a nip every now and then, without Sylvia knowing. There was a special feature he had me build into it."

He turned the contraption on its side, grabbed one end of the base and gave it a twist. What initially appeared to be a laminated seam slid apart, revealing a narrow cavernous space.

"Unless I'm mistaken, we're going to find a flask in here."

"Now just a minute," said Sam. "I've been carrying that thing all over. I'd hear it rattling or sloshing around if a flask was in there."

Stewy turned it on its side. Nothing fell out.

"See?" Sam was satisfied. "Like I said."

Stewy stuck his fingers deep inside, then looked up at Sam with a defiant twinkle. "It is too in here. It's just wrapped up. Maybe so Sylvia wouldn't hear it if she was dusting it or whatever." He pulled out an object wrapped in thick felted material. When he unfolded it, a pouch of some sort appeared.

"Don't look like no flask to me," Victor said.

Stewy loosened the drawstrings and dumped the contents.

The earrings fell out first. Then a few rings, and finally an ornate necklace.

"Why fry my fanny and call it Monday." Vic stared in astonishment with the rest of the men.

"Those must be Sylvia's heirloom pieces," said Sarah. "The ones they were looking for with their treasure hunt."

"These look for real." Vic took out a viewing lens and examined the stones. "This necklace alone is worth a pretty penny."

"Sylvia will be ecstatic," said Sarah. "She deserves this, with everything she's been through. Can we go with you when you take it back to her?"

We. It was music to his ears.

"Well, of course, honey. That would be fine. While we're at it, we'll figure out what she wants done with Charlie's 'folk art' here."

She threw her arms around her father. "Thanks, Dad. You've made my day. In more ways than you can imagine."

"Wish I'd known what I had here," he said. "Just got lucky."

"Maybe the rest of us ought to be taking a look at what all we got stashed in our vehicles," said Stewy. "Sure has been the day for it. I still haven't given old Green Gertie a decent lick and polish, after all the work she did for this flood."

"The wife's been bugging me to clean the junk out of my truck for months," said Victor. "Wait'll this story gets out. I'll be hearing about it all the more."

"Who'd have guessed?" said Chet. "Life just gets stranger and stranger, don't it?"

CHAPTER NINETEEN

Sunday, June 8ᵗʰ

"Sylvia is one of those matriarchal types," Paulson told Lacey. "She thinks it's her personal responsibility to shoulder the entire collective family burden, whatever it may be. Jimmy's screw-ups have been especially hard on her. We're going to stop by and see her this morning."

"Dad's going to bring over that jewelry," said Sarah. "That in itself will be a piece of healing. She's such a sweet lady."

"How's your father?" said Lacey.

"A little shook up. It was a blow, hearing about his shop that way. But you'd never know it. He's full steam ahead on house rebuilding. Nate said he'd be out to help sometime." She pressed her lips together, avoiding further comment. Her tone had probably said it all.

"We need to keep an eye on Sylvia in the months to come," said Paulson. "She shows signs of both depression and acute stress from time to time. Some of it was there to start with. This last week pushed it further along. I doubt she has the resources for treatment."

The phone rang. Lacey held up a finger, pointing at them to wait while she answered.

Sarah looked away, letting her gaze wander over the hive of activity she'd unexpectedly joined this past week. The public affairs team passed.

Stan was sharing a long story with Brian, embellished with his usual theatrics. She would miss Stan, when he returned to wherever it was he came from.

"I don't know which amazes me more." Lacey pushed away the phone. "Everything you two have been through, or that you keep coming back for more."

"I'll be leaving the operation today," said Sarah. "I have my own clients to tend to."

"I figured as much. Will I see you down the road? I wouldn't mind having you back."

A tall, stately woman approached. "So these are the two who've been having all the adventures."

"Sarah, Paulson—this is our job director, Nan."

"Thank you for your services." Nan shook hands with both of them. "I know you health professionals give up a lot to be here. So do your clients. I don't know how you manage it. But I'm glad you do."

"It's been well worth it," said Sarah. "I've learned so much. Not just about disaster response. I've picked up insights that I'm positive will benefit my own clients. It's all so new, so evolving. It really tempts the scientist in me."

"We're hoping to see both of them on another operation," said Lacey. "They're keepers."

"You never know," said Sarah. "But right now I have an out-processing appointment to keep. Nice to meet you, Nan. If you will excuse me."

*****

"I need to know what to tell the incoming manager about your intentions," said Lacey.

"Incoming manager?" Paulson had never anticipated this kind of development. "You're not staying?"

"The operation's up and running smoothly. This last storm system left a much bigger mess a couple of states over. Experienced managers are in even shorter supply than experienced DMH field responders. They need me. Someone else can take over wherever I leave off."

It was unsettling, how dependent on her he'd become. After the first storm, he'd thought he could handle everything on his own. *Just look at yourself, now.* "I appreciate what you've done. For us, and our community. I never knew how complex and involved these things could get. If you're going to do it right, that is."

"Consider coming along with the traveling show sometime. I could use you."

He shrugged. "I'm not good stock for handling the frustrations. It seems like that's the story no matter what field of mental health you're in. As soon as the administrative end moves in, you run up against something misguided. Or the system throws in some absurd monkey wrench.

"And then there's the Sylvia's—the clients who need traditional services, but the system isn't there for them. Same as her asshole son. Would he be sitting in a cage right now, costing taxpayers mucho bucks, if he'd had decent access to drug treatment?"

"Every mental health arena has challenges," said Lacey. "It's why we need dragon slayers."

Proverbial knights in shining armor—subservient, of course, to King Admin. *No, thank you.*

He crossed over and looked out the window, drawn to the familiarity of everyday life on Main Street. It was time to move on. "This little corner I've culled for myself out here—it lets me avoid a lot of that. It suits me fine."

"Don't forget about change coming from within," said Lacey. "I know that's a trite statement. But it really is the same in systems as it is for people. Healthy change happens because of those of us who've been in the trenches. Those who know first hand what goes on at ground level, and understand how to deal with ultimate consequences and challenges. And, most importantly, those who care."

"That's what you do, then?"

"It's an uphill battle. I began the same as you. Helping those who were finding their way through disaster." She got up and joined him in his assessment of Marshland's heartbeat. "Getting to know them. Seeing what it's really like for them. What they need.

"Then there's following the new research. Collaborating with colleagues, putting together a broader perspective. Incorporating what I learn into my own observations and efforts. And, of course, knocking on the doors of any higher-ups who've become unwitting impediments to what citizens need, or don't seem to have gotten the memo about what they were supposed to be doing."

"How do you do it?" He locked eyes with her, searching for the sense in it. "It's bad enough for day-to-day disasters. If I kept coming up against such idiocy while dealing with this level of suffering, I'd start tearing my hair out."

"Think back to yesterday, at that aid station. Who did you help? What was it like? Was it worth it?"

"More than worth it," he had to admit. "I made a difference that day, especially for a new friend. And he came through for me in a big way. There were others I'm sure I helped, too, one way or another."

"You became an important part of their personal journeys. You helped smooth the road before them."

"That aspect of it works for me. But that's not admin. That's doing what needs to be done."

"You'd most likely be doing just that, if deployed nationally. Only you can decide how deeply to get into the politics. Just know that there are lots of other Marshlands out there."

"I'll give it some thought." He fished around in his wallet for a business card. "Call me if something comes up. Who knows. The boss might let me off every now and then. At this point I think she gets it. Someone needs to be on board who knows their way around during disaster."

"This does seem to come naturally for you. Near as I can tell, you've spent the last few years setting up a psychological first aid program of your own for Marshland's everyday disasters."

He hadn't made that association. But Lacey's appraisal of the situation was true, as usual. The similarities between disaster mental health and how he practiced social work in this tight-knit community were undeniable.

"After you've got a few out-of-town assignments under your belt, there are paid positions that come up. For those, you'd have to get involved with admin. Of course, moneywise you'd make more per hour as a cart boy at IGA. But being broke doesn't seem to bother you any."

He laughed. *If she only knew.* "It's an interesting proposition. But a bit premature. For now, I think I'll take advantage of the extra help in town, and stand down a while."

"Any last questions, while I'm still here to answer them?"

He looked her up and down, so settled and natural-looking in her bureaucratic disposition. Proving to be a friend, in spite of their philosophical differences. "I hope you come back and see us sometime. When things are better. You'll see what a fantastic part of the country this is."

"It'd be a nice way to use up some of my frequent flyer miles. No telling when, though. There's always another disaster."

"I'll look forward to your visit, whenever. I'm sure Sarah will, too."

"When you sign off, you're offered the same mental health exit interview as everybody else. Let me know if you're interested."

He considered it. "I do believe I have that covered."

The area around the porch was adorned with broken limbs and other storm debris Harold hadn't gotten around to clearing. Squirrels and birds explored the habitat alterations, busily reinventing their circus routines. The porch itself and the bench it supported had been well protected, both still solid and welcoming. Splotches of sunlight found their way through to where they sat and rocked. Peaceful and content. It had been a long time since Paulson had felt this relaxed.

Sarah finally broke the silence. "Who wants to go first?"

"I will," said Paulson.

"Still the professional volunteer, I see. Your disaster relief experience must not have turned you off completely."

The offhand remark hit home. It did characterize much of the last week. Sarah had noticed. "I guess not," he said.

"You know, some would say we're the least appropriate for debriefing each another. We might overlook something, or overreact, because we've been through so much together."

"It's not that big a deal. Even married couples regularly debrief with each other. It's been going on since Adam and Eve."

"And we all know how things worked out for them."

"I have no problem with it. I've seen you in action long enough to know that if you doubted your judgment, you'd say so."

"We won't know until we try, I guess." She looked ready to listen.

He'd already spoken some with Lacey. What if anything was left to process? More concerns came to mind in regard to his status with Sarah than the disaster relief experience.

On task, dude. "I had a long talk with Lacey about my future. I'd do this again in eye blink, if it happened here. She mentioned opportunities elsewhere, doing the same thing."

"Does that interest you?"

"I jumped into it this time because this is home for me now. The people I've come to know, and care about. I couldn't imagine not helping out."

"But it would be different elsewhere?"

"I don't know. That's the big question. Was it rewarding because of who I was helping? Or because it's what I'm comfortable doing, anyway? Or did it only work out because Lacey was here, mentoring me? Then, what if it were something bigger, or even catastrophic, like Hurricane Katrina, 9/11, Superstorm Sandy. Would it still work out with something that extreme?"

"Do you think you'll try it?"

"It's a thought. I used to have the reputation of being willing to try anything. Once, anyway. Maybe resurrecting that attitude would work in my favor, if the right opportunity knocks."

"You do look natural in the field. You size things up so sensitively. You always seem to know just the right thing to say, even in unorthodox situations. I've admired that about you, both as a person and a professional."

It touched him someplace deep and warm. "That's high praise, coming from someone like you. Your competence, and professionalism."

She smiled at him. They returned to companionable silence, rocking the glider in tandem. He bathed in the tranquility of it.

What I really want is for this moment to go on forever.

*****

Sarah hesitated. "I guess it's my turn."

I shouldn't be doing this with Paulson. The more she analyzed it, the more conflict of interest spilled out. If only she hadn't been in such a hurry, and taken time to debrief with Lacey. It was too late to back out now. Not without causing hurt feelings. "I got more than I bargained for when I came looking for Dad."

"I'd say that's an understatement."

"There's something to be said for having the rug pulled out from under me. Putting pieces of my past together, in the here and now—in the middle of a disaster, no less. It's an eye opener."

"Post-traumatic growth, I believe it's called."

"I do feel good about getting involved," she continued. "I'd do it all over if, heaven forbid, disaster strikes here again. But what's more important for me is what I told you the last time we sat here. This is still home to me, no matter where I go, or what I do."

"Your early growing years were here. It can't help but be an integral part of who you are."

"Most people who helped mold me are still here, too. Dad, of course. But also Aunt Millie and Uncle Harold. Chet. Lil. Nate. Countless others."

She paused, then put the rocker back in motion, as if it somehow helped her arrange her thoughts. "The anger I felt over Mom's death, the guilt I felt over abandoning this place. Those feelings led me into the belief that people here were unhappy with me. Maybe even rejected me, because I'd left. That I no longer mattered. Nothing could be further from the truth."

"What does this new perspective do for you?"

"I feel better about my past, my choices. More at peace. Everybody here still accepts me for who I am, who I've become, what I'm doing with my life. I've missed out on so much, all because of my own misperceptions. I can blame no one but myself. I'll be back again, soon. I need to make up for lost time."

"The disaster operation will go on for a while yet. If you come out on weekends, maybe you could continue to help. I'll still be involved, on and off. I'm happy to keep showing you the ropes."

"I appreciate that, Paulson. Especially with everything I've put you through."

"After this grant goes through, there will be a new mental health position opening. It's not permanent. Lacey says it'll probably be available up to a year. Finding someone to fill it won't be easy. There aren't any other mental health professionals in the Marshland area. Maybe someone in Willsey, but that would be quite a commute for a full timer. It pays so little, the position won't attract much. The recession aftermath might shake loose somebody who's desperate. But if you want to apply, I'll definitely put in a good word for you."

"I know there's continuing need." She chose words carefully. "But I'm also a responsible professional. I've spent years developing my client base. I rebuilt that bereavement program from the ground up. Both clients and program administration are counting on me. Transitioning out would take months. Your new position will need to be filled long before that."

"The hospital won't have any trouble finding someone to step in for you. The mental health field is glutted over there. You could always commute one day a week for your private clients. If nothing else, you'd have a great excuse to get that dragster wannabe out on the road."

He was beginning to sound anxious. Those eyes disguised nothing. And at the moment, he looked more like a pleading puppy-dog than Paulson.

She stood and stretched, smiling at him. "Sounds like you're finished with being a therapist right now. You're being Paulson. The friend I've come to know this last week." Going into overdrive, trying to get her to hang around longer.

"It does make sense for you." He either hadn't picked up on it or purposely ignored the not so subtle hint. "You said it yourself, you want to nurture relationships here."

Including theirs, she tacked on in silence, since he was leaving it unspoken. Shelley's instincts had hit pay dirt again. Why was she always the last one to figure it out?

"And, the relationship we have," she stated, seeing no way around it.

"Well, yes. That would be part of it."

"I would enjoy continuing our friendship. But you have to understand, just friends."

His eyes briefly darted. "There's someone else?"

"No. But look at the two of us. We're as different as night and day."

"So were your parents. Near as I can tell they did all right."

She laughed. "It's different, with you and me. This . . . this place I'm in."

Yes. Where was she right now? So much had happened. "I've only just begun to process Mom's passing. Working it through will take time. Grief takes time. There's no way around it."

"Yes, but . . ."

"There's also where I'm at with Dad. We've finally had a little clearing of the air, after a decade of being at odds with one another. We've practically forgotten who we are as people. I've that bridge to continue mending. As well as the bridge to my very roots. When it's all said and done, things will change. I may well be a different person than the one you see before you today."

"But I can help you with that. I can support you through it."

"You mean a teddy bear relationship. You know how those end up."

"Teddy bear." His brow knitted, a flash of recognition registering. "You mean like when people jump into another relationship while they're divorcing, as a support net."

"Yes. How often do those work out? Occasionally. But it's the exception, rather than the norm."

He stood. "We're different, you and I. There's already something there. You can't deny it. We both felt it. Back at the Lone Pine. When . . . we comforted each other."

True. She remembered it—the warmth, the easy intimacy. She did. But her professional self found a different place on the shelf for it than did Paulson. "In all objectivity, during times like this it's easy for people to bond. This friendship we're forging. For all we know, it's just an artifact of survival strategy."

"It seems real enough to me."

She crossed the perimeter of the porch and gazed at the trees above. The woodland creatures continued to frolic, life going on as if there weren't a care in the world.

"Are you familiar with the neurotransmitter oxytocin?" She sat against a chipped railing warmed by the sun, facing him. "The one that promotes connecting with others."

"I've heard of it."

"It gets released in greater quantities during times of stress. It promotes attraction, attachments, bonding of various sorts."

"This sounds like another version of Lacey's song and dance."

"Even Lacey noticed?"

Paulson just looked at her.

She burst out laughing.

"What's so funny?"

"Nothing. Or me, I guess. Look. Lacey's right. How much of our friendship is lasting will prove itself over time. For now, I face other important beginnings. They need to be taken care of."

All the same, she couldn't keep from smiling back at him and watching the power streaming from those eyes of his—eyes that, at times, managed to see her even more clearly than she saw herself.

*****

Sam picked his way around the garage, shaking his head at the mess Jimmy had made. Having the last remnants of his footprint on this earth scattered like refuse was just plain aggravating, to say the least. Charlie should have slapped that kid up the side of the head when he had the chance. Too late for that, now.

He couldn't really get mad at the river for its version of Armageddon. It was just nature's way. But he sure could assign a little accountability to Jimmy for this.

He stepped out into the open. The potential lovebirds were still dawdling by her Miata, where they'd been ever since Paulson hauled out that box of toys for her.

These young people. Little wonder the world was turning to hell in a hand basket. Why do they have to make their lives so darned complicated? If they kept things a little simpler and paid attention to what really mattered, they would all be a lot happier.

And what's with that preposterous car? Couldn't hardly be practical.

He rocked on his heels and began whistling "Goodnight, Irene." They didn't take the hint.

Oh, well. From the look of things, it wouldn't be much longer before Paulson had her using that vehicle to tootle on back.

Sarah waved a final goodbye to go along with the one that had been going on for the better part of the afternoon. Sam pulled out the disposable phone she'd pressed on him and waved it back. Paulson stood there, watching her on her way, until the car was out of sight. Eventually it occurred to Paulson to consider tearing himself away the empty piece of road.

"I'm putting coffee on," said Paulson. "That garage job is going to take at least one brew."

On his way to the kitchen, Paulson stopped at the outlandish fishbowl in his front room. "Sorry, Junior. Almost forgot about you, didn't I?" He dropped some flakes into the water. The hungry fish darted up and snarfed them away.

"Who are you going to get to do this for you . . " Paulson said, ". . . during my jaunts to the big city?"

Does the future hold more disaster for Sarah and Paulson? If so, how deeply do they get into it—disaster politics, or their odd relationship?

Find out with the next installment of The Keepers Series:

KEEPERS SAVING THE WORLD

Available now at Amazon.com

Read more at www.keeperconnections.com

ABOUT THE AUTHOR

Laurel Hughes, Psy.D., is a licensed psychologist in Oregon. She has participated in over 50 disaster operations with the American Red Cross. Her experiences range from major catastrophes, such as the Events of September 11th, to minor local flooding. She also dabbles in disaster mental health program development and technical writing. Among such efforts are the Behavioral Health Emergency Response Plan and Field Guide for the Oregon Department of Human Services, and numerous materials for the American Red Cross—including joint efforts with the Substance Abuse and Mental Health Services Administration of the U.S. Department of Health and Human Services, and the U.S. Department of Defense.